STROKE OF MIDNIGHT

MIDNIGHT'S PAWN

HEATHER GREYE

Published by Black Sheep Media LLC

Editor: Elizabeth MS Flynn, emsflynn.com

Cover Design: Deranged Doctor Design, www.derangeddoctordesign.com

Formatting: Mayhem Cover Creations

To Mom and Thom, for always believing in me.
Love you!

CHAPTER 1

"I'M TEN BLOCKS AWAY." Dizzie spoke into the microphone embedded in her helmet.

"You've got plenty of time to deliver that package." The disembodied voice on the other end belonged to the dispatcher for Tremaine Corporation couriers.

"Sure, if I want to be *on time.*"

"On time" wouldn't cut it, not tonight.

"You and your bonuses, Dizzie." The dispatcher laughed. No matter how many times they'd worked together, the people on the other end of the line didn't understand what drove Dizzie.

Hell yeah, she wanted that bonus. Every extra credit got her closer to paying off her contract. Closer to freedom. Freedom from the corporation that had raised her and now owned her until she paid back every credit they'd spent on her over the years.

"I've got ten minutes to claim it. I'll contact you when it's done. I'm out."

Dizzie switched off the mic and hunched low over her motorcycle. She took the next turn faster than she should.

The bike responded like it was part of her. Adrenaline raced through her as she skimmed low to the ground. She laughed and enjoyed the rush.

Dizzie loved late-night deliveries like this—the city felt so much more alive. Neon lights reflected off hundreds of feet of glass buildings, creating the illusion of daylight on the city below. Rainbow-colored daylight. The colors danced across the people, the pavement, and puddles left over from the last rain, lighting the city streets up like a never-ending party.

Rounding the corner, she slowed down and popped back upright. A few feet ahead, a group of drunk street kids staggered off the sidewalk in front of a 24/7 convenience store. She slowed to avoid them, her hands and feet working in sync to downshift.

It was nearly midnight and people and cars still crowded the streets of downtown Seattle. Determined to avoid more careless pedestrians, she glanced over her shoulder before slipping through a break between cars and into the next lane.

Once she'd secured a place in the flow of traffic, she blinked slowly to activate the optic implant in her right eye. Instantly, a map with a small clock overlaid her normal vision.

A red light flashed right in the middle of her route. Her stomach sank. Dammit. That meant traffic. Traffic meant she might lose that bonus.

The distance between her and the congested streets was closing fast. She'd spent years riding these streets and knew their twists, turns, and hazards better than anyone. The only shortcut from here to the delivery point was through the next alley.

Ugh. She hated alleys. They were filled with unpleasant

things. Like drunks, drugs, and bodies.

A skeezy alley? Or a little closer to owning her future?

Easy decision.

Taking a deep breath, Dizzie glanced in the mirror and cut into the lane to her right, sliding between two cars. A horn blared behind her.

Calculating the distance that separated her from the next alley, Dizzie waved a hand over her shoulder in absent apology. "Sorry!" Checking her mirror one last time, she cut her handlebars to the right to make the turn.

The trajectory carried her into the dark gash between buildings. She shuddered when she nearly scraped one of the buildings that framed the alley. Dizzie held her breath until she sped out the other end.

Brakes squealed as she broke out of the darkness and back onto the brightly lit main road. Heart racing more from relief than excitement, she sucked in a deep breath and glanced at the clock in her display.

Seven blocks, eight minutes.

Speeding up, she pressed closer to the bike frame, sliding into the zone where she and the bike became one. Experience, instinct, and the optical implant guided her as she zigged and zagged across the lanes, dodging speeding cars and oversize trucks.

Two minutes later, Dizzie pulled up in front of the hotel and scanned for courier parking.

Nada.

Dammit. Valet it is.

She pulled off her helmet. Exhaust-flavored fumes replaced the stale recirculated air of her helmet. A valet hurried over to assist her. Dressed in tight black pants and a T-shirt that hugged muscles she didn't think came from a gym, he was the perfect eye candy for a high-end hotel like this.

"Take good care of my baby." Dizzie tossed him her keys as she slid her leg over the bike.

He snatched them out of the air with his good hand. The other was highly modified, fitted with a device that accessed the ignition of any vehicle. She winced. His implant didn't bother her. Whatever wiring or programming his bosses had added to it to keep him honest, did. Without that, he'd probably make a hell of a living on the street as a car thief.

His eyes flicked between her and her ride. She didn't give him a chance to argue. Moving through the front doors like she owned the place, Dizzie tugged off her gloves and shoved them into her bag.

She pressed her hand against a nearby scanner. "Urgent delivery for Portia Tremaine." A flash of heat warmed her hand as the system scanned her palm. She pulled away when she heard the familiar hum of her record being accessed as the computer confirmed her identity.

"ID verified. Dizzie, no surname. Tremaine Corporation courier. Access granted. Ms. Tremaine is in the penthouse. Proceed to Elevator 12."

Tucking her bag close, Dizzie checked her ocular display. Barely five minutes left.

Elevator 12 opened as she approached. Although the car was programmed for her destination, she pressed the button for the penthouse anyway. Though she knew it had no effect, Dizzie punched the close-door button repeatedly. Other passengers would only slow her down.

Hyperaware of the clock ticking away, Dizzie reached into her bag, double checking that the high-priority package was still there. Thicker than the average envelope, the squishy bubble wrap covered a solid core.

What was it?

Dizzie sighed. Not her business.

Finally—finally!—the elevator stopped. "Penthouse level," a computer voice announced as the doors opened into a different world.

Floor-to-ceiling windows ringed the perimeter. The inky darkness of Puget Sound bled into the riot of colors from the city. Of course the wealthy company owners and the uber-rich investors who ranked above them on the social ladder would party up here, where they could look down on all the little people.

Her nose twitched. Even the air smelled different up here, a heavy mix of perfumes that smelled and tasted worse than exhaust.

Zeroing in on the doors to the ballroom, Dizzie double timed it over the lush carpeting, her heavy boots not making even a whisper of sound. "Urgent delivery for Ms. Tremaine," she told the guards posted outside the grand wooden doors. Keeping a firm grip on her bag, she lay her free hand on another scanner.

After the scan cleared, a guard held out his hand for the package. "I'll take it to her."

Dizzie shook her head and tightened her grip. "Nope. Package says deliver to Portia Tremaine." A quick up and down look. "You're not Portia Tremaine."

He scowled. "Wait here. I'll send someone to find her."

Dizzie hated these power games. All she wanted to do was deliver the package, collect her bonus, and get back to her room. And none of that could happen if he didn't let her do her job.

She bit back a sigh and smiled instead of rolling her

eyes. "Of course. Though if this package is late, I'll be sure to tell Ms. Tremaine why."

The guy finally moved, but she was excruciatingly aware of her time—and her bonus—ticking away. He left the door cracked open.

She peered into the ballroom. The rich, the beautiful, and the weird mingled in the grand space. High and low tables were scattered around the periphery, covered by white tablecloths and floral centerpieces that each probably cost more than she'd make in a month. A band—a live band! —played on the far side of the room, while guests swayed and danced on the gleaming dark marble floor. Lights flashed here and there as newsies captured images of the event.

She surveyed the sea of guests with their bright, stylish clothes and outrageous body mods. Light from the chandeliers reflected off adornments created from base metals and circuitry. More than one person sported unusually colored hair, but her attention was caught—and held—by an elaborate updo sculpted from twinkling filaments.

Dizzie shifted her focus from the truly unique hairstyle. As much as she'd love to people watch, the package wasn't going to deliver itself. She had minutes to find the boss's daughter in this mass of people. Tall and blond, Portia Tremaine shouldn't be too hard to find. If only Dizzie could see over the crowd.

Still no sign of the guard.

Screw this. Dizzie slipped into the ballroom and took a hard left, putting as many people and plants as she could between her and the guards at the door.

Scanning the crowd for the Tremaine heir, she still couldn't get a good-enough view.

Dammit! She was *not* going to lose this bonus because

she was short. Dizzie scrambled onto an abandoned chair at one of the perimeter tables, ignoring the surprised looks of people nearby.

"C'mon. C'mon! Where are you?" She didn't have time for this.

Yes!

A familiar-looking icy blonde stood with a companion near the edge of the dance floor. "Gotcha!" Dizzie jumped off the chair and threw herself into the crush.

CHAPTER 2

KILLIAN ST. John stood near the edge of the dance floor with Portia, waiting for Tommy to return with their drinks. He stared into his empty glass. How to get that last drop of amber liquid from the bottom of the glass to his mouth? He'd once seen a girl with a tongue modification that curled out six inches. That would have been useful.

Portia slapped his arm.

"Ow!" He rubbed his stinging biceps. "What was that for?"

"You haven't paid attention to a word I said."

True, though he'd never admit it. "Of course, I was. Blah, blah, blah, Tommy. Blah, blah, Tommy's so amazing." Killian pitched his voice to a high falsetto. He'd teased her like this since the day she'd announced she was in love with his other best friend. A longing for simpler times flashed through him. He added "Tommy's so dreamy" and a fake swoon with his hand on his forehead.

"You're horrible." Portia smiled. "Horrible, but not wrong. He's *sooo* dreamy," she parroted his tone, "and great in bed."

"Stop, please stop," he cried, half serious, half not.

She laughed. Killian raised his glass to his lips, remembering it was empty too late. "Where *is* your handsome husband? He promised me another drink."

"You know him," Portia said. "Probably saying hello to everyone he sees." Still, she scanned the crowd around them.

Tommy Gilmore was flighty and flirty and the life of any party. Portia was the serious one in their close-knit trio, weighed down by too much work and too little appreciation from her father. And Killian? He was the one who just didn't give a damn anymore.

He loved his friends, used to love his life. Part of the investor class, he and Tommy had grown up with no responsibilities, as well as too much money and not enough sense. Unlike Portia, the only expectations Killian's family had ever placed on him were to sit back and enjoy the money that rolled in from long-ago investments.

That had been enough for his father and grandfather. Enough for him too. Lately, though, he was so fucking bored. What was *wrong* with him?

Killian eyed his empty glass. Wait for Tommy or fetch his own damn drink?

This was what his life had come to—an existential crisis around an empty glass.

"Excuse me, Ms. Tremaine?" The confident voice behind him was pitched loud enough to be heard over the music and the chatter. Probably some damn newsie wanting a photo. Another party, another front-page story about the rich and the beautiful doing nothing.

He pasted on his fuck-you-paparazzi smile. Next to him, Portia had done the same. They turned in unison to face the interloper. Bracing for a blinding flash and an obnoxious question or two, Killian came face-to-face with a stunning woman in black synth-leather—and froze.

"Well, hello there." He swapped his paparazzi smile for his most charming.

But her attention was on Portia, and she was completely ignoring him. That was unexpected. He blinked, but didn't dim his smile.

For a second, he almost wished she was a newsie. *They* never ignored him.

God, you're such an asshole, Killian. Make up your mind.

He watched the newcomer, envying her concentration. Her focus. He'd never been that intent on anything. He and Tommy had tried anything and everything. Partying. Drugs. Never a job, though—that seemed a little extreme. Was that all it took? Portia would laugh her head off if she knew what he was thinking.

Enthralled by the courier, Killian stepped closer. What would it take to get all that attention focused on him?

"Urgent delivery for you, Ms. Tremaine."

Before Portia responded, their trio was joined by a disgruntled-looking security guard. He was panting and his face glowed red. Exertion or embarrassment? Either way, Killian didn't appreciate the interruption.

"I told you to wait." The guard directed his ire at the lithe courier.

Killian turned toward the guard, intent on protecting the courier. Wait, what was he doing?

Portia waved the man off. After a burning glare at the courier, the guard stomped off.

Killian sighed. Sometimes, when people got between the Tremaine heir and company business, blood was spilled and lives were ruined.

Not tonight, though. Too bad—it would definitely liven things up.

While Portia attended to the ritual of accepting the package, he watched the courier. His interest in the woman far outweighed his curiosity about the package.

The courier wore her fair hair in braids. The simple hairstyle drew attention to her vivid blue eyes. Although surgery and modern lenses made any eye color possible, Killian was sure hers was natural. No one in her position would spend credits on such a useless upgrade.

She extended a scanner to Portia. Her bright red nails perfectly matched her tough-girl uniform. "State your name for the record." Her voice was cool. Confident.

Clearly out of place in this swirl of high society, she didn't seem bothered or intimidated. In fact, she appeared comfortable in her own skin in a way that Killian hadn't been in far too long. How did she do it?

Beside him, Portia placed her hand on the sensor, her pale pink nails a sharp contrast to the courier's fire engine red ones. "Portia Tremaine."

"Identity confirmed," the computer chimed. Portia removed her hand from the scanner and the courier looked at the screen.

"Thank you, Ms. Tremaine." She slid the scanner into a side pocket and reached into her messenger bag. Black synth-leather, like her outfit, and just as well-worn.

Extracting a bulky envelope, she offered it to Portia. "Here's your package. Have a nice night."

Portia took ownership of the package. The courier's gaze lost focus and flickered to the side. She must be using an optic display. Whatever she saw there made her smile.

Her entire face lit up, revealing dimples in her cheeks and adding a sparkle to her eyes. Her obvious joy sent a spear of envy through him. He wanted to get closer to her, experience that joy for himself.

"That will be all." Courier dismissed, Portia's attention turned to the package.

Killian kept his attention on the courier. She didn't look surprised by Portia's abrupt dismissal. Working for the Tremaine Corporation, she was probably used to it.

Transaction complete, the courier pivoted and walked away. Killian watched her go. Her leathers fit like they'd been made for her and her swagger gave movement to already dangerous curves. She paused and he held his breath. Maybe she'd forgotten something and would turn back.

Instead, one of those delicate, red-tipped hands snaked a glass of champagne from a passing waiter.

The move put her in profile and he watched as she took a sip, her nose wrinkling at the bubbles. He laughed. He'd done the same the first time he drank champagne. How had he forgotten such a simple pleasure?

Portia turned to look at him. He ignored her, totally focused on the courier.

She took another sip. Her nose was still wrinkled, but this time the bubbles brought another unguarded smile to her face.

Setting the unfinished glass on another waiter's tray, she caught him watching her. For the briefest second, she paused, her eyes wide. Then she smiled and gave him a brazen wink before turning away.

"Who was that?" He watched the courier weave through the crowd, her dark outfit a stark contrast to the other guests' colorful clothes.

"A courier." Portia responded, her tone conveying the unspoken *who cares*. "What has gotten into you?"

When Killian couldn't see the courier any longer, he lifted his empty glass to his lips again. Dammit. What *had* gotten into him?

"I have no idea." The absolute truth. The little blonde had been a bright spot in an otherwise boring night. One that beckoned him closer.

He wanted her to smile at him like champagne bubbles. Needing another distraction—this time from his imagination—Killian grabbed Portia's hand. "Dance with me."

Portia tugged her hand free and stared at the package, her expression troubled. "I need to deal with whatever this is. I should go to the office."

"Didn't you promise Tommy no business tonight?"

"This is an emergency." She didn't look up from the envelope.

For most of their lives, he and Tommy had tried to convince Portia that there was more to life than working. But she was determined to win her father's approval, to be the heir he demanded. Personally, Killian thought the old bastard would never be satisfied; he'd treated Portia badly her entire life. What did he know, though? His own parents had been dead for five years and he didn't have anyone to prove anything to.

To distract himself from the sudden ache in his chest, Killian shifted to peer over her shoulder. "Is it really? Who sent it?"

The package wasn't anything special as far as he could tell. The bulky yellow parcel had a shipping label with her name and a mark that indicated it had been processed through the company mailroom. Nothing about it looked urgent.

Then again, what the hell did he know? He was the one with nothing but time on his hands.

"It doesn't say." Portia turned the package over.

"You two have obviously forgotten how to have fun," a voice behind them drawled.

A new drink dangled over Killian's shoulder.

"Thought you'd gotten lost." Killian turned toward his other best friend.

Tommy shrugged, an effortlessly charming move that had gotten them out of more scrapes and tight places than Killian could count.

Killian grabbed the crystal tumbler with an eagerness that should probably worry him. Raising it with a nod of thanks, he took a long sip. Smooth fire poured down his throat.

A bit more than half of the golden liquid remained when he finally lowered the glass.

Tommy stared at the tumbler. "That's no way to treat good liquor. Next round, you can brave the mob at the bar."

Killian grimaced. Reason enough to savor the rest of this drink. He lowered the glass, dangling it from his fingertips.

"Yeah, that's what I thought." Tommy nodded and presented Portia a fresh glass of wine by the stem.

A server appeared, whisking away their empty glasses.

"Why so serious?" Tommy wrapped his arm around Portia's waist and pulled her close. They were a striking couple. Portia's floor-length dress was an icy blue, the perfect foil to her glittering diamond and sapphire jewelry. The sleeves were long and the neck was high, but the cut highlighted her figure. With her golden hair pulled into an intricate knot at the back of her head, she was the perfect embodiment of her Ice Queen sobriquet.

Tommy's tux, while similar to Killian's own classic black, reflected his playful side. The fine silver threads woven through the black caught the light and sparkled almost as much as her dress.

"Duty calls," she said, leaning into him, package in one hand, drink in the other.

Watching the easy way they fit together, Killian took another swallow of his drink. He told himself that the sudden burn in his system was the alcohol, not jealousy.

He wasn't jealous of Tommy and Portia.

They were the perfect couple. And so damn happy together. They didn't freeze Killian out. Totally the opposite. That almost made it worse.

Sometimes—like tonight—spending time with them nearly killed him.

Tommy plucked the package out of her hand and frowned at the Tremaine stamp on it. "They delivered this here?"

"Yeah." Portia nodded. "Headquarters wouldn't send a courier to an event like this if it wasn't urgent. I should open it. They might need me to go in."

Tommy frowned.

Killian knew what he was thinking. Portia practically lived and breathed the family business.

As a Tremaine investor, Killian appreciated the hard work she did to improve his bottom line. As a friend—one with more money than he could ever spend—he worried that she was putting herself and her marriage in jeopardy.

Portia and Tommy stared at each other. Tension gathered around them, making Killian twitch. Were they gearing up for a fight? Portia would never air her grievances in public, but Tommy didn't always have her restraint.

"They're playing our song, Portia," Killian said, hoping to distract the couple. Over the chatter of the crowd and the clink of glassware, he caught whispers of a familiar tune.

"Our song" was a revoltingly romantic ballad from Portia and Killian's one ill-advised date in high school.

"You were such an asshole that night, staring at other girls all evening," Portia said, her attention finally pulled away from the package.

"You didn't have to leave me stranded on the dance floor." The painful embarrassment of that night was a distant memory.

"Yeah, I did. You deserved it," Portia said, a smile in her voice.

He'd totally deserved it. His fifteen-year-old self hadn't known how to treat a woman.

"Hey, I thought you were glad he ruined your date. Otherwise you'd never have gone out with me." Tommy bumped shoulders with Portia. Her glare dissolved into a smile and the tension around them dissipated.

"I'm right here, you guys," Killian said. Thank god the distraction had worked.

"Dance with the man already," Tommy said. "You know how whiny he can get."

Portia's attention darted between Killian and the package.

"This will still be here when you get back." Tommy hid the envelope behind his back.

"Maybe they'll play *our* song next." The look Portia gave her husband when she said that smoldered.

Killian tugged at his collar and wished he wasn't witnessing this.

"I'll see what I can do," Tommy replied. Doubtless, Tommy would bribe the band as soon as Killian and Portia stepped onto the dance floor.

"Love you." Portia brushed her lips over his.

Killian turned away, giving them a moment of privacy.

He turned back when Portia slipped her hand into his. "Ready?" he asked.

"Fine." Portia glared at both men. "You can have your damn dance. After that, I'm leaving and taking my package and my husband with me."

"And your husband's package, too," Tommy added.

Smothering a laugh, Killian clasped her hand and drew her onto the dance floor before she offered up another excuse.

"Thank you, darling. You're the best friend ever." Killian smiled down at her.

Portia laid her hand on his shoulder while his arm circled her waist. She was the perfect height, nearly the perfect partner. Still, he imagined a different woman, one with golden braids and sharper edges, in his arms.

"Aren't you having the tiniest bit of fun?" he whispered as they swayed to the music.

"Are you?" She shifted so her gaze met his. "Tommy and I are worried about you. You haven't been yourself lately."

Damn. He'd hoped they hadn't noticed his boredom. Then again, Portia and Tommy were his closest family. Everyone else were either distant relatives, acquaintances, or employees.

"I'm right, aren't I?" she prodded.

He shrugged. This wasn't the time or the place to get into his issues. If he had them. Which he didn't.

"Just figuring some stuff out." A bullshit answer. Portia stared at him, but didn't call him on it.

Shit, she really was worried about him.

"We're here if you need us," was her only reply.

He exhaled, not realizing he'd been holding his breath. "What about you guys? Are you okay?"

He spun her out. When he reeled her back in, she said, "Fine. Just...figuring some stuff out."

The corner of his mouth curled up as she echoed his non-answer.

She looked over his shoulder for Tommy. Happiness flared in her eyes and Killian knew she'd found him. She always found Tommy in a crowd.

With that one look, the not-jealousy was back. It had always been the three of them, but now they were two plus one.

"Should I take you back?"

"What?" Portia shook her head, blue eyes dancing. Eyes that reminded him of the pretty little courier. "Oh no, mister. You begged for this dance. You're not getting out of it so easily."

"There's the hard-ass corporate bitch everyone thinks you are," he said with a laugh.

"Damn straight." She lay her head on his shoulder. For a minute, Killian wished she were his.

He didn't mean it—there'd never been a lick of attraction between them. That was all Portia and Tommy. He merely wanted what they had.

It was frighteningly easy to imagine the courier in his arms, her head on his chest, his hand tangled in her braids.

He shook his head to clear the ridiculous image. The courier may have been gorgeous, but she was completely unsuitable. His friends would eat her alive.

"What's the matter?" Portia lifted her head to look at him.

"A silly thought." He was reluctant to admit how much the mystery woman had intrigued him. Or how attractive he'd found her. Maybe he would seek her out. No one needed to know.

Portia stared at him a long moment. Finally, she smiled. "I'm glad. I didn't think you had silly in you anymore."

He didn't know how to respond to that. At a loss, Killian dipped her, needing distance. He pulled her up, back into his arms.

A sudden whoosh and deafening boom startled Killian.

What the hell—? Was that a giant firecracker?

The noise reverberated around the room. Had there been fireworks planned for the party? They sounded too close. Like they were in the room.

"What the hell?" Portia exclaimed.

Acrid smoke tickled Killian's nose and his nostrils flared. Around them, the other partygoers looked around, as puzzled as he was.

Then a bass rumble cut through the music. The band cut off abruptly, replaced by the shriek of metal on metal.

Everyone on the dance floor froze. Time stopped, then whirled forward. Somebody screamed. Then there was a burst of movement and noise.

Around them, dancers dashed every which way, terror in their eyes. Bodies swarmed forward, merging into an unmoving cluster.

He pulled Portia close as they were swept into the crowd. "We've got to get out of here."

The wave of bodies surged again, moving toward an exit.

Portia struggled to look around. "What about Tommy?"

"We'll find him." Tommy had been closer to an exit. Killian prayed he was already out of the ballroom.

Something crashed to the left of them. An agonized scream followed. Then ended abruptly.

The cluster of bodies condensed then exploded as people scattered.

In the chaos, Portia pulled free and darted back the way they'd come. "Tommy!"

"Dammit!" Killian raced after her. People had to be getting out, because the dance floor wasn't crowded any more. Broken glass and discarded shoes littered the marble floor. And chunks of—ceiling? He looked up at the flickering neon lights.

Where had those come from? The realization that he was looking at the neighboring skyscraper took too long.

This was bad. Really bad.

While he'd stared at the missing roof, Portia had stumbled to a stop a few feet away.

"Portia! We've got to go!" He lunged and wrapped his arms around her.

Then he noticed what had stopped her. Feet poked out from beneath a mass of metal and concrete.

He looked around. More feet. More legs. More bodies.

More screams.

He forced back nausea. He couldn't help them. He had to focus on Portia.

What was left of the ceiling creaked and shuddered. Pieces rained down on them. A fist-sized piece hit his brow. "Fuck!" Warmth trickled down his temple. He ignored it and concentrated on getting a struggling Portia to safety.

The next chunk—a bigger one—pummeled his shoulder. Tightening his grip around Portia, Killian lifted her off her feet and surged forward, ignoring the gasps and screams around them. The ceiling creaked again, the terrible noise reaching ear-splitting levels.

Suddenly, silence filled the decimated space. A palpable air of terror hung over the ballroom. Killian looked around the room at the destruction and the crush of people still straining for the exit. *Was it over?*

Killian looked up at the neon lights flickering against the night sky. With an ominous thunder, the remaining ceiling shuddered and collapsed.

Everything went black.

CHAPTER 3

"HEY, dispatch? Package delivered. I'm on my way home."

"You get that bonus, Dizzie?" Dispatch's question crackled over the comms.

"Hell yeah, I did." Her gaze flicked to the account notice on her implant screen and she grinned like an idiot.

She tipped the valet—habit, even without the rich bonus—and smiled when his thanks and phone number appeared onscreen. Dizzie threw her leg over her bike and slipped on her helmet.

"Congrats. Enjoy your celebration."

"Pfft, what celebration? I've got the early shift. I'll drag Alice out tomorrow after shift to celebrate."

"Roger that. Drive safe." Dispatch dropped off the line, moving on to the next courier and the next delivery.

Job officially completed, Dizzie started her bike. Her system buzzed with energy and she itched to spend a few of those shiny new credits. Next time she got one of these late-night requests, she'd trade away her six a.m. shift.

Alice wasn't going to believe how awesome her night had been. A fat stack of credits. The valet's phone number.

Fancy champagne. But her best friend was truly going to die of jealousy when Dizzie told her about the famous Killian St. John.

Slipping out of the hotel parking lot, she merged onto the main road. She wasn't in a rush now, so she obeyed the speed limit and replayed her interaction with Killian. He'd looked cool and aloof in his black tux and crisp white shirt. Her pulse had fluttered and she'd practically had to fan herself when he looked at her.

She'd nearly fainted when he said hello. Years of practice and a standard script were the only reason she'd managed to maintain a professional façade.

Killian's family had been a major investor in the Tremaine Corporation since the beginning. The St. Johns were Seattle royalty and she was a corporate courier. Killian had grown up in a fancy house with a fancy family, while Dizzie had grown up in a crèche, raised by the company. Whoever her family had been—the orphanage had no records of them—they obviously weren't on the same level.

How she'd managed a wink when he'd caught her nabbing that glass of champagne, she'd never know.

The smile that had crossed his lips in response? No wonder he'd been named Seattle's most eligible bachelor three years in a row.

Lost in that smile, she wasn't paying attention to the traffic. The squeal of brakes in front of her broke the spell. She slowed down cautiously, muscle memory coming to the rescue before she was consciously aware of what was happening.

She pulled up alongside a stopped taxi and flipped up her visor to look around.

Everyone was stopped. Her lane. The one next to her. "What the hell?"

Dizzie activated the traffic view on her implant. Black lines indicated blocked traffic all around her area, while red police activity lights formed a constricting ring around the hotel.

She blinked away the screen and tried to make sense of the stopped traffic and the ominous red and black map. Something must have happened at the hotel. She scanned the area, but was too far away to tell what was happening at the hotel.

All around her, car doors swung open and people spilled out, their attention focused on the giant screens mounted on the sides of buildings.

Shit. That couldn't be good.

Propelling her bike with her feet, she maneuvered until she was half on the sidewalk, half wedged between two parked cars. Whatever happened wasn't worth sitting in the middle of the road like a target.

"Hey! Watch it, asshole," she yelled when a pedestrian bumped her bike and snarled at her. Totally his fault—his attention was fixed on the news too, but he was the one moving.

Images of a building with half the top floor missing filled the screen. Giant white text identified the damaged building as the New Amsterdam Hotel.

Dizzie exhaled in a whoosh.

The time stamp on the never-ending loop of footage read 12:05. Minutes after she'd left.

Her stomach turned and she felt lightheaded. *That could have been her.*

The canapés had smelled so good and looked so pretty, she'd been tempted to grab one or two of the little nibbles from passing waiters after she'd delivered the package. Only a death stare from a security guard had stopped her. Her stomach roiled again. Just one of those delicious-looking finger foods and she might have been there when...

The screens changed, filling with images of the city's elite and powerful. Pictures taken as they had arrived earlier tonight. Beautiful people in their beautiful clothes.

God, she would have looked so out of place in the wreckage. An uncomfortable laugh bubbled out. She clamped her hand over her mouth and glanced around. Everyone else was still staring at the screens.

She swayed as her close call sank in.

An image of Portia Tremaine, Tommy Gilmore, and Killian St. John flashed on screen. Had they made it out?

Imagining them crushed under the rubble...

She barely managed to lean far enough away from her bike before she threw up.

On the jumbo screen, the images changed again. Lights bounced over and around the damaged floor, creating eerie shadows in the rubble. Footage from a news drone showed search and rescue helicopters circling the building.

Every major corporation, every news station, had to have aerial support on scene searching for their own people. Would they stop to help those they found buried? Or would they leave them and continue searching only for the ones who mattered?

Dizzie shifted on her seat, thankful another skyscraper blocked her view of the hotel.

The images shifted again and the screen split into quarters, each one featuring a single person. She sucked in a breath. Leopold Brunswick, the assistant to the head of the Tremaine Corporation, occupied the top right corner. The other three boxes featured the leaders of other companies or their proxies. The scrolling text along the bottom highlighted what was happening with the rescue efforts of each group. Corporate security would lead the investigation—they policed their own. Non-corporate law enforcement was left to handle tasks traffic and other "less important" crimes.

The newsies must not be able to get images within the wreckage. That was a small mercy. If there were bodies, they'd be shown over and over as talking heads rambled on.

She wanted out of here before that happened. She wasn't sure she would be able to look at the lifeless bodies and not remember the pulsing energy of the ballroom or Killian's disarming smile.

Dizzie put her helmet back on, tucking her braids beneath the hard plastic. All she wanted now was to get back home.

CHAPTER 4

KILLIAN DREAMED OF SUFFOCATION. Of a giant weight bearing down on his chest. Desperate for his next breath, he gasped awake. Darkness pinned him down. His arms and legs flailed but barely moved.

Nononononononono

"Mom? Dad?"

Silence.

His heart was beating too fast. He sucked in air with short, shallow breaths. The air was thick and gritty, carrying more particulates than oxygen.

Struggling against the panic, Killian struggled to remember what had happened. He and his parents had been vacationing in a distant country at a newly completed resort they'd invested in when the building had rumbled and collapsed.

Grief washed over him and he choked back a sob. And somehow, that familiar emotion allowed him to force back all his feelings and think.

He'd been with Portia and Tommy, not his parents. They'd attended a party in Seattle. There'd been a deafening, horrible sound, so like the one Killian heard in his nightmares. He'd caught up to Portia and pulled her close as the ceiling fell down on them before the world went to hell.

Portia! Tommy! Where were they? He had to find them.

Killian shot upright. Or tried to.

His eyes flew open. Darkness surrounded him. What the hell was going on?

He reached up to wipe the tears away, but his arm never reached his face. He tried again; it didn't move at all.

Was he paralyzed?

Panic swelled again and Killian sucked in air with short, shallow breaths.

Shit! At this rate, he'd hyperventilate and pass out. Again. He didn't want that.

Killian forced himself to take deep breaths. In and out.

In.

Out.

With each breath, his breathing slowed and his head cleared.

Suddenly, the darkness around him gave way to an eerie glow, the light made hazy by the bad visibility.

"I think...something...here."

Rescuers?

"Over here!" His shout dissolved into a cough from the fine particles coating his throat. The thick air burned his lungs. Was he loud enough to be heard?

More bits of muffled conversation floated his way. Pinned down flat on his back, in near darkness, Killian had no idea if they were anywhere near him. He had to try.

"Hey, over here!" That was louder. Maybe. His throat still burned.

He tried to raise his arm to wave them over but couldn't.

The light moved away.

"Dammit!" The only way to get their attention would be to make a louder noise.

He reached out for something—anything—he could use and discovered he could shift his left arm a little, but his right arm was completely immobile.

His fingers scrabbled over loose gravel-size rocks. If there were bigger chunks, they were out of reach.

The darkness was back. The voices gone. Had he imagined them?

He needed to take action. Rescue himself. Remaining here, trapped in the darkness...

Even thinking about it caused the panic to rise. He couldn't lay here and wait for rescue. Not again.

Gathering his strength, he tried to sit up and barely moved. He was pinned from at least the waist down and one arm.

"Fuck!"

A buzz echoed in the space around him and the emergency lighting kicked on. The pale light wasn't much and there was no way to know how long it would last.

Clenching his abs, Killian lifted his upper body up as high as possible—inches, maybe—and twisted sideways. He lifted his head, neck muscles straining to hold the position. In the dim, dusty light, he saw a metal bar above his chest. He wasn't dead, so something else must be taking the weight.

His head drifted back down to the ground and processed what he'd seen. The metal beam wasn't on his left arm. That was good.

Really good.

He didn't want a metal arm to match his metal leg. That shit was for either the kids desperate to turn themselves into cyborgs or for the super soldiers who had to have multiple replacement limbs. Not him. Never for him.

Small chunks of rubble were piled around him. He tugged his left arm, finally freeing it from the loose concrete, but the rubble demanded its price. His arm burned where the rough edges had ripped off the suit sleeve and scraped skin off.

Ignoring the flame of pain shimmering across his forearm, Killian tucked his arm close to his chest. With his left side free, he rolled as far as he could in the other direction. Although he didn't move far, it was enough to see why he couldn't move his arm—Portia.

Powdered concrete coated her skin and in the emergency lighting, she looked like a corpse.

Tears welled in his eyes. "Please don't be dead," he begged.

This was all his fault. If he hadn't demanded that dance. Hadn't encouraged her to stay at the party.

He tried to wiggle his arm, hoping the movement would wake her. Nothing happened. His arm wouldn't move.

Shit.

Muscles quivering, he lowered himself back to the ground, sucking in another mouthful of grimy air. He coughed, nearly choking on the fine particles.

"Portia!" he wheezed when he could breathe again.

No response.

With his arm pinned by Portia and the rest of him anchored down by the steel beam, there was nothing to do until help arrived. Unless...

He levered himself up again, his stomach muscles burning with fatigue. What was immobilizing his lower body? Grasping the far edge of the beam with his free hand, he pulled himself up as far as his trapped arm would allow.

It wasn't the steel support that held his legs down. It was a chunk of concrete several feet wide.

Killian lay back down. There had to be a way. The rescuers hadn't been back this way. Were they rescuing other people, like the pretty courier?

Irrationally, he hated the thought of her being trapped alone.

Don't be stupid, Killian.

He shouldn't even be thinking of her. Freeing himself and Portia had to be his priority. Then finding Tommy.

Where *was* Tommy? Had he made it out? Was he buried under the rubble somewhere?

Killian forced the worry away. He had to focus on the things he could control. Right here. Right now. That meant moving the slab of concrete.

There might be a way. A really stupid way.

He couldn't lay here and do nothing.

Hoping he wasn't about to make a fatal mistake, Killian released his breath and shifted until he was flat on his back. If he could move the slab out of the way, he might be able to slide out from under the steel beam.

By leveraging the power in his cyber leg, he might be able to get enough thrust to shift the slab and free them from this mess without waiting for rescuers who had already passed them by once.

Killian steadied his breath and blocked out all the distractions. The panic and terror. The overwhelming worry for Portia, Tommy, and himself. Even the ringing in his ears and the agonizing throb of pain from his entire body.

He forced it all out of his mind and concentrated on his left leg. Did he have enough range of motion to make this work? Straining, he rolled his ankle, tapping the side of his foot against the rubble. Sensation traveled up his leg.

That was good. That meant the circuitry was transmitting from his artificial leg to his nervous system and back again.

He exhaled in relief. Step one complete. If his cyber leg had been damaged, the whole plan would have failed.

Now the tricky part. Focusing on his knee, he pulled it toward his body. This was a finesse move. He bent his leg slowly. The metal might be willing, but the flesh around it was weak.

The line between shifting the concrete and undoing the painstaking cyberwork connecting his leg to his body was a fine one. One he couldn't risk crossing.

The knee joint creaked and rattled as his leg took up more of the weight of the concrete. Nothing to worry about. Yet.

Sweat beaded on his forehead as he slowly repositioned his leg. By the time he put his foot flat on the ground, it felt like hours had passed.

Breathing heavily, sucking in more dust with every gasp, Killian considered his options.

With the slab balanced precariously on his metal leg, he had enough room to slide his right leg so it was tucked under the stronger left. Some protection, not a lot.

The slab wobbled and tilted to the other side. "Shit!" he yelled.

If he couldn't control where the slab went, he'd fuck up his other leg. And maybe the rest of him.

This was the tricky part. His escape might mean someone else's death.

No. He couldn't worry about anyone else. Not right

now. He and Portia and Tommy had to come first, no matter what.

Ignoring the strain on his right shoulder, he wiggled and tried to scoot his hips closer to his feet. The closer he got, the better this would work. In theory.

Rolling his back over the loose rubble was excruciating. With every painful centimeter, he wanted to stop. When he couldn't go any farther, he pulled his left knee close to his chest while still trying to keep the concrete from falling.

He braced the sole of his foot on the underside of the concrete and took a last deep breath. "Please let me survive this," he said out loud.

"One."

"Two."

"Three!" Expelling the air from his lungs, he focused all his energy into thrusting his leg up.

The chunk of concrete flew backward nearly a yard, landing with a clatter somewhere past his feet. It set off a mini rock slide and flung more particles into the air.

Killian lowered his shaking leg to the ground. Until that moment, he hadn't truly believed it would work.

"What the hell?" The noise must have caught the attention of the rescue workers wherever they were.

Good. Maybe they'd be drawn back this way.

With the block removed, the only remaining impediments to movement were the beam, which he could work around, and Portia, who still pinned his right arm down.

She was still unconscious.

Killian rolled to his right side.

"Portia? Hey, are you okay?" No response. He pressed his fingers to her neck, not daring to breathe until her pulse fluttered against his fingertips. Relief surged through him. She wasn't dead.

Careful not to jostle her, after several long minutes he was able to slide his arm out from beneath Portia's torso. Arms and legs now free, he slid his body under the beam to reach her side. Every muscle in his body protesting, he sat up.

Killian shifted closer to Portia and took one of her hands in his. It was so cold. He squeezed it, trying to impart warmth.

He didn't pull her into his lap, not wanting to risk injuring her more. Medical science could fix a lot of things these days, but she and Tommy both took pride in being unaugmented. Of course, they'd never truly faced that choice like he had. Losing his leg had been nothing compared to the loss of his parents.

Now, where was Tommy?

He could be anywhere, buried under the rubble like Killian and Portia had been. Or maybe he'd escaped in the crush of people. Deep down, though, he feared Tommy's luck hadn't been that good. Bile surged up his throat at the thought of Tommy entombed alone under the collapsed roof.

Killian studied the area around him. The room was brighter. He might be able to stand now. Should he go look for Tommy or stay with Portia?

Lights bobbed around him, getting closer, and voices were just barely audible over the rush of his pulse.

"Over here!" he croaked. *Dammit!* Hacking up something unpleasant, he spit to the side and tried again.

"Over here!" He raised his free hand, waving into the dim light.

"Killian?"

He dropped his hand and leaned closer to Portia, his eyes closing briefly. "Thank god you're awake."

Her hand tightened around his as violent coughs racked her body. "What happened?" Her voice was raspy.

"I think the building collapsed."

"An earthquake?" she gasped.

He shuddered. "I don't know." Not entirely a lie—he didn't know for sure. It hadn't felt like the last one. Though the earthquake that killed his parents and trapped him in the rubble had happened five years ago, some days it felt like it just happened. He'd never forget the terrifying sensation of the ground rolling beneath him. That hadn't happened tonight. Recalling the fireworks and the chaos, he had a terrible suspicion.

Portia struggled to sit up.

"No, stay there," he said. "You might be injured."

"Where's Tommy?" Fear coated her words. Tugging her hand from his, she scrambled frantically to sit up. This wasn't the iron-willed woman the tabloids had dubbed the "Ice Queen." This was a wife terrified for her husband.

"Portia, let me help you."

Several slow minutes later, Portia was nestled in the vee of his legs.

"We've got to find Tommy," she sobbed.

Her tears broke his heart and echoed his own worries. Killian couldn't give in to those concerns now. He had to be strong for her.

"Listen to me, Portia. We'll find Tommy." He willed her to believe him. "We need to make sure somebody finds us, too, okay?"

She slumped against his shoulder and nodded. Whether in agreement or defeat, he didn't know.

Turning his head so he wasn't shouting in her ear, he tried again to summon help. "Over here!"

Nearby lights bobbled, then paused.

"What the hell?" someone said. "I thought you cleared this section?"

Shadows moved through the dense air. Rocks shifted around them with a clatter as someone came closer. A flashlight nearly blinded him.

Squinting against the bright light, Killian barely made out the two faceless figures beyond it.

"Can you shine that to the side?"

The light shifted. Killian blinked to clear the spots from his vision.

He curved his body protectively around Portia, unwilling to risk her life any further. "Anyone here from Tremaine?" he asked.

"Buddy, we got corporate folks coming out our ears." The second rescuer laughed. "What flavor did you want again?"

"Tremaine," Killian repeated. It was possible—but not likely—that his grandparents or maybe Tommy's family had sent someone to look for them. The Tremaine Corporation would definitely have sent a rescue team for Portia.

"Yeah, I think they're somewhere around here." Neither rescuer made any attempt to move.

"Go get them," Killian snapped.

"What's in it for me?"

Killian bit back a curse. Right now, these rescuers held all the power.

"I've got a high-level Tremaine exec here," he said—understatement of the year—"and I'm guessing you'll get some kind of reward for bringing them over."

Money was a great motivator. Both rescuers scrambled away. He heard them calling for Tremaine as they moved away. For rescuing Portia, they might even get their fifteen minutes of fame.

With rescue on the way, Killian wrapped Portia tighter in his arms and finally allowed himself to ponder what had happened.

He turned the last few minutes before the collapse over and over in his mind. No matter what angle he viewed the problem from, he ended up in the same place: a bomb had most likely caused the explosion and anyone could be responsible.

The caterers. Security. A corporate hitman.

As far as he knew, though, only one urgent delivery had been made right before the explosion.

His pretty little courier had smiled wide when she made the delivery. Had she been carrying the bomb? Had she known?

He closed his eyes. If the bomb had arrived with the courier, then the last time he'd seen the package was in Tommy's hands.

He cradled Portia close while they waited for the rescuers to return. Last time, he hadn't been able to save his family and there'd been no one to blame. Just a horrible accident.

If tonight hadn't been an accident... He'd go after the fucking courier and whoever had sent the bomb with every resource at his disposal.

CHAPTER 5

DIZZIE PULLED into her designated parking slot in the lower levels of Tremaine headquarters, almost collapsing from relief when she stopped. The ride home had been slow and stressful. Not due to traffic or others drivers, but because she couldn't get the images of the hotel wreckage out of her head. After a clipped report that she was on her way back, she'd ignored calls from dispatch, afraid she'd burst into tears if she tried to speak.

Metal claws rose from the ground and secured her bike. Her legs wobbled as she stumbled off the bike. She braced her hand on the seat to gain her balance before the system swept her ride into storage racks elsewhere in the garage. The motorcycle disappeared into the building as lasers flickered over the frame, scanning for damage.

Her pulse kicked up as she watched it disappear. Every time, she worried that she wouldn't get her motorcycle—her freedom—back. Being a courier suited her perfectly. She wasn't trained for anything else.

Dispatch and other desk jobs? Her idea of hell.

She slapped her palm on the scanner surface at the

entrance and walked into the lower levels of the building. She made her way on autopilot down the maze of corridors and to the dorms that housed low-level employees like her. When she finally slipped inside her room, she closed the door and leaned against it. She'd never been this happy to be in the safety of her quarters instead of on the road.

Her room was small, the smallest size available, but that was fine with her. The company might feed her and provide housing, but all those costs were rolled into the price to buy out her contract. When kids from the crèche turned eighteen, the company gave them access to their files —where they came from and how they ended up in Tremaine care—and a bill for their upbringing. Until Dizzie earned the credits she needed, the company owned her, body and soul.

Well, not so much her soul, but only because they hadn't figured out how yet.

She hung her jacket on a hook by the door and dropped into the chair in front of a small computer monitor. All she wanted was to go to bed and put her best-worst day behind her, but business came first.

Logging into her bank account, she moved quickly though the passwords and biometric scans until she got to the account screen. She stared at the deposit notice for the payment and the bonus in her account with mixed feelings. It was one of the largest payments she'd ever received, but the excitement she'd normally feel was muted by the terrible accident at the hotel.

"Just take the money," she muttered and started transferring funds around.

The bulk of tonight's earnings went to her corporate debt. It might take her years, but she'd buy her freedom or die trying. She may have spent her first twenty-three years indentured to Tremaine, but she wasn't going to spend her whole life here.

The remaining credits were spread out across a number of secondary accounts. Basic living expenses—like the clothes stacked haphazardly on the other chair against the wall and the rainbow of nail polish bottles on the dresser—she paid out of her account at Tremaine Banking. Next, she replenished the credit sticks she used for fun money.

The rest she very carefully transferred to the emergency fund she'd created outside the Tremaine system. A shady entrepreneur slash bar owner called the Jack held the account. For a small monthly fee, of course.

Logging off, Dizzie toed off her boots, crawled onto her bed, and flipped on the video screen.

Big mistake. The explosion dominated every channel. Over and over again, the screen showed the damaged structure and the steady stream of stretchers and body bags leaving the building.

Newsies on one channel called it a terrorist attack. On another, they claimed it was a corporate assassination attempt. Chyrons screamed things like "Industrial Espionage Gone Wrong?" and "Will Crash Crash Stocks?" Experts offered "proof" for their pet theories.

That could have been me.

The words looped through her head. The shakes started the moment the reality of the night's events finally hit her. She clenched her fists, but that wasn't enough to stop them.

The voices droned on, listing the famous people at the event—movie stars and corporate bigwigs she hadn't seen. Portia Tremaine and her husband. Killian St. John. With each name, she pictured the crowd in her mind and relived the swirling chaos of the party.

Dizzie wrapped her arms around her middle and focused on Killian. The way she'd seen him—alive.

He'd been even better looking in person. His smile a deadly weapon and his gaze a caress.

Had he been one of the people removed from the building on a stretcher? Or a body bag?

Her stomach roiled. She wrapped her arms tighter around her middle, willing the panic and nausea away.

Killian St. John's family was a big-time investor in the Tremaine Corporation. Surely he'd be one of the first people rescued.

Pounding on her door drew her from her thoughts and the news. "Dammit, Dizzie! Open the door!"

"Alice?" Dizzie unlocked the door remotely. "It's open."

A dark-haired tornado blew through the door and flung herself onto the bed. Alice was Dizzie's best friend and the most persistent person on the planet.

"Are you okay?" she said, her eyes wide.

"Why wouldn't I be?" Dizzie tried to sound normal. She was totally fine, if you ignored the trembling and the so-close-to-dying part of her evening.

"Dispatch said you weren't answering calls. I've been worried sick."

Dizzie leaned against the headboard. "Sorry. Things were..." She searched for words to describe the experience. "Overwhelming."

"What happened?" Alice propped her chin on her hands and stared at Dizzie.

How to explain to someone who hadn't been there? Dizzie didn't want to look too closely at the events of the night. What she had seen on the screens was probably enough to give her nightmares.

"You had a job tonight?" Alice prodded her.

Dizzie nodded. Alice knew about the extra jobs she took on, though probably not exactly how many. Though she might. As Alice was part of Tremaine Security, her job was to know who was doing what and why in the company.

Opposites in practically every way, Dizzie and Alice had maintained their unlikely friendship even when corporate life had taken them in different directions. According to the aptitude test every kid in the corporate orphanage was given at thirteen, Alice was a rule-follower. Her high scores for that and critical thinking had netted her one of the "glamorous" jobs: security.

Dizzie had scored high on balance and problems with authority, abilities that had gotten her assigned as a courier. The job fit her perfectly and she'd never regretted the assignment.

"I had a delivery to the party," Dizzie said. She had to tell someone.

Her friend took a deep breath. "The one in the news?"

"Yeah. I had a delivery for Ms. Tremaine." A vision of Portia in her sparkling blue dress rose to mind. Dizzie squeezed her eyes shut and willed it away.

When she opened her eyes again, Alice was staring at her. Alice quickly blanked her expression and sprang off the bed. Trepidation crawled over Dizzie's skin as her best friend transformed into Tremaine Security Alice.

"Don't say another word." Alice flicked her gaze toward a corner of the room. The corner Dizzie had always suspected held a surveillance camera.

Worry lay heavy in Dizzie's gut as her best friend acknowledged the camera. Her fight or flight instinct kicked in, narrowing her focus and drowning out the shakes. "What's going on, Alice?"

Dizzie pushed off the bed, careful not to make any

sudden moves. She wanted to pace, to shout, to act instead of waiting for an answer. Her fingers curled into her palms, her nails digging in hard enough to hurt.

Alice shifted, slightly changing her angle to the camera. *I'm sorry*, she mouthed to Dizzie.

Sorry? What the hell for?

Dizzie got her answer when Alice raised her wrist to her mouth. "This is Gartner. I've got a possible lead on the explosion at the New Amsterdam Hotel." She paused at whatever was being said in her earpiece.

"One of our couriers, sir." Her gaze met Dizzie's for a split second before she looked away. "On a routine delivery. She might have information we can use."

Well, fuck. Her best friend had just turned her in.

Dizzie struggled to process what was happening. The whole evening was a nightmare she couldn't escape.

No way was she sticking around and waiting for whatever happened next.

Barefoot, Dizzie took a small step backward, moving closer to the door. Not sure what she would do if she got there. Not sure what Alice would do. She'd never beat Alice to the door. Taller, heavier, and highly trained, Alice could take Dizzie down in an instant.

"I can bring her in the morning." Alice frowned at the response she received. "Sir, she's exhausted."

"But, sir—"Alice paled and broke off. "Mr. Tremaine's assistant, sir?" Dizzie's former best friend swallowed hard and nodded at whatever was said next. "Yes, sir. I'll bring her in."

Dizzie inched toward her boots, shoved her feet into them. If she had to run, she didn't want to do it barefoot.

"Yes, sir. We'll wait here for an escort." Alice frowned

and looked at Dizzie again. "I don't think that's necessary, sir. She's just a courier."

Usually, Dizzie hated that phrase. *Just a courier.* If those words got her out of this tonight, she'd never complain again.

Dizzie took another small step toward the door. Just in case.

"Yes, sir." Lips pinched, Alice dropped her wrist but didn't meet Dizzie's gaze.

"What's going on?" Dizzie wanted Alice to explain why she'd turned her oldest friend in.

Alice shoved her hands into her pockets. She hunched her shoulders and looked uncomfortable.

"Portia Tremaine, along with a number of high-level Tremaine Corporation investors, was at the hotel tonight."

Dizzie nodded. She knew this part.

"They're still digging out the rubble of the building's top floor. The security team—and Mr. Tremaine, of course —are very eager to discover what happened. Whether it was an accident or," Alice dragged the word out, "something else."

"All I did was deliver a package. Talk to biz services, check the logs. I wasn't around when the accident happened." Alice still wouldn't meet her eyes and the first tickles of panic colored Dizzie's words. "Why do they need to come get me now?"

Staring at the floor, Alice said, "Someone called in a tip. Said a bomb caused the explosion."

"*A bomb?*"

Alice continued as if Dizzie hadn't spoken. "The tip said it may have been an inside job."

Dizzie swallowed. "Inside what, the hotel?"

Alice didn't answer.

As the silence between them grew, Dizzie finally caught on. "*Me?* They think *I'm* the inside job?"

"They don't want you. They want whoever was responsible. Tell them what you saw and you'll be fine." Alice spoke in a rush, the words tumbling out.

That was when Dizzie knew she was lying. Alice didn't believe it would be fine.

"They'll be here in a few minutes, Diz. Go with them. Don't make a fuss. Don't piss them off with that mouth of yours. They're out for blood right now."

Dizzie didn't want to imagine how eager they were.

"I won't forgive you for this, Alice."

Alice swallowed hard. "I know." Now, finally, she looked at Dizzie. "This is my job, Dizzie. I didn't have a choice."

"OUTSIDE OF THE minor cuts and bruising, you're a very lucky man. However, the muscles around your implant are strained. Rest a few days, keep weight off that leg. That's a small price, I'd say, for saving Portia Tremaine's life." The doctor dropped his voice, aware of the possibility of eavesdroppers.

Killian tried to smile, but it didn't come. He'd saved Portia's life, but he hadn't been able to save Tommy. His remains had been pulled from the wreckage after they'd whisked Portia away to the Tremaine Corporation's private hospital.

They'd brought Killian there too, after he was safely removed from the rubble. In addition to medical care, he'd been offered any damn thing he wanted.

All he wanted was his best friend alive again.

He'd stood with Tommy's parents when the doctors informed them that he'd been dead on arrival. The damage from what Killian believed was a bomb had been extensive.

Each word had been a blow. He'd stood by them as they railed at the doctors, begging for transplants, drugs, even cyber enhancements. Any options that would save their son. Killian understood what they were going through. He'd done the same five years ago.

Though Killian had known the odds of Tommy surviving were slim, the loss hadn't sunk in until Tommy's father had wrapped his arms around Killian and he'd felt the other man's hot tears on his neck.

Killian hadn't lost it then. Wouldn't—couldn't—until whoever was responsible was punished.

No one had told Portia yet. He didn't envy the person who had that task. She was on a floor above him, in the family's private wing.

He couldn't visit. Not yet.

It should have been him. Tommy should have been on the dance floor with his wife. Killian should have been on the sidelines holding the package. His selfishness, his demand to dance with Portia, had destroyed her life.

She'd never forgive him and he didn't blame her.

"Are we done?" Brusque, but he didn't care. Maybe the doctor would write his rudeness off as grief and stress.

Stress—yeah, that was a perfectly valid reason. So was the fact that he hated hospitals. Had hated them ever since he'd woken up an orphan after the accident that had taken his leg.

The doctor frowned. His fingers brushed the screen as he scrolled though Killian's records again and sighed. "Yes," he said slowly. "I'd prefer to keep you for observation in case of concussion. But I imagine there are better places for you to rest and recover. Ones without all the attention from the newsies."

"Perfect." Let him think the paparazzi were the reason Killian didn't want to hang around the hospital.

"Not to mention we could use the bed," the doctor

continued. "They're still bringing in people who were hit by debris. Plus all the lookie-loos who got into traffic accidents from staring at the news when they should have been paying attention to their surroundings."

Killian raised a brow. The hospital was a private one, available only to Tremaine investors, employees, and people who paid dearly for access. "They're accepting outsiders?"

The doctor nodded. "I hate to say it, but it's good PR. And most of the injuries that occurred outside of the building won't require extensive medical assistance."

That made more sense. Tremaine never did anything without a reason.

Though Killian itched to leave, the opportunity to gather information was too good, especially since the doctor was in a chatty mood. "Were many other people injured?" Anyone associated with the big corporations would likely have been taken to private facilities the way he and Portia had been.

Everyone else? Normally, they'd need to make a deal with the devil to get care. Was the courier one of those?

As his head cleared, Killian had decided that if Tommy had been at the center of the explosion, the courier was the most obvious way the bomb had gotten into the building. But why would she do it?

Did it really matter though? If she were responsible for Tommy's death, he would make her pay.

Until then, he hated to think of her battered and bruised, dying in a dark alley. Nobody deserved to die like that.

He frowned. Why the hell was he worried about her? He must have hit his head harder than he'd thought. She was likely some kind of domestic terrorist or corporate assassin.

"A dozen, maybe two," the doctor said. It took Killian a second to remember what he'd asked. "The worst of it was within the hotel itself. As you know," he added.

Yes, he did. Killian pushed back the memories and slipped off the exam table. The pain in his leg caused him to bobble his first step, but he ignored it, pushed through the pain, and steadied himself.

The doctor frowned.

Killian stared back, daring him to say something.

Finally, the doctor dropped his gaze to his tablet. "Do you want a prescription for the pain?"

Hell, yes. His back and shoulder twinged. The strain in his leg where muscle and bone met metal and machinery burned. "A mild one." Killian waited for the usual raised brow, the sternly worded warning.

But there wasn't one. "Good choice." The doctor pressed his palm to a wall-mounted datapad and swiftly keyed in a request. Soft plinks followed. The doctor cleared and locked the screen. He pulled two pills from the dispenser.

"Here." He dropped the small white tablets into Killian's hand. "These should hold you for the next few hours, until you get your prescription filled."

"Thanks, doc." Killian popped them into his mouth and swallowed them dry. There was a lot to do before he visited a pharmacy.

CHAPTER 7

SECURITY HAD ARRIVED QUICKLY. Alice faded into the background when a team of two joined her in Dizzie's room. Two more waited outside. No one stopped Dizzie from grabbing her jacket, but she hadn't been allowed to bring any electronics with her. She hadn't made a fuss, still hoping it would be a quick meeting.

Yeah, that hadn't happened.

Security had tucked her into a cell on the lower levels of Tremaine headquarters. That had been hours ago. When security had first appeared, she'd been glad it was late and no one was around to see her being marched through the halls. She regretted that now. As far as she knew, only security knew her location.

Dizzie shivered. Until tonight, the cells had only been rumors. Tremaine employees whispered about them, but she never knew anyone who'd ever seen them. Until now. Wasn't she the lucky winner.

The cell was about ten feet by ten feet. Smaller than her room, but not by much. It hadn't taken her long to pace from one side to the other. Plas-glass walls kept the space from being claustrophobic, but it also allowed her to see into the cells either side of her and beyond. They were all empty.

The silence was unnerving. She'd pounded on the glass, just to see what happened. Nothing. No one came. She'd bet her savings that there was a camera in the room, maybe even more than one. Thank god she'd only had a sip of champagne—what if she'd had to pee?

Now she sat on a hard mattress, her back against the wall. The room was cold and she was thankful she still had grabbed her jacket. Her nails clicked against the bed frame, a steady rhythm that was the only sound besides her breathing. The flickering light in the hallway was giving her a headache.

She hated being closed in like this. The best thing about being a courier was working outside. Her friends teased her about the freedom of the open road, but they'd never spent hours with the wind rushing past and the world speeding by.

Minutes later—or was it hours?—voices echoed down the hallway and shadows crept along the wall.

Her throat was suddenly dry. Were they coming to let her go? Or was this the start of the interrogation?

Dizzie fumbled with her braids, pulling them out quickly. She finger-combed the loose strands, gathered them into a high ponytail, and quickly twisted the rope into a single thick braid. She'd seen the Ice Queen wear this style once and instead of looking like her normal bitch self, Portia had looked like a badass. Dizzie hoped the style did the same for her.

The shadows drew closer and she couldn't decide how she wanted to face them. When she was leaning against the corner, arms crossed over her chest was her first instinct.

Afraid she couldn't pull off intimidating, badass ponytail or not, she settled on nonthreatening.

So Dizzie perched on the edge of the bed, her feet pressed together, and her hands folded in her lap.

Four people stopped in front of her cell. Two wore Tremaine Security uniforms. Alice wasn't one of them and Dizzie didn't know whether she was relieved or concerned.

The third man was Phillip Tremaine's assistant. He wore the same suit he'd had on for the televised interview, but it looked rumpled now. It had been a long night. Jaw clenched and lips pressed together, the man looked angry. He glared at her and she sat up straighter. Even though Leopold Brunswick was the CEO's right hand, she wouldn't cower. She hadn't done anything wrong.

Her gaze swept to the fourth visitor. Her jaw dropped when she identified him and she was glad she was sitting down.

Killian St. John.

What the hell was he doing here?

Seeing that he wasn't in a body bag sent a rush of relief through her. She mostly ignored it while she tried to make sense of the unlikely quartet.

Security she understood. The CEO's assistant made total sense. But why was Killian St. John here? He should be in the hospital.

Dizzie had clung to the hope that they'd ask her a few questions, realize she didn't have any useful information, and let her go. Alice's warning about an inside job rattled around her brain, poking holes in her confidence. These were the big guns, people who didn't mess around. She swallowed hard.

Brunswick gestured toward the cell. "Is this the courier you saw at the Ocean Wilde Gala, Mr. St. John?"

Killian stared at her for a long moment. Dizzie stood still as he studied her. There was no trace of the flirtatious charmer from the party. No smile, no hint of laughter in his eyes. His expression was grim, his shoulders tense under the dirt- and blood-covered white shirt. His coat and bow tie were gone. Gray dust covered his dark pants and streaked his dark hair.

"Yes, that's her." Killian's voice was as cold as his expression. He and Brunswick shared a look she couldn't interpret.

Brunswick looked away first. He scowled and motioned to security. A guard stepped forward and waved his hand in front of the scanner. The cell door opened with a hiss.

Freedom was so close, but it was an illusion. No way could she elude them all.

She watched them, gaze flicking from one to the next to the next. Brunswick lingered near the open doorway, arms crossed. While one guard stood watch, the one who'd opened the door dragged a chair into the cell. St. John followed him into the glass enclosure, dismissing the guard with a nod.

Even though he was disheveled and covered with debris from the explosion—possibly even wounded—there was no masking Killian's strength and confidence. Or the power he wielded. He stood with his hand on the back of the chair, barely giving her a glance before he turned to the trio outside the door.

"I'll be perfectly fine." His tone brooked no argument.

"I'm sure Mr. Tremaine would prefer I question the suspect," Brunswick said. "He put me in charge of the investigation."

Dizzie would rather talk to Killian than the weaselly assistant. Not that anyone asked her.

"He won't mind if I take this," Killian said. "For Portia and Tommy."

Oh shit, oh shit, oh shit. Were they both dead? Dizzie gulped and gripped her hands tighter. Her knuckles whitened. This was going from bad to worse.

Brunswick and the guards didn't immediately move. "If I have a problem, I'll send for you. As we discussed." Killian's voice carried anger and an undercurrent of violence.

The guards looked from Killian to Tremaine's assistant and back again.

"We'll be right outside." Disapproval and something Dizzie couldn't identify dripped from the assistant's voice.

"The two guards are enough," Killian said. "I'm sure other matters need your attention, given tonight's events."

Leo Brunswick pursed his lips, but said nothing else. Apparently, he wouldn't risk pissing off one of the company's primary investors.

The guards positioned themselves a few feet down the hall on either side of her cell. Brunswick glared at Killian again. Killian looked back with no expression. With a huff, Brunswick tugged on his jacket and retreated out of sight, leaving her alone with Killian.

For the first time since they'd joined her, she understood that the real threat wasn't Tremaine Security. The man in front of her had power, with a capital P.

For all intents, she was alone with one of the most powerful—and handsomest—men on the planet. Under other circumstances—say, not locked in a glass prison—this might be a dream come true.

Instead, the situation was more like a nightmare. Ripples of fear coursed through her system and she struggled to maintain her outward appearance of calm.

Killian flipped the chair around and straddled the seat, resting his arms on its back.

She wasn't taken in by his casual demeanor. Too much blood and dust on his clothes for that.

He sat a few feet from her. His deep brown eyes held anger. Pain. And...was that concern?

Dizzie shivered and struggled not to fidget under his intense gaze.

She looked away, staring into the empty cell to the right while she waited for him to speak.

The guards weren't paying any obvious attention. The assistant had disappeared down the hall. Alone with Killian St. John and no one to advocate for her.

She should have run the first time Alice told her to stay put.

"What's your name?" Hardened steel replaced his usual silky-smooth tones. The urbane rogue she'd interacted with at the gala was gone. In his place was a coldly superior member of the ruling class.

Refusing to be cowed, she lifted her chin and met his gaze. "Dizzie."

"What's your real name?"

Dizzie bit back a snarl. "That *is* my real name. My only name. Check my records." Everyone called her Dizzie. They always had. If she had another name, she didn't think anyone knew it.

He studied her for a long moment. "You were at the gala tonight." A statement, not a question.

She nodded.

He raised a brow.

"Yes," she added, mortified when her voice squeaked.

"Why were you there?"

Dizzie looked over his shoulder. Why was he here, asking the questions she'd expect from security?

Killian repeated the question.

"I had a delivery." She wasn't going to make this easy for him.

"For?"

"The package read Portia Tremaine," she answered, her words clipped. "I delivered it to Portia Tremaine. You were there, you saw." Why was he asking questions he knew the answers to?

Killian tilted forward in the chair, balancing on its legs and the balls of his feet. The move brought him close enough that she could see the fine staples that ran along his brow line and the bits of dust clinging to his hair.

Her lips pressed together. She hated that he'd been hurt. And hated that she hated it.

"Yes, I was there," he ground out. "I'm the only person who seems to remember the mysterious courier who delivered a mysterious package right before the roof came raining down."

Why did everyone keep suggesting she was involved? Outraged and slightly sick to her stomach, she pushed to her feet.

The guards outside her door shifted. Killian raised a hand and they stopped.

"I had nothing to do with whatever happened at the hotel. They told me to deliver a package, so I delivered the package." She wanted to say more, but where to start? Why the hell would she do something to harm Portia Tremaine?

"For the money."

Her eyes flew wide. Crap, she'd said that out loud?

Killian stared at her like she was shit on the bottom of

his shoe. "You received a large payout following the delivery, didn't you?"

Dizzie nodded, too overwhelmed to speak.

"That was an awful lot of money for a single delivery. Money you were excited to receive."

She had been. But not for...for what he was suggesting!

"It could have been anyone!" Oh god, she'd shouted at a major investor. Instead of terror, exhilaration raced through her. Letting lose was freeing.

She took a deep breath. "The package came through Central Business Services. *Everything* goes through biz services. They assigned the delivery to me, but it could have been any of us couriers. Why aren't you talking to dispatch or the people who processed the delivery? Or who it was from?"

"There are ways around any system." Dropping the chair back onto all four legs, he stood suddenly, towering over her.

"I'm a courier." She held her ground and stared up at him. She could use a computer, but she was no hacker. "If I'd had the skills to get around computer systems, don't you think they would have put me in networks instead of on a motorcycle?"

He paused.

"Check with biz services," she snapped. "They'll have a record of the package. A scan, too. Nothing gets delivered to the Tremaines without going through a bunch of damn tests."

Remembering every step required to get a package to the executive levels, Dizzie felt a little better about her odds. But not enough to slow the pace of her rapidly beating heart.

Killian took a step back, giving her some much-needed breathing room.

For reasons she didn't understand, she took a step forward. "Why are you here? Don't they have people for this?"

That damn tabloid-worthy smile crossed his face. "What do you mean 'this'?"

CHAPTER 8

"WHY ARE *YOU* HERE? Why isn't security questioning me?" Dizzie no-last-name punctuated her questions with her hands, drawing Killian's attention to her brightly colored nails. Still red, they looked as pristine and undamaged as they had earlier.

His own were ragged from clawing at the rubble. Tucked away in this cell, she appeared untouched from the night's horror. His anger surged, battling back his grief in the emotional push–pull he'd experienced since the roof's collapse.

Anger, grief, and an inexplicable sense of relief that she was unharmed, which only enflamed his anger higher. Jaw clenched, he waited for her questions to end.

When they finally did, she stared at him expectantly, as though she were waiting for answers. No, not waiting for answers. Demanding them.

It was ballsy, given their difference in station. And in any other situation—even at the gala—he would've found it cute. But not now.

"Why am I here? My family is a major investor in the Tremaine Corporation and that gives me significant access."

She didn't react to that. That was fine. He had plenty of reasons. "Why am I here?" he repeated. "Because I was there."

She didn't speak, but her gulp sounded loud in the quiet room. Good, he was getting to her.

He continued, voice cold. "One of my oldest friends—Portia Tremaine—was injured in the explosion tonight. Her husband, *my best friend*, was killed." He paused, leaning in because he wanted his next statement to receive the attention it deserved. "You killed my best friend. I want you to pay."

His words took the fight out of her and she dropped onto the bed. Her fierce façade crumbled and Killian enjoyed the moment. Maybe now he'd get the answers he needed.

She opened and closed her mouth several times before speaking. "How many people were killed?" Her soft voice lacked the fire of her earlier questions.

Mere curiosity or was she judging the success of her attack?

"I don't know. Does it matter?" He hadn't heard concrete numbers. Only one number mattered to him: two. The two people closest to him had been in that blast. One was dead. The other would never be the same again.

He'd never be the same again.

Dizzie blinked up at him, her big blue eyes glistening with tears.

She looked almost innocent. Was it an illusion?

It had to be. She had delivered a package—a bomb! She was the least innocent person in the room.

"I'm sorry." Her soft apology echoed in the sealed cell.

"Sorry for what?" She had to say it. He needed her to admit that she'd killed Tommy. Wanted to hear her guilty confession so he could get over his stupid fascination with her and get justice.

"I'm sorry for your loss. I know you and Mr. Gilmore were friends." She paused. "The newsies always said how close the two of you were."

Her words struck nerves exposed and raw from the night's events. Pain, rage, and grief gnawed at his insides. He whirled away, needing as much distance from her as the cell could provide.

The urge to punch the glass was strong. He fought it back. All of it. He had to bury it all or he'd never get the answers he needed.

Killian stared unseeing out the glass wall, rebuilding his calm piece by piece until his emotions were back under control. Finally, he was able to face her again.

How could she sit there so calmly when he felt like a caged animal?

He crossed his arms, hiding his fists, and tried to project an image of calm. "Tell me what happened, Dizzie." He used her name deliberately to forge a connection between them. She had to admit what she had done.

Her posture softened and she eased back on the bed. Once her back was pressed against the wall, she drew her legs in close and wrapped her arms around her knees, looking young and vulnerable.

A clever trick or the real her? If he convinced her to talk, he'd know.

The buzz of his phone broke the silence. She tensed. Whatever she might have been about to confess was lost.

Fuck.

"Yeah?" Phone to his ear, he never took his eyes off her.

He studied her, noticing details he'd missed before. Dark circles marred the skin under her eyes. She looked exhausted.

Dammit. He shouldn't care.

"They're coming for the girl." A not-quite-human voice spoke through his phone.

What the hell?

"Who is this? What girl?" Okay, stupid question.

"If you want answers, get her out of there. They're watching you. You're running out of time." The call ended with an abrupt click.

Killian stared at his phone. The caller ID screen was blank. Not unknown. Not blocked.

Just...nothing. He'd never seen that before.

A chill crawled up his spine.

CHAPTER 9

A TAP on the glass made Killian jump. A guard stood in the doorway, watching him closely. "Is there a problem, sir?"

Killian thumbed the phone off and slid it into his pocket. He hoped the cell's cameras had missed the weirdly blank screen.

He forced a smile and lied. "No, it's fine."

Nothing about this situation was fine. He'd barely made it through the worst night of his life. Now he was getting cryptic calls? He was tempted to ignore the warning, but every time he considered it, another shiver of unease ran through him.

"The press looking for a quote." The ever-present newsies made a perfect scapegoat.

He dismissed the guard with a nod. *Scapegoat.* An interesting word.

Why was he getting warned that someone was coming for the courier? Who was coming? Had Dizzie been set up? Could he really trust the voice on the phone?

Too many questions and not enough answers. The mysterious phone call roused his curiosity.

Her story about the package made sense. The Tremaine Corporation was a business and a solidly run one, based on the dividends he received. Of course, there would be a process for delivering packages. He could request the records, check her story.

But for a bomb to make it through the system, someone on the inside had to be involved. And Tremaine Security obviously considered her a person of interest.

He shoved his hands through his hair. Fuck! He wanted answers. Justice. Revenge.

Take Dizzie and run.

If she was innocent, he'd be saving her. And if she wasn't...well, he'd deal with that too.

But run where? And how? Killian had bullied his way into the holding center, but he doubted he'd be able to talk his way out with her.

Two armed guards were the first barrier to getting out of there. They needed a distraction. Or...

Dizzie perched on the edge of the cot, carefully watching him. He dropped into a crouch in front of her. The strained muscles in his hip flared in pain.

"When's the last time you ate?" She wore the same clothes he'd seen her in at the party and looked as grimy as he felt.

She must have been locked up soon after getting home. The explosion had been hours ago. He hadn't stopped for food—wouldn't be able to eat if he did.

Dizzie looked at him warily then shrugged. "I don't know. Yesterday?"

"Have they fed you?" He spoke quietly, not wanting the guards to overhear his half-assed plan.

She laughed bitterly. "They locked me in this room and

left. I don't know how long it's been." Her body radiated suspicion. "Why?"

"You must be starving." It was crazy to think this would work.

She didn't respond.

"*Faint* with hunger?" Killian emphasized the first word. Would she understand what he was asking?

She shrugged in response, her expression asking why he cared.

He wanted to tell her he didn't. That was another lie, though he still didn't understand why her well-being mattered. He stared at her, willing her to understand.

Her eyes widened. Her gaze held a million questions, but he ignored them.

"It's been hours." She collapsed, sliding off the bed and onto the floor gracefully. A perfect landing.

"Help! She's collapsed. I think she hit her head. We have to get her to the clinic. Now!"

Her eyelids fluttered, then she winked and he flashed back to the fun part of the gala.

Killian exhaled, relief replacing some of the tension he'd carried since the bombing. Her acting skills concerned him, but not enough to stay here in the bowels of headquarters. For the moment, she'd chosen to trust him.

Too bad he didn't trust her.

He scooped her up and stood. His hip ached as the metal leg took most of the stress. She might be short, but she was a solid weight in his arms. Not too heavy. Not too light. In his arms, she felt...right.

CHAPTER 10

DIZZIE LAY STILL, trying to wrap her head around her current position in Killian's arms. His arms wrapped around her, creating a sense of safety. Despite the comfort, it was hard to remain limp. Tension rode her body.

After that call, his need to leave had been palpable.

His shirt smelled of dust, blood, sweat, and fear and she shivered. Beneath her cheek, his heart beat loud and strong, but fast. He wanted out of her cell.

At first she hadn't understood why he was asking her questions about when she'd last eaten. It had finally clicked that he *wanted* to her to faint from hunger. She didn't understand why, but if he wanted to get her out of the cell, she was more than happy to play along.

It wasn't as if she trusted him. She didn't. But if it came down to being with Killian outside this box or with security inside it...that wasn't a hard call.

Why was he helping her? Who had called him?

"It could be serious," Killian said, probably to a guard. Opening her eyes now might get them both caught, so she forced her body to relax. It was harder than she expected, probably due to her proximity to Killian.

Killian St. John was holding her! Wait 'til she told Alice... Dammit. She wouldn't be telling Alice anything ever again.

She exhaled slowly to ease the tension from her shoulders and tuned back in to the conversation.

"With head wounds you never know. She needs to be checked out in the clinic immediately."

He used his most arrogant voice to make it less a sentence and more an order.

"Sir, I don't have that authority."

Killian shifted his weight. His chest moved beneath her and his shoulders rolled back, lifting her closer. She pictured how intimidating he looked, covered with visible reminders of the bombing.

The guard didn't say anything, but she imagined she heard him gulp.

"As a major Tremaine investor, *I* authorize the visit." He paused and she imagined he was choosing his words carefully. "She witnessed the explosion that put Ms. Tremaine in the hospital and killed her husband."

Pain coated his words and she swore she felt his heart break beneath her cheek.

"The courier may have information vital to the investigation," he continued. "If she's injured or sick, we may never know the cause of the explosion."

"That, um, that wouldn't be good. Sir."

If she weren't supposed to be unconscious, Dizzie would have laughed at the panic in the guard's voice.

Tense silence filled the air. Dizzie held her breath.

Finally, the guard choked out, "I'm sure it will be fine if

you take her to the infirmary. Wouldn't want anything to happen."

Probably his first command decision. Would he end up in one of these cells for making it?

"Glad we understand each other." That powerful rumble of Killian's voice again. "Which way to the clinic?"

Based on the guard's stuttered directions, they were a few floors below the infirmary level. Was Killian really taking her there?

Killian's weight shifted again and then he was moving. No one else tried to stop them.

Eyes still closed, Dizzie considered what she'd just witnessed—a rare opportunity to observe investor power in action. Impressive.

She'd never understood the people who said power was an aphrodisiac. In her experience, power turned people into assholes. Still, it had been compelling to listen to Killian throwing his power around. For her.

Killian turned left outside the cell, then right, following the guard's directions. The next turns veered from the precise instructions. She was pretty sure Killian was taking random lefts and rights.

She tensed, sure that he wasn't taking her to the clinic. Should she speak up? Leap from his arms?

"I know you're awake." His voice rumbled beneath her cheek.

"Okay." Dizzie didn't open her eyes. Once she did, the reality of the evening would intrude. Until she did, she remained in the space between knowing and not knowing. Safe and unsafe.

"Why are you doing this?" She waited for him to stop, to set her down and demand she walk, but still he carried her. It should bother her, but it didn't.

There was no answer for a long second, his breathing and the echo of his footsteps the only sounds around them. "I don't know."

Her eyes flew open and tilted her head to look up at him. She hadn't expected such honesty. "Was it the phone call?"

He shrugged. Muscles rippled across his chest. Where their bodies touched, it felt…intimate. "The phone call warned me that they were coming for you."

"What?!" *Oh shit. What did that mean?* She struggled in his grasp, until he finally stopped. "Put me down!"

His grip loosened and she slid down his front. The hard strength of his body revved up the part of her that remembered how long it had been since she'd been this close to a guy.

The rest of her, the completely panicked, who's-coming-for-me part, was too busy deciding which way to run.

Once she found her footing, Dizzie stepped back and looked around to get her bearings. They'd stopped in an empty corridor. Multi-colored stripes decorated the walls.

Planting herself in front of one of the walls, she dredged up long-ago memories. It had been a long time since she and the other corporate-raised orphans had played down here.

"Where are we?" Killian asked.

"You don't know?"

He shook his head.

"This was your big plan? Wander aimlessly around the bowels of Tremaine headquarters?" *Save me from clueless rich people.*

"My plan was to get you out of that room. So you're welcome." Killian shoved his hands into his pockets and glared at her.

For some reason she found that hilarious. Dizzie struggled not to laugh. She didn't think he'd appreciate that. Or he'd think she was hysterical.

"I figured once we were clear of the dungeon, you'd lead us out of here." He stood stiffly in front of her, almost daring her to laugh.

Still, he was *almost* asking for directions, so she'd cut him some slack. She gestured to the wall. "See the colored lines? They provide location and directional information. Once I know where we are, I can figure out how to get us out of the building."

Dizzie tugged him into an alcove. "I don't know if there are cameras," she said, pressing close to him. She studied the color coding, air tracing her fingers over the lines and dredging up old memories.

"We're still a few levels below the clinic. It's the red and white stripe." She twisted to look at him. "We're not going to the clinic, are we?"

"We're not going to the clinic."

"Okay, good." Avoiding the infirmary was fine with her. "When we don't show up at the clinic, they'll come looking for us, you know."

Killian didn't respond, but tension radiated off him, filling the tiny alcove around them.

Okay. Fine. She could plan her own rescue.

She focused on all the colors and what they represented.

"Blue is the dorms. They're probably watching for us there. Purple is the main offices. Definitely not going there." A handful more colors and matching locations and none of them presented a good option. Except...

"Green it is," she murmured.

"Where does green go?" Killian asked.

His breath fluttered over her nape, caressing the

exposed skin. She exhaled slowly and reached deep for her focus. "Green will get us out of the building." She grimaced. It wouldn't be pretty. "Let's go. The sooner we're out of here, the sooner I can go my way and you can go yours."

She'd barely stepped into the corridor when Killian grabbed her elbow and pulled her back into the alcove. Not expecting the move, she stumbled into him, hands pressed against his chest to stop her momentum.

Do not lean into him, Dizzie.

Proximity short-circuited her brain. "What are you doing? We need to go!"

With his free hand, Killian tilted her chin up to meet his gaze. "You can't seriously think I'm letting you out of my sight."

It took her a moment to realize he'd meant to intimidate her. Dizzie laughed.

They were on her turf now, in the halls she played in as a child. Down here, his glower was cute but ineffective.

"What's so funny?"

"Nothing." She settled her hands on her hips. "Let me go. I'll disappear. No muss, no fuss. You can focus on who actually sent the bomb."

He shook his head before she stopped speaking, his lips pressed together in disapproval. "Not going to happen. I didn't rescue you from that cell to let you disappear. You have answers I need."

Answers? "I told you everything I know."

"I don't believe you. I'm not letting you go until I do." His voice had taken on that investor imperiousness again.

Dizzie stepped backward. She'd been wrong. It wasn't hot—it was actually kind of scary. If she made a break for it, could she lose him?

She knew how to get out, but Killian still had a grip on

her elbow. She could hurt him, but that would only get her in more trouble. Better to make him want to be rid of her.

"Say we do get out of the building. Where are we going?" She tugged her arm free.

He opened his mouth. Closed it.

"Shit. You don't know, do you?" She was sure he was going to deny it. But he didn't.

"I hadn't thought that far. Getting you out of the building was my top priority." Killian swiped a hand through his hair, briefly exposing an angry red cut before his hair settled over it again.

Some of her frustration evaporated. She was running on fumes and wasn't injured. He had been in the middle of the collapse at the hotel. Dizzie was impressed that he was thinking and speaking at all.

Still, that didn't solve their problem. "Some rescue this is."

Killian flinched like she'd hit him. Then he pulled his phone out of his pocket and stared at it, as if willing it to ring. "Look, I was expecting him," he waved the phone in emphasis, "to call again and provide more instructions. We need to get out of here."

"Fine. I can get us out. Follow me. And do exactly what I tell you to."

This time when Dizzie stepped out of the alcove, he let her go. She took off, following the faded green stripe on the wall.

She didn't look to see if he followed. His footsteps on the floor behind her said he was.

Memories rushed back as she led them deeper into the depths of the building, the rights and lefts almost automatic.

His long legs brought him even with her in no time. "How do you know where to go?"

"I grew up in these hallways." Dammit, why had she said that?

"In the hallways?"

"Playing in them," she clarified. "All of us did."

"Ah." He said it like a lightbulb had gone off in his head. "You grew up in the corporate orphanage. How did you end up there?"

Dizzie flinched. She didn't like to talk about her childhood with outsiders—or anyone, really. They asked invasive questions like that one, never realizing their curiosity picked at open wounds.

"Orphan, orphanage." Seemed self-explanatory to her.

He must have heard the warning in her tone. His next question wasn't rude, just stupid. "You're sure you know where you're going?"

"Yes, we're getting close to the exit."

Even if the signs didn't tell her where she was, her nose did. Couldn't he smell it?

There was only one exit that was never covered by guards and had limited cameras.

Waste disposal.

CHAPTER 11

THEY KEPT to the green route Dizzie remembered, rounding two corners before the questions started.

"What is that smell?" The words sounded harsh in the eerie quiet of the hallways.

She didn't answer right away. She was too busy trying to block her nose. "Lots of people."

"We're heading *toward* people?"

"Not exactly." Oh, was he going to be surprised when they got there. "We're almost there."

"Almost where?" His voice was thick as if he was holding his nose.

"Shhh!"

He grumbled and she smiled. Who knew that bossing around an investor would be this much fun?

Though the questions stopped, she heard him thinking loud, loud thoughts.

A lifetime of tabloid stories hadn't prepared her for the real Killian St. John. The arrogance, sure. Exactly as expected. Good looks that grime from the bombing couldn't hide? The only surprise was that he was even better looking in person. But the willingness to follow her lead was completely unexpected.

They turned the final corner and she stopped. "Stay here," she whispered. "I'll make sure it's clear."

"I'm coming with you," he insisted.

She shook her head. "You don't know what you're looking for. Or where to hide while you do."

She did. Or she had. Dizzie ran to the end of their short corridor. The space opened up exactly the way she remembered.

Deep in the basement, a complicated series of bins and conveyors collected the building's trash and carried it to the landfill. Those transfer bins were her escape plan.

The trams ran like clockwork, automatically controlled from elsewhere in the building. Security monitored the area —sort of—but never paid close attention. Corporate espionage was a huge concern for the company. The trash was searched and sorted before it reached this point. Not to mention, the smell was a strong deterrent.

She watched the system, silently counting the timing of the transfer for two full cycles. Nothing had changed.

She returned to their hiding place.

Killian was practically shaking with impatience. "Where were you?"

"Making sure we don't get killed. C'mon."

Retracing her steps, she led him to the edge of the platform.

He paled as he caught on to her plan quicker than she'd expected.

"We're going out with the trash?" he asked with a gagging noise.

"You didn't have a better idea," she whispered, then shushed him again as he began to object.

She grabbed Killian's hand. He stiffened, but didn't pull away. If he had, she'd have left his sorry ass to face Tremaine Security alone.

"Leaving the building this way is tricky," she warned. "We need to time the jump perfectly. There's a narrow window of time after one train leaves and before the next one arrives."

His grip softened and his fingers curled around hers.

The synth-skin bandages that covered his palm were rough against hers. The artificial skin was intended for quick fixes. Doctors could heal wounds easier, but it took longer.

Was the rest of him as banged up as his hands? She rubbed her thumb over the back of his hand. She meant it as a comfort, but when he flinched, she regretted it.

Keeping her grip as businesslike as possible, Dizzie leaned close. "We need to get over there," she said, pointing across the tracks, "quickly and quietly."

The rattle-rattle of the next cart got louder. They didn't have long.

"C'mon!" She tugged his hand and raced forward. Thankfully, he followed without hesitation.

She ran toward the tracks and stopped at the edge. Killian pulled level with her.

It was all coming back to her. "Steady. We have to let the first one go by."

The incoming tram whizzed by, nearly smothering them with the stench. Her stomach clenched.

"Oh god, that's awful." Her hold on Killian strained as he leaned away from her and puked over the side and into a bin down below. "I should take you back to the cell for this," he rasped.

He sounded so traumatized that she struggled not to laugh. "I doubt you could find your way back," she teased.

Sobering, she studied the tracks again. As soon as the outgoing tram raced by, she started counting. "One Tremaine sucks, two Tremaine sucks, three Tremaine sucks." She chanted under her breath, the rhyme and the rhythm familiar and soothing. She and her friends had yelled it when they snuck down here to play.

"What are you saying?" he asked.

Without breaking the pattern, she squeezed his hand to silence him. She passed twenty-nine and stepped to the edge. "Okay, now!"

They jumped.

Killian hesitated, but she was already moving. Her momentum pulled him down with her.

Oof! Not the best landing or the softest, but since they ended up inside the tram the way she planned instead of under it, she considered it a win.

The smell, though, was worse close up. Rancid food and things she didn't want to think about.

Releasing Killian's hand so she could ready herself for the next step, she missed the contact as soon as it was gone.

"We need to get to the side of the car." She spoke loud enough to be heard over the rattle of the tracks.

"We have to go through the *garbage?*" Killian gagged.

Oh, sweet spoiled rich boy.

It took both hands to work her way toward the edge of the metal car, practically swimming through the garbage. The surface shifted constantly and crossing it required slow and cautious movements.

With each move, Dizzie tried not to think of all the horrible things under her. As kids, they'd come up with the scariest possibilities. Bodies of Tremaine enemies had been the worst.

She shuddered. It still was.

No signs marked the transition from Tremaine headquarters to garbage tunnel, but the sounds around them changed. "I think we're outside of headquarters," she told him.

They'd made it to the outside edge of the car.

"What now?" Killian was inches away from her. Like her, he'd crawled on his hands and knees over the rotting mess, his distaste written on his face.

She was surprised and impressed how he did what needed to be done.

"It'll dump us in a landfill a couple minutes away from headquarters. We have to jump when the tram starts to tilt. We need to clear the rest of the garbage, instead of being buried under it."

"Are you sure about this?" His disgruntled tone told her exactly how much he disliked her plan.

"Too late now." She scanned their surroundings, terrified at the possibility that there had been changes to the system. It would suck if the dump had been concreted over. "On three."

The car passed a familiar landmark. "Get ready," she told her reluctant shadow.

She slid into position, her hands on the railing and her feet braced best she could.

"One." With a deep breath, she drew her legs up and perched on the metal rail in a deep squat.

Next to her, Killian copied her movements with a groan of pain. No time to ask if he was okay. They had to move quickly.

"Two."

She tensed.

"Three!"

Something caught her eye as she sprang into action. A ledge.

Making minute adjustments to her body position—the way she did on the bike—Dizzie aimed for it instead of the garbage below.

The ledge was farther away than she'd anticipated. Her hands slammed onto the flat surface and she scrambled for purchase. Her fingers dug into the shelf and her nails scratched along it as she started to slip.

Killian hit the garbage pile with a curse. The pounding of her heart and the rush of blood in her ears drowned out whatever he said.

Abs and arms straining, she pulled her knees toward her torso. She had to stop the rocking that threatened to send her into the dump below.

"We were supposed to get out through the garbage." Killian was pissed.

Dizzie couldn't blame him. She'd changed plans on the fly.

She glanced down. He'd landed on top of the unstable pile a few feet below her. Judging by all his cursing, he must be scrambling to stay on the surface.

"The plan's changed," she yelled. "You can still get out. Turn left and head toward the wall."

Dizzie tried to indicate the direction with her head without swinging again. "The door in the corner will lead you to an alley a few blocks from Tremaine headquarters."

His glare was like daggers. Hanging from a narrow ledge above a massive pile of garbage was infinitely safer than being near him at the moment.

"I'm supposed to get *you* out of here." That wasn't worry in his voice.

"I can get out from here," she called. "Thank you for getting me out of the cell, though."

A safe place to sleep was her priority. As soon as she got out of here. Tomorrow she'd focus on proving her innocence.

"You're not leaving me here!" His roar echoed in the space around them.

Definitely time to go.

"You'll be fine. Thanks for your help!" She infused her voice with perkiness. At the same time, she threw an elbow over the ledge and tried to pull herself up.

"Not. Going. To. Happen." His voice came from below her. Around her, the wall rattled with each word, generating bigger and bigger ripples that rocked the ledge.

By the last word, she'd lost all her progress and hung by her fingernails.

Shit!

Her arms trembled. If the metal wall didn't stop shaking soon, no way could she hang on, much less pull herself back up. "Stop it! I'm going to fall."

"That's the point," he growled.

Was he trying to get her killed? Okay, the fall wouldn't kill her. Probably. "Why are you doing this to me?"

"I'm not letting you out of my sight until I get answers about what happened at the party."

"I told you before, I don't have any answers." Her throat was sore from shouting. Muscles straining, she couldn't hold on much longer. "Just let me go. I'll disappear far, far away."

"It's me or Tremaine Security. The longer I have to stay in this pit, the more willing I'm gonna be to pick security."

"I can stay up here all night." She was such a liar. She had minutes left. Maybe.

"Get down here now or I'm coming up and getting you."

"You and what army?" The words slipped out. *Dammit, Dizzie!* Taunting the angry man in the garbage dump wasn't a smart move.

Something wrapped around her ankle. She screamed.

She tried to jerk her leg away, but whatever had a grip on her wasn't letting go.

"Get it off." She shook her leg. "Get it off."

Laugher, rich and deep.

"Why are you laughing? Get it off me!" She kicked wildly again.

"I told you I wasn't letting you go." His voice was gruff.

"That's you?"

"What did you think it was? Some kind of garbage monster? That only happens in the vids." Laughter made his voice sexier. Damn him.

Dizzie tamped down the flicker of attraction. She was in the middle of a nasty garbage dump, running for her life. She didn't have time to find Killian St. John massively appealing.

Killian grabbed her other ankle and pulled.

Poof, attraction gone.

She had to let go or she'd hurt herself.

"I hate you," she hissed as she released her death grip on the ledge.

"Wait!" Dizzie flailed in midair as Killian's hand let go of her ankle.

She landed hard on the garbage. Her head bounced on something hard under the pile and everything went black.

CHAPTER 12

THE SMELL of garbage hit Dizzie in the face. "What the hell?" She reared back, her body sinking into something squishy, but the smell followed her. The smell...was *her*! "Gross!" Exhaling through her mouth, she tried to get a breath of fresh air, but everything was tainted.

"You're awake."

Startled, Dizzie looked toward the voice. Killian sat to her left. Beyond him, city lights sped by. They were in a vehicle, heading...somewhere.

"What happened? Where'd you get the car?" The last place she expected to be was in a spaceship-sleek car with Killian St. John.

"You hit your head when you fell. I got you out and had the car meet me at our location." He recited the facts, but she was sure he was leaving things out. In fact...

"I hit my head when you *made* me fall, you mean." Her voice rose in outrage. She remembered losing her grip and falling toward the garbage. Nothing after that, though.

She studied his profile. Hands on the wheel, he held himself rigid.

"I didn't mean for you to fall. Honest."

He sounded sincere, so she moved on. "Where are you taking me?"

"Does it matter?" He glanced over at her. In the flickering streetlights, he looked as tired as she felt.

Did it? Well, yes. And no.

"Yeah, it does." The whole night had spun out of control and she needed to take some back.

Killian slid his thumb over the touchscreen on the steering wheel and put the car on self-drive. He shifted to look at her.

She tensed. All she'd wanted was a simple answer. Instead, he studied her like a bug under a microscope.

Dizzie shifted her gaze and studied the road in front of them. It looked as though they'd left Seattle proper and entered the outskirts of town. Given the city's sprawl, it didn't look all that different. Skyscrapers filled the horizon, reflecting the glow of the early morning light.

"From the moment I saw you at that party, I knew you'd be trouble."

His words hit like a blow. "Whatever." She bit her lip and stared straight ahead.

"Not in a bad way. Well, not mostly."

"Wow, you're a real smooth talker." The words slipped out, but she didn't care. She should've stayed at headquarters. Whatever the corporation wanted from her couldn't hurt this bad.

She attempted to relax into the cushy passenger seat with its high-tech filler, but she was too tense. Fingers laced to keep from lashing out, she turned to look out her window. She needed out of this car. It was too confining, too confusing to be enclosed in here with him.

She rested her cheek against the seat. If she could smell

anything over the reek of garbage, she bet it would smell like real leather. Or money. Cars this nice didn't use synthetic leather. They didn't use synthetic anything.

That perfectly described the differences between them.

Neither of them attempted to fill the silence between them.

Until Dizzie gasped.

Killian rolled up to an ornate set of gates.

She recognized the entrance to Killian's home immediately. If she hadn't, the throngs of newsies outside it would have clued her in. Never in a million years had she imagined they'd end up here.

His purchase and restoration of the stately old home had made headlines for months. The finished product had been featured on at least two architecture sites.

"This isn't a good idea." She pressed back in her seat. She was dying to see inside, but if the newsies saw her, the corporation would soon know where she was.

Would they recognize her? If they didn't, the men and women clustered around the gate would dig for information. Anyone seen in public with Killian St. John was subjected to intense public scrutiny. The thought of people focusing on her life made her skin crawl. Dizzie envied him his wealth and power, but she didn't envy him the lack of privacy.

Killian's sigh echoed in the small space. "I was hoping they wouldn't be here yet." He pressed a button on the dash.

Ejection seats? Her tired brain conjured up the ridiculous thought. Then again, they wouldn't be out of place on this surreal day.

Instead of shooting the two of them into the air to who knew where, the windows darkened.

"Pretty nifty trick." The automatic window tinting was some straight-up cool tech.

"Thanks." His reply carried a hint of amusement.

She leaned closer to the glass, studying the slightly darker surroundings outside, then pulled back. "Can they see in?"

"No," he said. "Not yet."

"What do you mean?" she asked.

"The cat and mouse games never end. You figure out a way to block them, they pay big credits for workarounds."

That made her anonymity seem downright attractive. "Sounds awful. You run them over?"

"Not yet," he repeated.

She laughed. If this were her life, she'd be damn tempted. "Are they here all the time?"

He shrugged and focused on steering through the cluster of people outside.

The gate opened just wide enough for Killian to steer the car through. The newsies pressed forward, trying to squeeze in through the nearly nonexistent space between the car and the gate. Forget her running them over—they seemed willing to do it to themselves.

The crowds outside stressed her out, so she focused on Killian's hands. He handled the steering wheel with skill, his movements strong and confident. Steady. He'd be masterful on a bike.

Who was she kidding? He'd be magnificent no matter what he did with those hands.

Once they were through the gates, she relaxed enough to take in their surroundings. No way was she going to miss this. Her deliveries tended to be in downtown Seattle. She rode by apartment buildings and slums, high rises and penthouses. Never out here.

She strained to take it all in. "Can I roll down the window?" Her finger was already on the button.

"No."

Dizzie stifled a laugh. She hadn't expected running for her life to be fun.

Though the driveway was short, it curved enough to create the illusion of being set farther back from the road. The corner lot and the landscaping around the drive helped. There were more trees on either side of this car than she usually saw in a week in downtown Seattle.

Killian passed the side of the building and curved around to the back. The drive sloped downward into an underground garage that looked newer than the house. The car slowed and he pressed a remote on the sun visor—garage door opener, probably—and the car rolled forward again. "We're going in through the garage."

She didn't see much as he pulled in. The garage was smaller than the one at Tremaine headquarters, but that wasn't a fair comparison. The company was a huge multinational.

As soon as they were under cover and the garage door closed, she rolled down her window.

Dizzie whistled. They drove past a number of cars. Big cars, little cars. Cars she'd never seen before. She wasn't a car girl. Bikes had always been her thing, but his garage could change her mind.

Then she saw it. "Holy shit."

Killian pulled into a parking spot and she jumped out of the car. Momentum carried her past a half-dozen cars. Awe carried her past the rest until she stood in front of it. *Her.* Nearly four hundred pounds of gleaming metal and high-tech components.

Her body vibrated with barely contained excitement.

Killian stopped next to her, but she couldn't tear her eyes away from the masterpiece. "Is this what I think it is?" Her voice was quiet, almost reverent.

"The Turbosmith Excel." He whispered back, amusement threaded through his words.

"Damn." One syllable became three.

The motorcycle was top of the line, extremely expensive, and, next to its owner, the most beautiful thing she'd ever seen. Drawn to the sleek silver lines, she stretched her hand out. Snatched it back. This work of art deserved more respect. "Can I touch her?"

Killian let out a strangled sound.

"I wasn't going to hurt her." It was insulting he'd think that. She shoved her hands in her pockets.

"No, no, it's fine. I wasn't expecting that," he croaked.

Tearing her attention from the bike took an act of will, but she checked to make sure he was okay.

Slouched against a support post and despite the ruined suit and dregs from the dump, Killian looked every inch the rich playboy. She'd seen that damn amused half-smile in countless tabloid stories.

Screw him. He could afford toys like this, but to her they were dreams. Ones that appeared in celebrity lifestyle vids or billboards ads. She wasn't about to pass this opportunity up.

She stepped closer to the motorcycle. To the Excel. A bike this beautiful deserved to be called by her proper name.

Aware that she was just as grimy after their misadventure as Killian, she traced the curves of the motorcycle in the air, her finger hovering just above the sleek machinery. "Aren't you a beauty," she cooed. "So damn pretty."

CHAPTER 13

WATCHING Dizzie trail her fingers over the bike's shiny finish was the hottest thing Killian had ever seen. He imagined her fingers stroking over his skin. His metal.

He shifted uncomfortably, his pants tighter than they had been minutes ago. This attraction was damned inconvenient.

Don't be stupid, Killian. She might appreciate a well-made machine, but that didn't mean she felt the same about cybernetic enhancements. His limited experience over the last few years had proven the opposite.

"Leave the damn bike alone," he said with more bark in his voice than he'd intended. "We need to get inside."

"In a minute." She ignored him. Again.

Being ignored was a new feeling, one he didn't like. His cars and other toys usually enhanced his appeal. They didn't negate it.

Jealous of a fucking motorcycle. That was a new low.

Killian straightened and stepped away from the concrete pillar. He battled back the urge to pull her away from the motorcycle, to pull her to him.

"Can I take her for a ride?" Her blue eyes pleaded with him.

An image of her riding him flickered in his primitive brain. Desire flooded his system, nearly short circuiting his ability to form rational thoughts. She was going to be the death of him.

She nearly had been.

That sobered him the way nothing else could have. "No. We've got to go."

That got her attention. She tipped her head back and turned those eyes on him. "You said we'd be safe here."

"We are." Probably.

"C'mon." Killian grabbed her wrist and tugged her away from the motorcycle. She followed, taking one last look.

Then Dizzie tugged her arm free and he let it drop. Gesturing for her to walk in front of him, he herded her toward the elevator that would take them upstairs. To his home.

Built in the early 1900s, the house had originally been a single-family home. In the intervening years, it had also been a bed-and-breakfast and then a bookstore with a small café on the first level. It had sat empty for years, its old-fashioned charm turning brittle and worn. Though his realtor, as well as Portia and Tommy, had tried to talk him out of the purchase, the upper floors and the view had called to him.

The elevator from the garage to the home had been designed to hold six to eight people, but now, it felt too small, too close with just the two of them. The ride felt as if it took hours and Killian regretted not taking the stairs. Surely the stairwell wouldn't be as oppressive.

The sudden rush of nerves surprised him. He'd brought women here before, rarely and only after long internal debates. Yet when he needed a safe place to hide the courier, home had been the first location that came to mind. That was...concerning.

Still struggling to understand why he had brought her here, Killian was slow to exit the elevator behind Dizzie.

The first floor held his office, the library, and the formal dining room. The middle floor currently served as storage. The top floor, though, was a masterpiece.

The former servants' quarters had been given new life. His architect had removed most of the walls to create one large apartment, with three spacious bedrooms and a state-of-the-art kitchen, as well as a variety of other living spaces. The elevator opened into the living room, with views out over the city.

"This is amazing." Dizzie stopped abruptly and stared out the windows.

Warmth rushed through him. Pride in his home, he assured himself. "Thank you."

Tommy and Portia had said he was nuts when he'd bought the old building. He had his pick of places to live in the city, but the high-tech metal-and-glass towers left him cold.

He still wasn't sure if he'd chosen this one or if it had chosen him. Maybe it was the old brick exterior or the price or the distance from the city center. Whatever it was, he'd spent a small fortune updating the interior while maintaining the original fixtures, hand-carved woodwork, and ornate fireplaces. He loved it.

She crossed the room to the wall of windows. "This is some view."

"Yes, it is." What the hell was he doing, wanting to show off his home like she was a guest? She was his... He exhaled sharply and crossed the room to stand by her. He had no idea what she was, except here.

Perched on a hill, the house overlooked the city in all its chaotic glory. The view was better at night, when neon signs painted the buildings in rainbow-colored light and tail-lights turned the roads into ribbons of red.

Only his bedroom had a better view. Killian swallowed hard. It was folly to think of her and his bedroom.

"I didn't bring you here to admire my home. We need to continue our conversation."

"You don't know how lucky you are, do you?" she admonished without looking away from the window. "I bet you never take the time to appreciate all this. The opportunities you have. The freedom."

The last was added in a whisper.

He wouldn't have heard her, wouldn't have seen the puff of condensation on the window, if he hadn't been at her side.

"You're wrong." He appreciated it. Had since the accident.

What she saw as freedom, he sometimes saw as chains. Duty and fear and the past bound him so tightly he might never escape. The urge to share was strong, but he buried it deep like everything else.

None of which he would ever share with the woman who had killed his best friend.

With anyone.

That was what she did to him. She drew him in until he ignored his best interests and his common sense in order to get closer to her.

He needed to get away from her, if only for a little while, to rebuild his armor and recommit to his plan.

"We need to talk," he repeated. "But I don't want you—us—ruining my furniture with this stink." Their clothes were coated with reminders of the garbage dump and the smell returned with a vengeance. "I'll have someone show you where you can clean up."

CHAPTER 14

"HOLY CRAP!" Dizzie blurted like an idiot.

Killian's housekeeper glanced around the guest bathroom. "Impressive, isn't it?" Her smile was serene and the look in her dark eyes was friendly. Dressed in a stylish pantsuit and with her gray hair in a pixie cut, she didn't look like the housekeepers in the vids.

"Um, yeah." That was one word for it. *Huge* was another. The bathroom was bigger than her entire quarters at Tremaine.

It was pretty, too. Not girly pretty. More like everything-matches-but-isn't-tacky-and-must-be-super-expensive pretty.

Even if she weren't covered in garbage, Dizzie would be extremely out of place.

"You can clean up in here," the housekeeper said kindly. "Take your time. There's a robe behind the door and a selection of loungewear in the bathing area. Use whatever you need. Leave your clothes outside the door and I'll..." she paused, nose wrinkling. "I'll see that they're taken care of."

Dizzie's cheeks burned. She smelled bad and, from

what she could see in the bathroom mirror, looked worse. "Thank you, Mrs. ...ah..."

"Call me Elsa, dear," she said. "All Mr. Killian's friends do."

Should she tell the other woman that she and Killian weren't friends? No, that would make this whole situation more awkward.

"Okay. Thank you, Elsa."

The woman smiled and left, closing the door behind her. Leaving Dizzie alone in a room that probably cost more than she'd earn in her lifetime. Her circumstances had changed so fast—too fast—and Dizzie found it hard to catch her breath.

She washed her hands multiple times and swished her mouth with water. Finally she felt almost human and calm enough to take in her surroundings.

In addition to the sink and a gleaming toilet, the bathroom contained a shower and the largest tub she'd ever seen. The white porcelain and shiny fixtures gleamed in the light, straight out of a homes-of-the-rich-and-famous profile.

The tub called to her.

Killian's housekeeper said she could use this room. But she hadn't meant the tub too. Had she?

No. She should shower. It would be quicker.

Before her internal debate escalated, Dizzie turned on the water for the tub. The old-fashioned fixtures flummoxed her for a moment while she tried to adjust the water temperature. The dorms didn't have fancy bathtubs. She wiggled her fingers under the faucet and finally managed to get the water a few degrees below scalding.

Deciding she'd left good manners and probably self-preservation far behind, she opened cabinet doors. Bottles of bubble bath and other toiletries neatly lined the shelves.

She grabbed a bottle of shimmery orange liquid labeled "citrus blossom." She opened the bottle and sniffed.

Oh, it was perfect!

She tipped half the bottle into the water, laughing in delight when it foamed into fluffy bubbles.

Breathing in orange-scented air, she dropped her jacket on the floor. She kicked her boots off, leaving them in a haphazard pile next to her jacket.

She toed off her socks and braced for cold against her feet. They met warm tile instead and she sighed. A girl could get used to this.

While the tub filled, she stripped down to her bra and underwear, feeling too exposed to take off all her clothes, and turned on the shower. There was no way she was soaking in that tub with any trace of the garbage dump still on her.

Adjusting the temperature was easier this time. She grabbed the citrus blossom bottle and stepped under the water. It was like being caught in the Seattle rain, but this water was warm and welcoming. Unweaving her braid, she tilted her head back to let the water soak in, then poured the bath soap into her hands. She lathered up her hair and body, grateful to smell something other than the sour stench of garbage.

She rinsed and stepped out, worried that the tub would overflow while she was in the shower. Stepping carefully so she didn't slip, Dizzie crossed to the tub and turned off the water.

With a death grip on the railing, she climbed the two steps that led up to the tub and dipped a toe into the water.

Perfect.

Steps led down into the tub as well. Water covered her ankles, then her knees. She lowered herself the rest of the way until her butt hit the tub floor. She rested her head against the water-warmed porcelain, leaning against the ledge.

The warm water and quiet room were unbelievably peaceful. She'd love to stay here forever. But she couldn't. Places like this weren't made for people like her. Orphans. Couriers. Murderers.

Her breath caught in her chest. Killian thought she was a murderer. And maybe he was right.

Ever since she'd seen the news, she'd tried to keep the delivery separate from the bombing in her mind. They were the same thing, she knew that now.

Everything she'd told him had been the truth. All she had done was deliver a package, the same way she'd done for the last eight years. She never knew what was in them, only where to take them and when the deadline was. She'd delivered thousands of packages and parcels and whatever else the Tremaine Corporation needed delivered.

This was the first time anyone had been hurt by it.

The images she'd seen on the big screen right after her delivery replayed like a sideshow. The destruction and the faces of the people who'd been there. She still didn't know how many people had been injured—had been killed!—because of her.

Reality hit, washing over her. The sob burst out of her with a wail.

Dizzie pulled her knees up and wrapped her arms around her legs. The water sloshed around her as she rocked back and forth, making no effort to keep the tears under control.

Where did she go from here? Should she turn herself in?

If she were a better person, that was what she would do.

But during those hours in the cell, the walls had closed in on her. If she turned herself in, it would surely be worse.

And what about whoever had sent the bomb? Dizzie stopped rocking and sat up, leaning back against the tub. She sniffled hard and willed the tears to stop. What about the actual bomber? If she was in custody, would they stop looking?

Of course. Nothing in all her years at the company indicated they would do anything else. They had a culprit, no need to do more.

Why should she give up her freedom when there was someone out there who had done much, much worse?

"What do I do?" she said aloud. Self-sacrifice wasn't her style. She'd carry guilt from the delivery forever, but she wouldn't carry the blame. Survivors like Killian and Portia wouldn't see the distinction.

She dropped her head back onto the rim of the tub. So how did she find the person behind the package?

Alice was right. It had to be an inside job. No way had someone gotten that package through Business Services without assistance.

Her eyes drifted shut as the water and the bubbles pulled her deeper under their spell and twenty-four hours without sleep caught up with her.

Half awake, half asleep, Dizzie thought she heard her name.

The rap on the door startled her. She jerked and water sloshed around the tub.

"You okay in there?"

Even muffled by the door, Killian's voice caused her warm and relaxed muscles to tense.

"Yeah, I'm, uh, fine," she called out. Her voice was throaty from her crying jag.

No response. Maybe she'd imagined him.

She closed her eyes and the soft swish of the water and the crinkle of popping bubbles worked their magic again.

"You've been in there a long time. Do you need anything?" The door swung open.

Dizzie squeaked and slid down until her chin brushed the water's surface and the bubbles provided camouflage.

"Oh! Sorry." Killian cleared his throat, but remained in the doorway. "I didn't realize you were still in the bath."

She appreciated that he turned away from both the tub and the mirror. "Sorry. I..." With no idea what to say, she trailed off.

Awkwardness hung in the air. An unexpected sense of intimacy lay beneath it.

"Do you need anything?" he asked again.

She was nearly naked and the hottest man she'd ever seen was a few feet away. His hair was damp and he'd changed into jeans and a shirt that emphasized his physique.

Did she need anything? Him. In the tub. With her.

Embarrassed by the direction of her thoughts, she tore her gaze from him and cast around for something to request.

"Elsa mentioned cleaning my clothes? I've been wearing the same ones since they detained me. They've seen better days." Dizzie wasn't sure they were even salvageable, but they were the only clothes she had right now.

Killian didn't respond.

Oh god. She'd asked Killian St. John to do her laundry. She'd fully submerge if she thought it would do any good. "Never mind," she mumbled.

"This pile?" He pointed to the filthy clothes she'd scattered on his pristine bathroom floor.

She nodded. "And, um, these too." Before she could convince herself it was another bad decision, Dizzie flicked open the front clasp of her bra and shrugged out of it.

Her movement shifted the bubbles, turning her camouflage into a peekaboo show. She kept an eye on the door, but he acted like a perfect gentleman. Slipping her panties down her legs was more difficult. Sudden moves would send a tsunami of water over the tub's edge, flooding the floor, and leaving her more exposed.

She stretched her arm out over the tub, her underwear a wet, pathetic pile of white fabric in her hand.

Killian stepped into the room. Tension met humidity, thickening the damp, orange-scented air, making it hard to breathe.

The once-perfect water was now too warm as her body overheated. Her heartbeat grew louder. Surely he could hear it. Color flooded her cheeks.

If Killian experienced this same sudden physical reaction, he didn't show it. He scooped up her outer layers, then approached the tub. He reached for her dripping underwear.

She held still as he approached. His fingers brushed hers, the slightest slide of flesh against flesh. More than enough to make her skin tingle.

Their eyes met. Her lips parted. Heat flared in his gaze. He tamped it down and retreated, taking his touch and her clothes with him.

What had just happened?

All she knew was that she could breathe again.

"I'll have someone take care of these for you," he said stiffly. "I'm sure Elsa told you where to find a robe."

"Um, yeah, thank you." Tongue-tied, she struggled for words. It didn't matter, though. She was talking to his back.

He walked away without another word. The door closed behind him with a soft click.

Her breath whooshed out, sending bubbles dancing into the air.

Reeling from the intensity of the encounter, she took a deep breath and slid under the bubbles.

CHAPTER 15

"SHIT." Killian rested his head against the closed bathroom door.

He'd knocked on the door with the purest of intentions. When Elsa had mentioned Dizzie wasn't out yet, irrational worry had kicked in. Whether he was worried she had escaped a windowless room or worried something had happened to her... Well, he hadn't considered too closely.

None of the scenarios he'd imagined had come close to what awaited him in the bathroom.

Fucking bubbles. He'd glimpsed smooth pale skin and the curve of her breast in between those bubbles as she'd handed him her wet underwear.

Dammit.

Cold water trickled down his wrist. He'd tightened his grip around her wet clothes. Time to find someone to take care of this.

"Elsa." The internal communication system transmitted his call.

His housekeeper hurried around the corner. "Yes, Mr. Killian?" She was a small woman but a force to be reckoned with when it came to taking care of his home. Killian didn't know what he would do without her.

"Have these cleaned, please."

Elsa nodded and took the pile of clothes.

Killian thought about what he'd done with his own clothes after his shower. "On second thought, dispose of them. Clean the synth-leather, but if you can track down the same thing in real leather, get it. In black. And get, say, two weeks' worth of clothes for our guest. Put a rush on a few outfits for today. Within the hour, if possible."

There was a robe and some simple pajamas in the bathroom, but the thought of Dizzie traipsing about his house in a robe made his pulse race.

"Anything specific, sir?"

Picturing Dizzie in the stark colors that Portia wore, he decided they wouldn't suit her personality. Her bright red polish indicated she didn't shy away from color. "Bold colors. Blues and greens. Maybe purple. And probably some black," he added, given that the clothes she'd shed were in dark, serviceable colors.

Except her underwear. The virginal white made him feel almost ashamed of the things he'd been thinking. Almost.

Elsa coughed delicately and nodded to the damp items on the top of the pile. "And undergarments, sir?"

His imagination served up an image of Dizzie in deep jewel tones that would stand out dramatically on her pale skin. Pale pinks would make her look almost ethereal.

His breathe caught. Both would be stunning on the dark sheets of his bed.

Dammit. "Pretty, but functional." He'd let Elsa choose and perhaps retain some sanity.

"As you wish. Will she be staying with you?" she asked delicately.

Killian ran his hands through his hair. Everything in him wanted to say yes. Keep your enemies closer, right? And what was closer than skin to skin?

Fuck! The events of the night and the lack of sleep were getting to him. This attraction was proof he was losing his goddamned mind.

"Give her the room across from mine." The one where she'd already made herself at home in the bathtub.

He rarely had guests. Even Portia and Tommy usually chose to return to their condo in the center of the city, close to Tremaine headquarters, instead of staying in his guest room.

Tommy.

Grief kicked him in the chest, the reminder he needed.

This wasn't sleepover. It wasn't a date or a booty call. It was an investigation. He had to get his head back in the game.

Dismissing Elsa with a nod, Killian turned back toward the living room. He needed to get an update on Portia.

CHAPTER 16

KILLIAN SAT at his desk and called Portia. It rang several times. The video screen flickered to life as he was about to hang up.

"Hello, Killian." A close-up of her face, then the view changed to a wider angle.

"How are you feeling, Portia?" She looked better than the last time he'd seen her, lying on a stretcher as the medics maneuvered her out of the ballroom, her skin ashen, her eyes wild with fear. Onscreen, Portia was still pale, but she was in her own bedroom, leaning back against a mound of pillows. Even through the screen he could see her eyes were red from crying.

"How do you think I'm feeling?" Her voice was gritty and carried signs of strain.

Killian rubbed his chest, aggravating the bruised skin. The pain brought back memories of the entire awful night. As did the evidence of Portia's grief.

"At least a little better, since they let you come home," he said.

"Let me? Nobody *lets* me do anything. I demanded to

come home." Despite the weakness of her voice, her waspish tone carried hints of her old self. Then her face crumbled. "Tommy's dead and I'm in our bed alone."

He watched her weep, unable to do more than murmur consoling words. "I know, I'm sorry." Inadequate words.

He'd done this to her. He shouldn't have called.

God, he was such a selfish bastard.

Tears streamed down her face. His gaze blurred and he brushed the first of his own tears away with the back of his hand.

He hadn't grieved yet. He wouldn't until Tommy's killer was brought to justice. Then he'd crawl into a hole with his memories and pain and maybe not come out.

"It's my fault." Her voice was thick with emotion. "I should have been with him instead of dancing with you."

Her words hit like a blow.

"Don't say that! If you'd been with Tommy, I'd have lost both of you." His stomach turned. Without the two of them at his side, he'd be all alone. "I miss him too, but he'd want you to go on."

He sounded like a fucking greeting card, when in reality he was being torn apart inside.

"There was no way to know that would happen," he went on. If threats had been made, Tremaine Corporation and the other big players would have kept their people away. "It was a terrible accident."

"Unless it wasn't." Portia wiped away her tears. "It was the courier, wasn't it?"

Shit. How was he supposed to answer that?

He still believed the courier had delivered the bomb. He was sure of it. But her arguments last night had raised questions. Who sent the package? Was she only a pawn?

If so, he was willing to move her around the chessboard.

Portia took his silence as assent. "You think so, too, don't you? That's why you went to headquarters last night."

"You know about that?" He brought his head up.

"Of course I do." Her look chastised him for asking a stupid question. "Security brought me everything they'd gathered on the explosion. Including your very interesting visit to the holding cell."

"When? They told me you were out of it most of the night." Either unconscious or inconsolable.

"After they..." Her voice broke. With a deep breath, she rebuilt her composure. "After they told me about Tommy, I demanded to be kept in the loop. My father agreed."

That was a surprise. Portia's father—Phillip Tremaine— was a pure bastard. To everyone, including his daughter.

"Who's leading the investigation?" Every company that had lost personnel or property in that explosion would want that role.

"My father wants Tremaine Security running the investigation. His assistant will coordinate with any other companies."

Having seen her father in action, Killian couldn't imagine anyone else winning that battle. "I'm glad Tremaine will be running it. For Tommy's sake." His hand hovered over the hang-up button. "I should let you get some rest."

"You're not getting off that easy!" Her voice rose with each word.

Killian froze. "What do you mean?" He'd hoped to hang up before she focused on his visit last night.

"The report says you helped her escape." Betrayal was etched into her expression and her voice.

Fuck. She wasn't wrong. He couldn't defend himself,

because he still didn't understand why he'd trusted that cryptic message.

He chose his next words carefully. "She passed out. I was afraid we were going to lose our best and only witness, so I took her to the infirmary. How is that helping her escape?"

Killian hated how easily the lies came together. Deceiving Portia this way made him ill. But it wasn't all a lie. Dizzie was their best chance at finding the truth. This way, he could protect both women.

Onscreen, Portia was so quiet, he wondered if he'd accidentally muted the phone. The longer she stared at him, the worse he felt. He faked a yawn to end the call. "You need to rest, Portia. Let the investigators do their jobs. I'll tell them whatever I learn."

Portia ran a ragged nail over her lips. Never one to appear in public looking less than her best, that nail told him more about her state of mind than anything else. "Don't manage me, Killian. I don't need to rest. I need Tremaine Security to bring her to headquarters. I need her to pay for killing my husband."

"What if she's innocent?" Had he really said that out loud? He winced, ready for Portia to swipe at him.

Instead, her voice was pure Ice Queen. "She delivered the bomb. She's guilty. What else do I need to know?"

Killian rubbed his eyes. He was exhausted, his brain too fuzzy to have this conversation.

Even at his best, he didn't think he could break through Portia's grief and change her mind. The bitch of it? If Tommy were alive, he'd know exactly how to get through to her.

CHAPTER 17

DIZZIE KNOCKED on the door of the office. Killian looked up, startled.

"I'm sorry, I didn't mean to interrupt. Elsa told me to come here...?" She studied him from the doorway.

Killian sat behind a piece of furniture that was half desk, half sculpture. The base was a half-cylinder of gleaming metal, rising in a graceful arch from the ground. The dark bronze glowed with warmth. A slab of dark wood balanced on the top of the curve, the surface polished to silky smoothness. The mix of old and new suited him. Just like the building and the rest of the room.

"I asked Elsa to bring you here." He waved her in and gestured to the chair opposite him.

Dizzie sat carefully on the edge of the chair. The frame was the same metal, but dark leather that perfectly complemented the desk covered the seat and back. "Thanks for the clothes." Several outfits had been waiting in the bedroom after her bath.

A flush crawled up his cheeks. "I had Elsa dispose of the ones you were wearing. It was the least I could do."

She inclined her head and waited for annoyance that he had destroyed her clothes to hit her, but it never came. She'd miss her jacket and boots, but the rest of her clothes wouldn't have survived the last twenty-four hours. Not to mention, she'd forever associate them with the events of the night.

The black leather pants and a deep blue shirt that she'd paired with high black leather boots at least somewhat looked like "courier" clothes. If the courier was on a high-fashion runway. Underneath she wore cute blue panties and a matching bra that had been impossible to resist, especially since she'd rather burn the ones she had been wearing for two days than wear them again. Softer than the leather pants, these made her feel girly and powerful at the same time.

Now, knowing the man in front of her had purchased them for her, she tried not to squirm.

Elbows braced on the desk, Killian studied her. "Portia Tremaine knows I got you out of headquarters."

Dizzie shot to her feet. She'd expected Tremaine Security to be after her, but not Porta herself. "I can't stay here." For a few minutes she'd let herself believe in the fancy fairy tale that Killian and his home presented. His words had stripped that option away. The only options left were to prove her innocence or get out of town. Not that she had any idea how to accomplish either.

"Where do you think you can go that the Tremaines won't find you? It's a global company with resources you can't imagine," he asked, his tone matter-of-fact.

Oh, she could imagine the resources, all right. One didn't grow up in the company, literally, without understanding how vast and heartless it was.

Once she'd been clearheaded enough to think again

after Killian's interruption, she'd spent her time in the cooling bath drafting a plan. It focused mainly on the savings she had with the Jack and the bar owner's reputation of being willing to take any job, for a price.

"I have some money set aside. I'll pay for protection until I find a way out of the city." Hysterical laughter bubbled up and she forced it back down. Her savings might cover a few hours of protection, especially against a corporation.

Killian looked at her. "Do you think it will be that easy? Portia's out for blood. Whatever you pay, she'll pay double or triple to track you down."

"What do you care?" she lashed out. "You had your own plan when you barged into the cells last night. What changed?"

"I...don't know." He sighed and settled back in his chair. "I can't help feeling that there's something bigger at play here."

"Then let me go," she pleaded.

"I can't," he said, shaking his head. "Portia would never forgive me."

Dizzie paced back and forth. There had to be a way out of here, but she wasn't seeing it right now. She needed more information.

"Then at least tell me what Portia's planning. Is there a reward?"

"There's no reward," he said. "Internal resources only, so probably a lot of Tremaine Security."

There was no reason for Killian to share information, but he had. Did he think it would intimidate her into staying? She parsed his answer, but it didn't make sense. "Why would she do that?"

"Asking any other company for help will damage the Tremaine reputation."

"No." Dizzie shook her head. Still-damp strands of hair tickled her neck and she shivered. "Internal resources. Why would she do that when it was an inside job?"

Killian paused, his dark gaze turbulent. "What do you mean?"

"Something Al—" Nope, she wasn't saying that name. "Something a Tremaine Security guard said as much before they put me in that cell. They thought it was an inside job." She pinned him with her blue stare. "That I was the inside job."

"What do you think?" His jaw was clenched, but the words were clear.

She clicked her nails together and shook her head. "It doesn't matter what I think. I'm screwed any way you look at it."

"That's why you should stay here."

She snorted. That made as much sense as Portia's decision to ignore an internal threat.

"What if I can help you?" he asked.

"Why would you do that?" She stared at him suspiciously. "*How* would you do that?"

"I don't know how, but Tommy would want me to do the right thing."

He sounded sincere, but she couldn't shake her suspicion. Investors didn't help people like her for no reason. She had nothing of value to offer in exchange. Well, not nothing, but that option seemed unlikely. "I don't think so," she said. "I think I'd rather take my chances on the run."

Killian stood abruptly. He planted his hands on the desk and leaned over.

Dizzie took half a step back, then gritted her teeth. She would not let him intimidate her.

"If I find you're guilty, nothing will stop me from handing you over to Portia wrapped in a big bow. If we can prove you had nothing to do with it, I'll get you safely out of town myself."

"How?" she asked, weighing her options. "I swear I didn't know what was in the package. I can't prove it, though." That was the problem in a nutshell. She couldn't prove it and her word wouldn't count for squat against the Tremaine Corporation's heir.

"We need to discover who sent the package."

She rolled her eyes. "Oh, was that all? Can you use your status to get data on the package? The way you got into detention last night?"

"I don't think that will work a second time. They're pretty pissed about last night. I burned some bridges with that. I wouldn't be surprised if they limited my access for a while." He circled the desk and leaned against it.

Her sudden awareness of his proximity was a problem she didn't need right now. "Can they do that?" she asked. "Don't you own most of the company?" It was ridiculous that someone with that much money and influence couldn't get access to those records.

"I don't own even close to most of it." He laughed and the warm rich sound sent inappropriate tingles through her body. "In fact, I usually don't have much to do with the company at all."

"Except cash their dividend checks." Oh, shit. She'd said that out loud. Dizzie tensed, waiting for his response.

"Close enough." His tone was more sad than mad. "Unless we can get someone in the company to check those records, we'll have to explore other options." He studied her. "Can you get someone from Tremaine to help?"

She focused on her nails. "I know lots of people there, but no way to know who would help and who would turn me in." If her best friend was willing to betray her, why trust anyone else?

"What about the guy on the phone?" Dizzie asked.

"What guy on the phone?" Killian's expression shuttered. He'd ignored two calls from Leopold Brunswick, Phillip Tremaine's assistant. He didn't know what the man wanted and he didn't care either. Was she asking about those?

"You said someone warned you to get me out of the building." It had been cryptic, but she knew someone had called him.

He shrugged. "I don't know who it was or how to reach him. Her. Whoever."

"Can't you call the number back?"

"Gee, why didn't I think of that?"

It wasn't fair. Killian even looked good exasperated.

Dizzie raised her hands in mock surrender. "Just trying to help."

He sighed and rubbed a hand over his face. "What would help is if you hadn't delivered the bomb in the first place."

She flinched. "I'm sorry. I've got to go." Stomach churning, she turned and raced out of the room.

CHAPTER 18

DECORATED in tasteful neutrals that complemented the burnished wood trim, the guest bedroom had every comfort Dizzie could imagine. A huge, comfortable bed dominated one wall and faced the windows, which provided another dazzling view of the city. If you didn't want to lounge in bed, there was also a sofa tucked in front of a fireplace, and a small stylish desk with a matching chair in another corner. There were two doors, one of which led to a humongous closet and the other opened into the bathroom she'd used earlier.

After fleeing Killian's office, she'd found her way back here. Once the door was locked, she'd thrown herself on the bed and cried her eyes out, then fallen into a fitful sleep.

That had been hours ago. Too embarrassed to face him, she'd gratefully accepted Elsa's offer of dinner in her room.

Now the isolation and solitude closed in on her and she felt trapped by the four walls.

Her pacing circuit took her past the window once more and she stopped to peer out. Night had fallen while she hid in the room. White headlights and red taillights created elaborate patterns on the streets. Her fingers traced the designs on the glass.

She longed to be out there.

Needed to be out there.

She craved the freedom of the open road.

Just freedom, really.

For all its beautiful views and comfortable furniture, the room was still a prison. One stocked with amenities that would make it easy to stay forever. The cloud-soft bed. Clothes appearing magically.

Killian.

She couldn't stay.

"Standing around won't clear your name." Saying it out loud gave her the push she needed to get going.

Her first priority: Get out of here.

Dizzie had delivered to a lot of buildings over the years. It was second nature to memorize routes from door to delivery and back again. Getting from the guest room to the garage would be easy. If Killian had any security measures like retinal scans or other biometric identifiers, they weren't obvious. Or else he'd used his body to block her view.

Oh, his body.

Every time they sparred, her pulse fluttered and her knees weakened.

Stupid hormones.

She'd hoped it was proximity. Or the adrenaline rush of running for her life. In the calm of his house, Dizzie worried that it was something more intangible.

Something irrational.

Argh. Definitely time to leave. Staying here was bad decision central.

She'd need a ride and she had the perfect candidate in

mind. The Turbosmith Excel was made to be ridden, not tucked away in a garage.

If Dizzie owned that Excel, the exceptional machine would be on the road every day, not hidden away in a lonely garage.

Owning an Excel may have been out of her reach, but "borrowing" it wasn't.

Okay, next. Killian's point about tracking down the person behind the delivery made sense. Ideally, she'd hire the Jack to help with that. Her entire savings would be wiped out and her ability to buy out her contract would be set back years. It would suck, but not as much as being dead or locked away. Given the last few days, buying her way out might not be an option anymore.

Dizzie dropped onto the bed and considered her plan: get out of house, steal motorcycle, and pay the Jack to help her. Easy-peasy, right?

Who was she kidding? It was a stupid plan, but it couldn't be worse than staying here. She didn't belong in this world. The complete absurdity of being in Killian St. John's house was messing with her head. Not to mention the luxury that surrounded her.

Her hands smoothed over her new leather pants. Butter-soft, they fit like a second skin. She'd nearly had a heart attack when she'd seen them laying on the bed. The high-end brand promised protection and freedom of movement as long as you were willing to pay for it. That promise would forever be out of her reach.

Although it wasn't a fair trade, she had no problem keeping the outfit, since Killian had ordered her clothes destroyed.

Dizzie looked at the closet, filled with brand-new

clothes all in her size. Grab the matching leather jacket and go. That's what she should do.

She looked at the closet again. Each piece of clothing was pretty and functional, simple but not plain. Things she might have chosen with an unlimited budget. It would be a shame to leave them here. Wouldn't it?

Refusing to second-guess her decision—she'd need new clothes on the road, maybe even sell them if she needed to—Dizzie grabbed the stylish messenger bag that had accompanied the clothes. It was probably as crazy expensive as everything else in the closet.

She stuffed underwear, a few tops, and a couple pairs of pants into the bag and started to slip the strap over her head before remembering the gorgeous leather jacket. If she survived this, maybe she'd be able to repay Killian someday.

Stop procrastinating, dammit.

The longer she mooned over Killian St. John's amazing taste and unexpected generosity, the less time she had to escape.

Escape was what she needed—*wanted*—to do.

Donning the jacket and slipping the bag strap over her head, Dizzie took a deep breath and opened the door. Anticipation swirled in her gut as she waited for...what? An alarm? A guard?

Nothing happened, so she stepped into the hall. The door closed behind her with a near silent click. Moving slowly and keeping her steps light, Dizzie paused every few feet to listen for people coming her way.

She didn't encounter anyone. Not Elsa. Not any other servants. Not even Killian himself.

That was good. Right?

Finally, she stood in front of the elevator. The arrows emitted a subtle glow and she stabbed the down button.

Dizzie leaned against the wall, trying to blend in with the shadows.

She'd made it this far, no need to get sloppy.

The doors opened silently. No one entered or left. She waited a few heartbeats, just in case, before slipping into the car.

"Now or never," she whispered and pressed the button for the garage.

The doors closed around her and the hum of the elevator told her it was moving, but she didn't relax until the doors opened again.

When she stepped out of the elevator, the door closed behind her, cutting off her main source of light. Like upstairs, the call button glowed faintly, not nearly enough to navigate by.

Dammit. The garage was dark and kinda scary.

Would the lights kick on for her or were they keyed to Killian?

Did it really matter? She had two choices—forward or back.

With a deep breath, she stepped away from the closed elevator and into the dark.

Lights sprang to life above her. Although she'd been expecting it, she still jumped.

Dizzie waited for her breathing to settle. Waiting until she was sure that her presence hadn't been detected. Then she took another step. And another.

The light above her flicked on. Step by slow step, she tested the timing of the lights. Three lights were lit at a time —one above, one in front, and one behind.

Now that she understood the pattern, the garage didn't feel quite so spooky.

As Dizzie crossed the garage to where she thought the

Excel was stored, lights popped on and off with each step. The uneven lighting both illuminated and hid Killian's car collection. Some vehicles she recognized from the gossip sites, though the articles had usually focused more on the beautiful women at his side than the horsepower he arrived in.

That was why the bike had been such a surprise.

She'd never seen a photo of him in leathers with that gleaming chrome beauty. That image would be unforgettable. What woman would turn down that ride?

As much as Dizzie wanted the bike for herself, she wouldn't say no to having all that power—man and machine—between her legs.

A quiver of excitement raced through her and heat pooled low in her belly.

Focus, Dizzie. Find the bike.

The next light flickered on and there she was. The Turbosmith Excel.

Sitting in a pool of light, the motorcycle gleamed. And really, there should have been a choir of angels singing, because the bike was a beautiful blend of art and science.

"Hi, gorgeous," she whispered. "You are I are going to take a little ride."

Slipping to the side, Dizzie heaved a sigh of relief when she saw the key was still in the ignition. When she'd noticed that earlier, she'd almost pocketed it, but she worried that Killian would see. He'd watched her carefully the whole time she explored the motorcycle.

She circled the motorcycle, looking for advanced security measures. If they existed, they were very well hidden and she wouldn't know about them until it was too late.

"All right, baby, let's get you out of here." She wrapped her hands around the handlebars and disengaged the brake.

Lifting the kickstand, she began her career as a bike thief. Nerves twitched in her belly.

Was she really doing this?

Rolling forward, the garage door opened as she neared. She jumped. These damn motion sensors were going to be the death of her.

Cool air rushed into the temperature-controlled garage. She zipped her jacket up all the way, thankful for the new clothes. The night air would be even colder when she was whipping down the road on this beauty.

When she'd cleared the garage by several feet, Dizzie paused and waited for the garage door to close behind her. And waited. She re-engaged the kickstand and walked back toward the garage.

Nothing happened. The door remained open.

Dammit. What did she do now?

Leaving it open was an asshole move. One that would leave Killian vulnerable to the newsies who swarmed his house.

She couldn't betray him that way. There was probably a way to close the garage from the inside, but how was she supposed to find it when only three lights at a time worked? If only she'd paid attention when Killian had driven them into the garage. He had to have a way to control it from outside. She'd thought there was a remote...

Of course there was. "Oh, Dizzie, you idiot," she muttered aloud.

She pulled the key out of the ignition and studied it. Dangling right next to the key was a small black fob. She pressed the button and held her breath. *Please don't be an alarm.*

The garage door slid closed as quietly as it had opened. *Yes!*

She settled the bag against her back. The bike was nearly too tall for her, which, given the height difference between her and Killian, wasn't a surprise. She could still ride it, though.

Dizzie stood on the foot peg and swung her leg over the seat. She shifted her weight to the right until the ball of her foot reached the ground, then raised the kickstand with her left.

She donned the helmet that sat on the rear of the bike and tucked her hair out of sight. Instead of heading directly to the front gate, she rolled the Excel forward with her feet, exploring the rest of the driveway. A rougher gravel spur branched out toward the back fence. She followed it carefully and was rewarded with what looked like a construction fence. Probably from the renovations.

This gate wasn't electronic the way the front gate was. There also wasn't a cluster of newsies outside this gate either. Parking the motorcycle, Dizzie dismounted and tugged at the gate, creating enough space for her and the Excel to slip through.

She turned the key in the ignition and pressed the starter. The bike sprang to life with a throaty rumble. It was absolutely perfect for Killian. Commanding enough to make you get out of the way, but not the "look at me" of insecure boys.

"Let's rock and roll," she said aloud, her heart racing.

CHAPTER 19

WHERE TO GO?

Staying with friends was out of the question. They all lived at headquarters and after Alice's betrayal, Dizzie didn't want to risk another friend turning her in to Tremaine Security.

Razor Jack's had been her original plan and it was still the best choice. Her money was there and she might be able to buy protection from the Jack.

Killian's warning about the corporation outbidding her echoed in her mind. Had spurning his aid been a huge mistake?

She couldn't forget that he'd blamed her twenty-four hours ago. His kindness could have been a ploy to get her to trust him.

It was late and she was tired. Tired, overwhelmed, and way out of her depth. Her training hadn't covered running from a major global power.

She looked back toward the house. Warm bed, good food, hot man. All that waited for her if she went back. But what would it cost her?

Fear, uncertainty, and a lifetime on the run waited for her on the road. Running would cost her friends, her job, and her home—everything. Except maybe her freedom if she stayed at least one step ahead. Stay in a gilded cage or risk it all for freedom?

Forward it was.

A block from Killian's, she opened the bike up. The tension riding her eased and her laughter rang out into the night as she and the bike pivoted around curves and corners as though they were one. This was where she belonged.

Damn, this was one beautiful bike. *So much power!*

Dizzie held to the speed limit, although it nearly killed her to do so on a few wide-open stretches. She couldn't afford the kind of attention the Excel at full force would bring.

She aimed for Razor Jack's. The bar was located on the seedier side of town, a part of Seattle that had resisted change and gentrification, no matter how hard the corporations tried.

Toggling her optical display on, she cycled through the traffic screens. Her current location was quiet and there was no unusual activity between her and the bar. As she zoomed out, a cursor blinked in her field of vision.

What the hell? That had never happened before.

She flipped through the traffic screens again. The blinking cursor showed up on every single one.

Fuck! It had to be some kind of glitch.

Her stomach sank.

The only way to fix it or reboot it was back at headquarters. The one place she couldn't go.

Maybe the Jack knew someone who could fix it. More money flowing out of her account. She sighed. Not something she could worry about right now.

The flashing white bar was distracting, but she was afraid to turn the system off. What if it never came back on?

The cursor moved in her periphery, leaving letters in its wake.

STOP. No RZ. TC waits.

Her breath caught.

What the double fuck?!

Completely freaked out, Dizzie swerved out her lane and nearly got squashed by a semi. She didn't have the focus to flip him off when he blasted his horn. Her hands were trembling as she pulled off to the side of the road and turned off the bike. Shaking too hard to keep it stable, she flipped the kickstand down.

She fluttered her eyelids, like she had a piece of dust in her eye. That only made her eyes water. It didn't get rid of the letters.

Her pulse thudded in her ears and her rapid breathing sounded loud in the confines of her helmet. She tugged it off and sucked in deep breaths of cool night air. The additional oxygen helped quell some of her panic and she could think clearly enough to decipher the warning: don't go to Razor Jack's because Tremaine Security was waiting.

Who had sent it? And how?

Someone had hacked her implant. It was the only answer that made sense.

Someone had *hacked* her implant and was using the fucking thing to communicate with her.

"Who the hell are you?" Her words were quiet in the night.

Like K phone

The moving type was disorienting. Her stomach rolled. She stared at the words only she saw. Words someone was typing *inside* her body.

"Killian's phone?" She'd watched him take a call. He'd told her it was a warning. "You sent that warning? Who are you?"

Yes. The cursor blinked in place for several long seconds before another word appeared. *Friend.*

A friend? Right. Her laugh was only slightly hysterical.

Her friends were low-level corporate drones, not hackers. Especially not hackers of this caliber.

Oh shit. He'd *heard* her.

Only one way that could happen. He hadn't just hacked the implant. He'd hacked *her.*

Dizzie barely got off the bike before she puked into the bushes. She wiped her mouth with the sleeve of her new jacket and winced. Gross.

"You owe me a jacket, you brain-hacking bastard!"

She stepped away from the bushes and dropped to her knees. Wrapping her arms around her stomach, she closed her eyes, hoping to stave off the sense of violation.

Instead of the darkness she sought, the blinking cursor waited for her.

Fingernails digging into her palms, she fought the impulse to claw out her implants. It wouldn't do any good.

She fought back a second wave of nausea, then flopped onto her back. "What the hell do you want from me?"

Help.

She barked out a laugh. "You've got the wrong girl. I can't even help myself."

Help you.

"How?" Why did she keep answering out loud? Did that make her more or less crazy?

Need safe place. Can help. An address in the same stark white as the cursor skittered over the screen. *Safe house.*

"Why the hell should I trust you? And how do you

know what I'm saying? Are you reading my thoughts?" What the hell else had the Tremaine Corporation done to her during her implant surgery?

There was a long pause. Long enough to wonder if she was imagining this whole interaction.

Lips.

She exhaled in a rush. Not the answer she was expecting. But for the first time since the cursor appeared, it was easier to breathe.

"You're reading my lips? How?"

Satellite.

Holy. Shit.

If this guy had the skills to hack a satellite, hacking her ocular implants would be easy.

She tilted her head up toward the sky. "Why are you hacking satellites? Or me?"

Something big. You=center.

Dizzie scrambled to her feet. "This isn't my fault! I'm not at the center of anything!" she yelled at the sky.

Except a big fucking mess, but she wasn't about to admit that to the creepy hacker in her head.

Not fault. But you=center.

Great. Either something was seriously wrong and she was hallucinating a conversation or a rogue hacker believed she was at the middle of a conspiracy. And she'd thought her life couldn't get any more complicated. Dizzie waited for option C, none of the above.

Blinking words interrupted whatever she was going to say next.

Need to go. Now.

"Why?" She didn't know whether to trust her mystery hacker or not.

Newsies.

"I didn't see any when I left."

Saw you. Know not K. Want to know who.

Well, shit. She thought she'd avoided them. They must have had a news drone above his house.

She looked up at the night sky. Was there one watching her now?

"Are you a newsie watching me with a drone?"

The cursor blinked at her, somehow looking offended. More letters flickered into her field of vision.

Rude! A pause. *Move!*

"Why do I need a safe house?"

Mystery lady + distinctive bike + KSJ. Do math.

Yeah, pretty much catnip to the twenty-four-hour news cycle. Ugh. More people looking for her.

A low rumble signaled an approaching vehicle. Dizzie tensed. Normal middle-of-the-night traffic? Or a horde of people searching for the next story?

"I'll be fine at the Jack's," she said, not sure if she believed it or not.

No response from her mysterious intruder.

She swung her leg over the bike. If the newsies were hot on her trail, she didn't want to be found in the middle of nowhere. She slipped on the helmet, slightly miffed that there'd been no response to her plan. For a second, she hadn't felt alone.

What would happen if the newsies caught her?

If they were desperate to identify Killian's mystery lady, she might be able to safely tell her side of the story.

Dizzie grimaced. On the other hand, if they found out she was inadvertently responsible for delivering the bomb, they'd sacrifice her for the story of a lifetime, then turn her over to the Tremaines for whatever punishment they would mete out.

She started the bike again. The blinker moved again.

Safe house! The same address followed.

Both Razor Jack's and the safe house were near the south end of the city. She'd decide which destination later.

CHAPTER 20

"WHAT THE HELL were you thinking, Killian?"

Killian's bedroom door slammed against the wall. Either that or Portia's accusation had woken him. One minute he was dreaming about dancing with Dizzie at the gala. The next he was bolting upright in bed. "What the hell, Portia?"

"I'm sorry. She used her code." Elsa hurried into the room on Portia's heels, her robe a marked contrast to Portia's severe black suit.

"It's okay, Elsa," he told his housekeeper. He'd given Portia and Tommy codes to the house—and permission to use them—when he'd purchased the place. This was not exactly what he'd had in mind.

"If you're sure?" She looked ready to defend him from Portia's wrath.

"I'm sure." Killian appreciated the thought, but this was outside her duties. He kept a wary eye on Portia while he ensured Elsa was out of the line of fire. "Would you please make some coffee?"

She studied him a moment, then nodded abruptly, tightened her robe and marched out of the room.

There was no time for relief. Portia was waiting to pounce. "What are you doing here, Portia?" This wasn't the way he'd planned to start the day. Was it even day? No hint of daylight peeked through the curtains. "What time is it?"

"It's time for you to tell me why you let her go," she snarled.

Hurry up with the coffee, Elsa. This conversation made no sense and he needed clarity.

"Let who go?" He studied Portia. Dressed in head to toe black, the lack of color emphasized her paleness and made her look tired. Drawn. Desolate.

"That damn courier," she snapped.

"Dizzie—" He broke off when she glared at him. "The courier is down the hall."

Killian rubbed the sleep from his eyes and tried to follow Portia's comments. What was she talking about?

"Your little courier," the words carried a sneer, "isn't down the hall, Killian. She's out there." She waved toward the covered window.

His heart stopped. What the hell was Portia talking about?

Feeling too vulnerable to have this conversation in bed, he swung his legs over the side of the bed. His shorts left his cyber leg uncovered and he stared at it. The metal casing wasn't shiny chrome like the Turbosmith Excel. It was a duller graphite, cast into the shape of a leg. Brighter silver provided the definition for the muscles, while black composite materials formed the joints.

While high quality, the leg was simple and functional. He'd been offered the best money could buy: a realistic-looking limb that matched his remaining leg almost exactly. He'd refused, telling everyone that the synthetic skin bothered him. In reality, he kept the plain metal as a reminder of what he'd survived. And what he'd lost.

Portia was one of the few people he trusted enough to reveal the synthetic leg to. How would Dizzie react if she saw it? Would she turn away in distaste?

Why was he even thinking about this now? He had to deal with Portia. Needing time to think, he stood, shouldering past Portia to the closet.

"How do you know?" He yanked on pants and a long-sleeved shirt, ignoring the aches and pains from the explosion. And how would she know if Dizzie was gone? The urge to cross the hall, to verify that Dizzie was where he expected her to be, was intense.

He'd planned to keep Dizzie away from Portia and the corporation as long as possible. He needed time to win her trust. With Portia's arrival, whatever slim chance he had of making that happen had evaporated.

"The newsies are interested in your new *girlfriend.*" Ice coated the word and she threw a tablet at him.

Killian snatched it out of the air before it hit him in the head. Man, she was pissed.

He flicked the tablet on, his fingers moving over the screen as he did a quick search. Portia followed his every move like she was watching a bug. The shadows under her eyes didn't hide her fury.

"My father's assistant brought your betrayal to my attention. He didn't want me to see it without warning. How could you?"

Her words hit home and Killian struggled to keep his breath even. How did he explain that everything he'd done was for Portia to bring the person or persons who killed Tommy to justice?

Dizzie was just the first piece of a larger puzzle. And if

he were starting to believe her, starting to feel things about her, well, this wasn't the time or the place to be thinking about that. And Portia certainly wasn't the person to share it with.

Shoving those thoughts deep, deep down, Killian focused on the tablet. It didn't take him long to find the story. Dizzie's "visit" topped several local news outlets, bumping the bombing from the top headline.

Fucking newsies.

He cringed at the headlines.

Late Night Escapade...or Escape?

The Playboy and the Mystery Lady

He flipped between screens, studying the accompanying images. The pictures showed a rider on a bike—his bike!—outside his home. Silhouetted against the night sky by the perimeter lights, the rider was obviously a woman. "When were these taken?"

"A few hours ago. Techs are running down the exact time. They're checking for any satellites in the area, too." Portia smiled her corporate-shark smile.

Damn. She was expanding her manhunt. He had to fix this, but he didn't know how. "You could have had your techs email this to me, Portia."

She tore the tablet from his hand. "Maybe I wanted to see your face when I met your new girlfriend, Killian. How long have the two of you been involved? Did you plan the bombing together?"

Such pain and venom in her voice. All directed at him. His shoulders slumped, his hands dropped to his sides. "How could you even think that? Why would I do that? You and Tommy are, were, the most important people in my life!"

That she believed he was involved in the attack that

killed his best friend ripped a hole in his heart. Her attack reminded him where his loyalties lay—with Portia and Tommy.

"I have no idea what's going on, Portia. That bomb turned my life upside down, too."

"Your life was turned upside down? *Your* life?" The shattering of her icy façade was such a surprise, he didn't see the slap coming.

The sting of his cheek shocked him. "He was my best friend too." The words slipped out, proving what a selfish prick he was.

"He was my husband," she choked out the words, her voice thick with emotion. Her eyes glistened and she blinked, fighting back tears. "Tommy was the only good thing—the best thing—in my life. Now he's dead. Because of that bitch courier you're hiding."

Her words gutted him. Killian stumbled back a step. She closed the distance between him and smacked the tablet against his chest.

It didn't hurt as much as the gaping hole where his best friend used to be.

Tommy. Portia. Dizzie. He wanted to do right by them all, but didn't know how. Suddenly it was all too much. "I loved him too, Portia!"

She stopped hitting him. Stood too close and stared up at him with big blue eyes that reminded him of the courier.

"He was my best friend." His voice was softer now that he had her attention. He curled his hands around her upper arms. He had her attention, but he needed to keep it. "He was a victim of the bombing, like we were. Like Dizzie was."

She sucked in a sharp breath. Her muscles tightened

and she tried to pull away. "Why do you keep protecting her?"

"It's not her fault. It's yours." *Fuck! Why had he said that?*

She wrenched free, hitting him with the tablet and her fist. "How dare you?"

This time he threw his arms up to block her blows. They hurt, but not as much as her words and the pain in her voice. "Dammit, stop! That's not what I meant. It's the corporation's fault—Tremaine Corporation—not yours."

"She delivered the bomb!"

"Yes. A bomb she picked up from inside *your* company. A delivery that somehow made it through your screening system to your courier."

She stopped swinging and stepped back, wrapping her arms around her waist. The tablet dropped to the floor.

He wanted to make it better, but didn't know how. She opened her mouth, but Killian spoke first.

"It all comes back to the Tremaine Corporation, Portia. Someone inside the company is behind this." When he said the words out loud, it was the only thing that made sense.

"You're thinking with your dick, Killian. She must have been a damn good lay for you to believe her lies in such a short time." Her sneer was diminished by the tears sliding down her cheeks.

"Your grief is blinding you to other possibilities." The words escaped before he could temper them.

She recoiled as if he'd struck her and dropped onto the bed. Wrenching sobs escaped her as she buried her face in her hands.

Fuck. Tommy would kick his ass for making Portia cry.

Killian sat next to her. "I'm sorry, Portia." She flinched

when he wrapped his arm around her shoulder, so he pulled back.

His own eyes welled with tears as he listened to her cry.

He should give in. Give Dizzie up and let the corporation deal with her.

He'd known Portia and Tommy his whole life. They should be the ones he chose. They were the obvious answer.

But the thought of throwing Dizzie back to Tremaine Security turned his stomach. She didn't think she'd make it out alive. He agreed with her.

There had to be another option.

CHAPTER 21

THE BUILDING LOOMING out of the dark alley wasn't a house. It didn't look all that safe either. Dizzie double-checked the address before rolling to a stop in front of a warehouse that had seen better days in a part of town that had seen better decades.

She checked the address again. Still a match for the one that hovered at the bottom of her field of vision. Why was she following the mysterious white text?

Oh, that's right, she was out of options. Razor Jack's had been too crowded to risk tonight.

"Put up or shut up," she muttered to herself. She slipped her leg over the bike.

Gentrification had hit Seattle's warehouse district hard, starting with the buildings closest to the waterfront. Now called lofts and retreats and suites, the refurbished buildings were sold to wealthy corporate types who could afford a view of the water.

Bracketed between the city and the waterfront were clusters of buildings like this one. Somehow they never succumbed to the developers and remained derelict. Still standing but abandoned. Was that why the hacker had sent her here?

Dizzie flipped her visor up. A rusty chain looped through the handles of equally rusted front doors. The windows were covered with years' worth of dirt and grime.

Yippee! She felt safer already.

Wind whipped through the space between buildings and she shivered. She didn't like being out in the open like this. Too exposed. She needed to get into that building. She looked up, waiting for instructions from her new...friend? Foe? How did you classify someone like that?

First, she had to deal with the bike. It was too damn shiny to leave sitting in front of the building.

"I'm sorry, baby." She stroked her hand over the chrome. "I've got to hide you while I check out the inside. I'll be back for you as soon as I can."

She grabbed the handlebars, took a deep breath, and rolled the motorcycle into the shadows to the side of the building. The smell of rot emanated from the dumpsters that lined the walls. Maybe this area wasn't as abandoned as it looked.

She tucked the bike into a corner behind one of the dumpsters. She hated to leave it out here. What if it got stolen?

A laugh bubbled out. She clapped her hand over her mouth. Talk about irony.

The shadows should provide protection for the motorcycle, at least until daybreak. If she hadn't accessed the warehouse by then, she'd move on.

Once it was hidden, she returned to the front of the warehouse. Dizzie kept to the shadows. This place gave her the creeps. It was too quiet. Too far from the hustle and bustle of the city.

Standing in front of the big warehouse doors, she studied the rusted panels and the worn siding.

How was a building this decrepit still standing?

She shook her head. Maybe this place wasn't as bad as it looked. Not that it mattered if she couldn't get inside.

Shivering, Dizzie removed her helmet and tucked her hair into the neck of her jacket. Her hair would be a beacon in this dark corner of the city, but the helmet covered her mouth, so the hacker couldn't read her lips. "A little help here," she said, tilting her head back so a satellite, if there was one up there, could see her.

She ran her hands over the doors. Fully expecting rusted paint, she was surprised by the smooth metal under her fingertips.

That was interesting. She peered closer.

Clever, clever hacker.

Despite its appearance, the door wasn't as old or as worn as it looked. It was cleverly painted to conceal the truth. Whoever owned the building had secrets.

Now that she knew the door's secret, she swept her hand over it again, seeking...what? A handle. A lock. Step-by-step instructions.

Nothing popped. Of course it wouldn't be easy.

There had to be a way in.

For a minute she considered pounding on the door or rattling the chain. No, that would be too loud and might give her presence away. She wished her guardian angel had provided more than an address.

As if reading her mind—and she hoped he hadn't been lying about that—a string of numbers appeared in her line of vision.

A keycode?

Which meant a keypad. But where?

Her fingers passed over one of the grimy windows. A pale light flickered in response. A keypad disguised as a window? Pretty fucking clever.

She pulled her hands away and stared at the dirty glass. The numbers floated in her field of vision. But no instructions.

"If I hid a keypad in a window…"

It should be easy to access, because standing out here too long would draw unwanted attention.

Dizzie turned halfway, scanning the area. She'd been out here too long.

She traced around the edge of the window with her nails, sliding them back and forth over the seam. One caught on a seam where the surface of the window was slightly higher than the frame.

"Aha!"

She held her breath and slid the tip of a nail under the thin edge. Praying she didn't break a nail, she braced a knuckle against the window frame. With the added leverage, the glass plate inched up with a creak.

Slowly, with as much finesse as possible, she lifted the grimy glass plate. Blue light appeared in the crack. She braced the panel open with her free hand. Once the plate was lifted all the way, a keypad was visible. The gap was wide enough to slip her hand in.

"Here goes nothing," she whispered.

She entered the string of numbers slowly, each move in the tiny space deliberate. Would it lock her out if she entered the wrong code? After the final number, she pulled her hand away and waited.

The double doors—which were actually one big door—opened with a groan. The entry was to her right.

Dizzie closed the glass panel. The fake dirt remained

unsmudged, with no indication it hid a keypad. If there were this many tricks on the outside, what would she find inside?

The entryway was dark when she stepped into it. Nothing happened until she tugged the door closed behind her. Lights flickered on, reminding her of Killian's garage.

Was he the hacker? He had money and liked his toys...

"You're being silly, Dizzie." She turned in a circle, studying the entry. It was a small room with concrete walls. With the door behind her, a narrow hallway led in the opposite directions. The air was musty, as if someone hadn't been here for a while, but the air didn't carry the smell of rot the way the alley did. The faint hum of electricity—from the lights?—was the only other sound besides her breathing.

She paused where she was. Would there be more instructions?

When none appeared, she adjusted her grip on her helmet, ready to use it as a weapon, and followed the hallway. It dead-ended at another heavy steel door. At least this one had an embedded keypad.

She typed in the door code. Nothing happened. Afraid she'd made a typo, she typed it in again, double-checking each number before she pressed each key.

Nothing.

"Are you fucking kidding me?" She kicked the door, tired of all the games.

Here she was, no sleep, no bed and, apparently, no code. And no help. So much for the promised safe house.

"I want to go home," she announced to the empty room. "Why did I listen to you?"

She dropped her head against the door and closed her eyes. Sleep loomed, just out of reach.

Numbers skittered across her implant. Her eyes flew open.

2*nd* *code. Was delayed.*

She punched in the numbers, reining in her anger for fear of damaging the thin plastic.

Twenty-six mini stabs later, the door opened with a soft whoosh, revealing a thin line of light. The air that escaped through the slim opening smelled of disuse. Wherever she was, it had been closed up for a while.

She pushed the door open and stepped over the threshold, her helmet in a death grip.

The light in the next room had a bluish cast. A few more steps and she learned why.

Filled with enough computers to rival a corporate control room, this room was obviously a hacker's playground. Monitors covered nearly every inch of wall and every flat surface was buried under other electronics. The contents had to have cost a fortune.

Two chairs—tricked out with more equipment—sat in front of the desks. The room looked empty, but she couldn't tell if the computers were actively in use.

She stopped where she was, makeshift weapon ready. "Hello? Are you here?"

Dizzie spun in a slow circle, taking in the entire room. It was huge—at least four times the size of her quarters back at Tremaine Corporation. Dust coated every surface. The room gave off big missing-mad-computer-scientist vibes.

Why had she been brought here? Not for her computer skills. Coding and hacking weren't part of her skill set.

She trailed a finger through the dust on one of the consoles, revealing a logo that made her gasp. This was top-of-the-line equipment, the kind that cost a fortune. It was probably cutting edge when it had been installed. The security made sense now, but the dust didn't.

A cloud of dust erupted when she dropped her bag into a chair, triggering a series of sneezes. God, this place might kill her before Tremaine Security did. She backed away from the chair.

Time to kill two birds with one stone. Explore her temporary lodging and track down some cleaning supplies. She couldn't stay here if she was going to sneeze the whole damn time.

Two rooms branched off the main room. The first was a small bedroom, with two narrow beds and a small attached bathroom. Compared to Killian's guest room, this was more what she was used to.

The second door led to a tiny kitchen. The kitchen was the complete opposite of the main room, with low-tech appliances including a hot plate and fridge.

Dizzie opened the cupboards. They were filled with canned goods. She pulled a few off the shelf and studied them. The expiration dates were close, but they should be fine. At least she wouldn't starve.

She found basic cleaning supplies under the sink. The cleaning cloths were dusty. She shuddered. When was the last time anyone had been here?

Dizzie pulled her shirt up over her mouth, bandit-style, and marched back into the main room.

Working quickly, she started with the chair in front of the main terminal. Billowing clouds of the dust filled the air and she sneezed again and again. Ugh. She felt grimy and disgusting. What she wouldn't give for Killian's big bathtub now.

When the chair and screen were as clean as they were going to get, she sat down gingerly, careful to avoid the neck support and the scary-looking port that jacked a hacker into the computer.

She jabbed the power button. This was her first chance to get online since Killian had carried her out of Tremaine headquarters. It shouldn't make her nervous, but her clenched stomach proved otherwise.

The terminal flickered to life quickly. The screen brightened on a surge of power, then faded to black with a blinking cursor instead of the standard user-friendly interface.

She stared at the screen. Couldn't this be easy for once?

The stress of the last few days finally overwhelmed her. "Dammit!"

The room muffled her shout.

All she'd wanted was to do her goddamned job and buy out her damn corporate contract. It wasn't fair. Who the hell charged orphans for the food they ate and the clothes they wore?

"Fuck you, Tremaine Corporation!"

Yelling felt good. Better than good. It felt like freedom.

The dam broke and the words flowed out. Things she could never say in her room at headquarters.

Dizzie surged to her feet, hands clenched into fists, and shouted at the ceiling. "Who the hell made you god?"

It was a stupid question with an easy answer. Money. It always came down to money.

She railed against all the corporations and investors she could think of. The Tremaines and the St. Johns, the Comforts and the Triplets.

When her voice got scratchy, she used the keyboard. FUCK YOU. FUCK YOU. FUCK YOU.

The stark white letters gave her almost as much pleasure as shouting.

Different letters flickered to life in her implant. The sudden double vision made her eyes cross.

See you made it to safe house

"Goddammit, you bastard!"

No response.

Her fingers clicked angrily over the keyboard. ANSWER ME YOU ASSHOLE

Stop shouting. Don't have much time

"Can't you see me?" She typed as she talked.

Not there.

"This is your place? Why haven't you been here lately?"

The answers were as terse as they'd been on the road. *Yes. Been busy*

"Why am I here?"

There was a pause. One long enough that she didn't think he would answer. That pissed her off.

Keep you out of the way. While fix this

Dizzie closed her eyes and stared at the stark white words on her implants. Who would have guessed the hacker's answer would be worse than his silence?

CHAPTER 22

KILLIAN RUBBED the sleep from his eyes and programmed the coffee maker for another cup. His third since Portia had left fifteen minutes ago.

The steaming liquid was bitter and black and burned on the way down. Exactly what he needed. A massive caffeine boost before he searched for his missing courier.

His courier.

That was what Portia had called Dizzie. She'd meant it as an insult.

She'd been wrong. Dizzie called to something deep and possessive in Killian. He couldn't explain it. Wasn't sure he wanted to. Not yet.

He wasn't sure what he would do if his feelings were nothing but an unhealthy obsession with the girl who'd killed his best friend.

Tremaine Corporation security might have the skills and the tools to find her, but he couldn't let that happen. She'd caught his attention and he wasn't letting go. Not until he got to the bottom of this.

With the last of the coffee burning through his system,

Killian continued to search his office. He could call the company, but that would bring attention that he didn't want. No, better to keep searching.

The Turbosmith Excel was equipped with a state-of-the-art tracking system, designed to locate a stolen motorcycle in situations like this. Unfortunately, he'd installed the software on a tablet forever ago and never bothered to add it to his current phone. Why should he, when he didn't ride anymore?

Killian found his old tablet buried under investor reports and company profiles on one of the bookshelves. He'd ignored his email and his staff had printed them off. Still, he had let the papers pile up the last few months, too out of sorts to deal with any of it.

They were all the same, nothing new, nothing to spark his interest.

He powered up the device. An older model, it still had a functioning touch screen and a camera. Swiping to open the tablet, he pressed his finger onto the biometric scanner.

The screen was cluttered with apps and notifications of events long passed. A number of updates automatically loaded. "Son of a bitch!" he muttered. They took time he didn't want to waste.

He drummed his fingers on the table, then stopped because it reminded him of Dizzie. She did that when she was bored or waiting.

The realization unnerved him. How was it possible that he knew her movements so well in such a short time?

A small beep broke into his thoughts. The updates had loaded. Once he refreshed the screen, the app was simple to use. A single dot flickered on the map. Pinching the screen, he zoomed in until the address appeared.

Dizzie and his bike were on the south side of town.

Closer than he'd expected, given her head start. The satellite map revealed a cluster of warehouses around the bike's location. What the hell was she doing there?

He'd warned her that Portia was throwing unlimited resources into tracking her. If she'd wanted to run, Dizzie should have kept going. The warehouses were too close to the city.

Killian threaded his fingers into his hair. It didn't make sense. Nothing about this whole situation made sense. What was he missing?

CHAPTER 23

DIZZIE ROUSED from her doze with a start. The room's dim blue light was disorienting and the artificial lighting made it difficult to tell what time it was. It took too long for her to recognize her surroundings.

The hacker's lair.

What had woken her?

She inched to the edge of the bed and stuffed her feet into her boots, keeping every movement as quiet as possible.

Dizzie grabbed a metal pipe she'd found when she'd gone out to retrieve the motorcycle. She swung it a few times, then twirled it around with her wrist. She didn't want to go exploring, but it beat huddling in the small room terrified.

Barely daring to breathe, she prowled the kitchen and main room. Nothing was hiding under the desks or in dark corners.

Maybe a bad dream had woken her.

She jumped and spun around when booms echoed through the building. Muscles tensed, she held her makeshift club at the ready. *What was that?*

The sounds came again, but this time she was ready for it. She closed her eyes and focused. Was that...someone pounding on the outer doors?

She should ignore it.

The pounding came again and her indecision was countered by the realization that whoever it was wouldn't give up.

The hacker would know the code, so it had to be someone who didn't belong. Tremaine Security? Had Killian sold her out? Her stomach churned. Had sending her here been an elaborate plan to turn her in?

Shit!

Clutching the pipe, she retraced her steps to the front door. Even on her tiptoes, she wasn't tall enough to see out the windows.

Dammit. This was a bad idea.

Dizzie secured her grip on the pipe, stepped behind the door, and pushed it open.

It swung open with more force than she'd expected.

Blinded by the early morning light, she raised the bat to her shoulder as a shadow fell across the threshold. Not willing to leave without a fight, Dizzie swung the bat.

A solid hit, followed by a yelp of pain.

Taking her frustrations out on Tremaine Security felt surprisingly good. She swung again, but hit the door instead.

"Dammit, Dizzie! Stop hitting me!"

Holy. Shit.

She knew that voice. It had haunted at least one of her dreams last night. "What are you doing here?"

Killian took advantage of her surprise. He trapped her behind the door and pulled the pipe from her grip. Too surprised to stop him, it slid out of her hands.

"Did he send you?" She stared up at him.

"He who?"

"Never mind." She shook her head.

She couldn't force him back outside. He had her weapon and outweighed her. Resigned, she closed the door, hyperaware of his presence.

The moment the door shut, she whirled around. In the hallway's dim light, he looked more dangerous than she'd ever seen him. Dark clothes, slight scruff on his jaw.

Well, damn. Trapped in the safe house was looking up.

Adopting a calm she didn't feel, Dizzie leaned back against the wall and crossed her arms over her chest. "What are you doing here?"

"You asked if he sent me. He who?" His expression was shadowed but his voice held curiosity.

"Nobody." If the hacker hadn't sent him... "How did you find me? Give me back my pipe!" She extended her hand.

"I think I'll hold on to this for now. Wouldn't want you to take another swing at me."

Smart man.

"Tell me what you're doing here or get out." She stood straight and tall, her hands on her hips, trying to look more imposing.

"You think I'd let you run away again?" His lips quirked.

He was laughing at her. She narrowed her eyes. "You don't 'let me' do anything. I'm not going back with you."

"Did I say you were?" he countered. "We need to talk. Here in the hallway or back wherever you came from. Your choice."

He wasn't going to leave, not until he wanted to. She

read it in every muscle. For a useless playboy, he sure had a stubborn streak.

"Fine. Follow me." She turned and walked away. His presence filled the small hallway. Solid. Reassuring. Overwhelming. She shivered. Nerves, she told herself. It was just nerves.

Killian trailed her. She knew he would. "What is this place?"

Dizzie shrugged and quickened her pace. If she put enough distance between them, maybe she'd shake off her response to him. Her fight-or-flight response from earlier had transformed into an emotion just as primal.

Her nipples tightened and she was intensely aware that he had purchased the lace underwear she wore.

Dizzie sped up, trying to quell the throbbing between her legs. She needed distance.

She was already on the far side of the computer room when Killian entered.

He whistled and shifted his attention shift from her to the equipment. His change of focus left her strangely disappointed.

He studied the computers. "Pretty intricate. Yours?"

She shrugged again. She didn't owe him answers—not until she knew why he was here—and maybe not even then.

"Your partner's?" he asked, when she didn't respond.

"What?" She was getting damn tired of his accusations.

"You just happened to run to a secure and untraceable warehouse? A partner is the obvious answer." Dizzie couldn't decipher his tone.

"No! I..." There was no way to condense everything that had happened into a reasonable explanation. Especially when she didn't understand it herself. "I've never been here before. It's a place to stay."

"Right." Killian gave her a sidelong glance and prowled around the rest of the room. Arms crossed, she watched him circle the room once, and then again. Then he dropped into the main chair in front of the computer and started typing.

Whoa. Was he *the hacker?*

Though he appeared comfortable at the keyboard, the custom-made chair didn't fit him like she'd expect. Which made sense if he hadn't been here in a while.

Then again, he hadn't known—or used—the code.

Pretending to look over his shoulder, she stepped closer and studied the back of his neck for a port. She didn't see one, but maybe they were like her optical implants—you couldn't see them from the outside. Without thinking, she swept her fingers over the back of his neck. He shivered beneath her touch and turned to look at her. She jerked her hand back.

"What are you doing?"

"Just checking," she said.

"Checking for what?" he asked, staring at her. When she didn't answer, he shook his head. "I can't do this with you hovering over me. Take a seat." He tilted his head toward the other chair.

"I'll watch from here." She rested her hands lightly on the back of the chair.

His fingers flew over the keyboard. The blank screen was suddenly replaced by a variety of news sites. Some were less newsworthy than others, but almost all splashed his name across the tops of the screen. She read the headlines and gasped.

He turned suddenly in the chair. Dizzie stepped back, but not in time.

Knocked off balance, she wobbled and grabbed at his

shoulders. Before she steadied herself, his hands were on her waist and he tugged her onto his lap.

Her breath whooshed out and she wasn't sure it was from the fall.

"I'm fine," she said. Stay or go? Her brain whirred frantically as she tried to decide.

"Sit still." Killian wrapped his arm around her waist. "Now I can keep an eye on you."

With the decision made for her, she regained enough awareness to catalog her new position. Killian's firm chest was behind her. His breath was warm on her neck. And his lap was solid and warm. And cold.

Wait, what?

She shifted. His left side was slightly cooler than the right. And harder. She wiggled. His warning growl reverberated through her entire body.

Now that she knew what to look for, she dropped her hands to her sides and trailed her fingers along his outer hips and upper thighs. Warm flesh under one hand, smooth metal under the other. "You have a cyber leg."

Her pronouncement hung in the air between them while beneath her his body tensed. He whirled her around until she was practically cradled in his arms.

"You have a cyber leg," she repeated. "How did I not know that?"

He cocked a brow.

Wow. She was taking stupid questions to a whole new level. Swatting him on the shoulder, she said, "You know what I mean. The newsies never reported on it."

"It's none of their fucking business."

How did one of the most watched men in the country keep a secret like that?

"What happened? When?" The questions tumbled out.

"Not your business either, Dizzie." Their eyes met.

Abruptly, he spun her back around.

Okay, true. That didn't stop her from trying to remember every article she'd ever read about him. Girl-friends, dates, parties. Every aspect of his life seemed to be fair game or the newsies—but never a whisper about a cyber leg.

Dizzie couldn't imagine having your privacy violated constantly. The small taste she'd gotten yesterday was enough. More than enough, when she focused on the computer screen.

Pictures of her escape accompanied the headlines. She leaned in for a closer look and Killian scooted the chair forward. As she flipped through the different pages, half her attention focused on the screens in front of her. The rest was still processing the press of his body against hers. His whole body, not just his leg. Though she was aware of the subtle difference between his two limbs, it didn't bother her. Like her, a lot of corporate employees weren't 100 percent human.

A sudden thought occurred and she wiggled again. More experimentally.

"Focus on the screen." Again that growl. The hairs on the back of her neck stood up and other parts of her tingled.

She didn't hold back her smile. Yeah, his parts were in working order.

Her smile dimmed as she read the stories. So far she was only identified as a mystery girlfriend. Better than a mad bomber or corporate courier. "Do they call any woman you come in contact with your girlfriend?"

"Pretty much."

"That's got to suck," she said.

"It does."

"Can we use that? They don't know who I am. I'll disappear from your life and they'll never know."

"You might be able to avoid the newsies, but Tremaine Security won't stop. Portia won't stop." Exhaustion and sadness filled his voice. "I think revenge is the only thing keeping her going."

"Did they follow you?" She twisted to face him, straining against his tight hold around her waist. "I'll get out of here."

"No one followed me." A thread of uncertainty ran through his words.

"Why did you come? What do you want?" She was tired of unanswered questions.

He was quiet. Probably wishing he was somewhere else. "I'm here because you stole my bike. I'm here because I was worried about you." He paused. His hands grasped her waist and his eyes met hers. "Because I can't stop thinking about you."

His hand slid up her back and he lowered his lips to hers.

CHAPTER 24

HIS LIPS WERE soft but firm. He brushed them over hers in feather-light kisses that were gentle yet demanding.

She started in surprise, then sank into the moment. Dizzie wanted more, so she leaned into the kiss.

Killian tightened his arms around her. She melted into him, losing the ability to think. She could only feel.

The warmth surrounding her. The pressure of his lips on hers. The strength in the body beneath her. It felt like heaven.

Killian's lips played chase with hers. But it wasn't enough.

She wiggled closer, seeking a better angle. She nibbled at his upper lip. A little nip. A playful demand.

His hand cupped her neck. Like his kiss, his touch was firm but gentle.

She didn't want gentle. She wanted more of the fire that raced through her veins. A fire that had sparked to life when he'd winked at her at the gala.

Her arms slid from his neck to his shoulders.

He tensed beneath her, waiting.

She nipped again, harder than before. His bottom lip this time.

Killian pulled back, his grip on her waist loosening. He sucked in a deep breath.

Dizzie took advantage of the pause. Using his shoulders and the chair for leverage, she lifted up and changed position, nestling her legs in the space between Killian and the arms of the chair. Her knees bracketed his thighs before he'd had time to blink.

She pulled him closer.

His eyes searched hers.

"Yes," she said. Her passion-hazed gaze met his.

Answering desire flared in his eyes. He leaned in toward her mouth, fingers digging into her hips as he pulled her closer.

When his lips met hers this time, it was no chaste closed-mouth kiss.

His kiss bundled all the danger and passion, fear and mystery of the past days into one explosive concoction.

She met him kiss for kiss. Nipping and sucking. Tongues tangling.

Push. Pull.

Give. Take.

The play of their lips more intense than anything she'd experienced before.

Scooting closer on her knees, she pressed her center against his arousal. Moaned into his mouth.

Closer. She had to get closer.

On her hips, his hands exerted enough pressure to angle her pelvis closer to his.

Hell yeah.

She squeezed her thighs together, trapping him beneath her. Her hips took on a life of their own, rocking back and forth, and pressing her heated core to his hard length.

Killian groaned and tugged her shirt free of her pants. When his hands slipped under her shirt, his palms heated her skin like a brand.

She hissed and he captured the sound with his mouth.

He traced delicate lines over her lower back. The restrained power in each touch made her shiver.

Dizzie pressed her breasts against his chest. The heat of him burned her inside and out.

She tore her mouth away from his and fought to catch her breath.

"You feel amazing," she gasped. She dipped her head for another kiss.

He traced another design on the small of her back, with his nails this time, and she almost came out of her skin.

Blood rushed to her nipples. The stiff peaks strained against her lacy bra and her brain nearly short-circuited.

She ground her pelvis against his, the delicate lace of her panties providing another layer of sensation. The warmth of his arousal was just out of reach, the barriers of their clothes too much, and she whimpered against his mouth.

Hips swiveling, she braced her hands on his shoulders, exerting more pressure in her quest to get closer.

He growled.

The sound called to her primitive side. She nipped at his lips again and gripped his shoulders.

His muscles tensed under her touch and she reveled in the movement, knowing she had caused it.

His lips pulled away from hers. "Ow!" He pulled his hand from beneath her shirt and she immediately missed his warmth.

Dizzie stared at him. *Why had he stopped?*

Killian gripped his shoulder, tugging his shirt forward, providing a glimpse of torn fabric. He reached back and his fingers came away slicked with blood. "What the fuck?"

Oh, shit.

She scrambled off his lap, putting space between them. "I'm sorry. I didn't mean to." Her cheeks burned with embarrassment and her stomach churned. She never lost control like that.

"What the hell happened, Dizzie?" Killian sounded confused, but not mad.

Hands clasped behind her back, she trembled while she looked everywhere but at him. "I, uh, I lost control."

Dammit. She wouldn't cry.

"I know what losing control is. That was way more than losing control." His voice was calm. Gentle.

"It was the chair." She blurted out the first thing that came to mind.

Killian pushed up from the chair. Hand on the backrest, he spun it in a slow circle, then studied his fingers again. "It wasn't the chair."

He turned sideways and looked around the room, presenting her with a clear view of his ripped shirt. Four holes edged with blood were clearly visible.

She made a cry of distress. "It wasn't the chair," she admitted.

"What happened? I thought you were into it." He advanced toward her, steady and calm.

"I was. I was totally into it." Her voice cracked. She took another step back, looked behind her. She was a few steps from the wall.

He took another step. She countered by stepping to the side.

Tension crackled between them.

Killian closed the distance between them with long steps.

Dizzie stepped back until she hit the wall. She wasn't afraid of him. Not really.

She feared his reaction. The questions he'd ask.

His arms reached for her and she tensed. He rested his hands on her upper arms, then slid them down toward her wrists.

Her body trembled with the urge to run, but she tamped it down. His rejection would come soon enough. Why waste time trying to run?

His grip was gentle as he tugged her arms forward.

She didn't resist. That would only postpone the inevitable. His hands cleared her wrists and then he was lifting her hands. Turning them over.

Dizzie tensed and tried to pull them back.

He paused, watching her.

She sucked in a deep breath, released it slowly. Nodded.

Palms up, she relaxed her clenched fingers. Her right hand was streaked with blood.

Killian freed her left hand. The only difference between her hands was the blood staining the palm and nails of her right one.

"You okay?"

She shrugged.

Ignoring the blood, he kneaded her palm, pressing on the bones. He worked his way up her fingers, repeating the process on each. Apparently satisfied with what he didn't find, he moved on to her nails.

His fingertip trailed lightly over the end of a nail. The

blood wasn't nearly as noticeable on the painted side, the red of it blending with her polish. "Titanium?"

Dizzie nodded, barely able to swallow past the lump in her throat. When people learned about her nails, they weren't usually quite so...calm.

"Why?" His hands cradled hers. Her hands trembled as they rested in his.

Embarrassed, she dropped her gaze.

"Security," she said. "Protection." They were literally her secret weapon. Now, she'd lost one of her few advantages against this man. If she'd ever had any.

Silence fell between them again.

She had his blood on her hands. It made her sick.

"I've gotta go..." Words failed her. She tugged her hand from his and dashed from the room.

CHAPTER 25

KILLIAN PERCHED on the edge of his seat, keeping pressure off the gashes on his shoulders. They'd probably stopped bleeding, but he couldn't check until Dizzie came out of the bathroom.

The way she'd stared at him—like he was about to kick a puppy.

He rubbed his chest. Thinking about it made him feel like a monster.

She'd looked so scared and small, standing between his body and the wall. Facing off Tremaine Security hadn't fazed her, but revealing her modifications had made her tremble like a rabbit. How many people had judged her for them?

Surely, after discovering his leg, she realized that he wouldn't be one of those people.

Easy for him to say—he hadn't exactly gone public with his own replacement limb.

After the earthquake and building collapse that had killed his parents and taken his leg, he'd been too fucking traumatized to do much talking. By the time he'd returned to a semblance of his former life...well, how did you drop that into conversation?

He didn't blame her for keeping secrets. Or for camouflaging her nails with brightly colored polish. Metal talons for fingernails made perfect sense for a woman whose life required visiting every part of the city, good and bad. They were the perfect weapon. Completely invisible, but hidden in plain sight. Security. Protection.

Killian stared at the closed bathroom door. What was she doing in there? He wanted to make sure she was okay, but also feared it would be awkward. If her claws hadn't come out, who knows where they'd be now.

A bed. This chair.

The way Dizzie had settled onto his lap...they'd have made it work.

"Are you going to turn me in?" She had slipped out of the bathroom and now stood in shadow on the other side of the room, hands clasped. At least she wasn't trying to hide them.

Keeping his voice quiet, hoping she didn't bolt back into the bathroom, he didn't answer immediately. "We can't stay here forever."

She didn't respond.

He didn't know what he was going to do. He should turn her in. Forget his grand plan to bring Tommy's killer to justice. Let Portia have Dizzie and call it good enough.

Who was he kidding? "No," he admitted with a sigh.

Now that he'd discovered that her only protection against the big bad corporate world was titanium nails? The only thing he knew for sure was that he wouldn't let her face this alone.

That shouldn't surprise him. He'd been doing the unexpected around this woman since he'd first seen her. She'd turned his whole world upside down.

"What are we going to do?" Fear didn't cling as strongly to her words.

"No fucking clue." He rubbed his hand over his jaw, the prickle of whiskers reminding him how out of his depth he was. "What's your plan?"

"Still working on it." She'd taken the second chair. Drawing her feet up, she wrapped her arms around her knees. She looked so small. Was she trying to appeal to his protective instincts or was this the effect she had on him?

"Two heads are better than one." He tried to lighten the mood.

Not even a smile.

He didn't know how to do this, how to break the awkward silence. They weren't friends or lovers. Just two strangers bound together by an awful moment and an amazing kiss. What did you say in that situation?

"How'd you find this place?" He asked the question that had plagued him since he tracked the motorcycle.

Her eyes widened.

Fuck. That was obviously the wrong question.

Stretching out his leg, he hooked his toe under her seat and swiveled her until she faced him.

She met his gaze. "How did you know to break me out of the cell?" she countered.

Killian stared at her, processing her question. What did that have to do with his question? "I got a phone call," he told her, curious what she'd do with the information.

"Anonymous?"

He nodded. "Beyond anonymous. Completely blocked."

"Me too."

"Anonymous call?"

She bobbed her head yes–no. "Not exactly. Anony-mous...text."

"You have your phone?" There hadn't been one in the clothes he'd collected during her bath. And he hadn't thought to have Elsa get her a replacement.

She shook her head. "It's back at headquarters. I think."

"You're lying." She couldn't get a text without a phone.

"No, I'm not. He..." She paused, lacing her fingers tight enough over her knees to whiten her knuckles.

"Don't do that. You'll cut yourself." Oh my god. Where had *that* come from?

Dizzie gave him a funny look, then dropped her feet and pushed out of the chair. She paced the room in small circles, her nails clicking together as she moved. Each time she passed him, she slowed and studied him. Then she was off to make another circuit.

He watched patiently, letting the silence stretch between them. Inside, he was dying to know what was so terrible she had to build up to telling him.

Finally, after a dozen laps, she stopped in front of him. Her hands dropped to her sides. Whatever she'd decided, she looked less stressed.

"Hehackedintomyimplants."

Okay, maybe not.

"What?" He tried to parse out the words. Someone had...*hacked* into her implants? That didn't make any sense. How could someone do that to fingernails?

Standing between his outstretched legs, she didn't meet his eyes. "After I left your house last night, someone—guy, girl, I don't know!—hacked into my implants. Told me that the newsies were watching your place."

"Too bad that warning didn't come a bit sooner." Whoops. He hadn't meant to say that out loud.

Dizzie glared at him. "*You* took me home," she snapped. "Of course, they think I'm one of your girlfriends."

"It's not my fault they're camped out at my house." He put his hands on her hips and pulled her closer. She didn't resist, but she didn't fall into his arms either.

She sneered. "Right. It's not your fault that you're hot, rich, and single."

Killian smiled. She thought he was hot. Ridiculous given the situation, but he didn't care.

"Get that stupid grin off your face, Killian. This is serious." She punched him in the shoulder. His wounded shoulder. He bit back a wince. He didn't want her to freak out again.

He tried to tone down the smile. "You're right. Super serious. But I don't understand how he hacked your implants." He nodded toward her hands.

She followed his gaze. "What are you—oh. No, not these," she said, wiggling her fingers. "These." She pointed toward her eyes.

"He hacked your *eyeballs*?" Saying that out loud made him queasy.

"My optical implants, yeah. It was...disturbing."

Killian shuddered. He'd seen a lot of gross stuff in his life—hell, after the accident, his mangled leg was one of the worst—but he'd always had a special thing about eyeballs. He didn't want to know any more. But he had to. "How?"

She shrugged. "He didn't say. And it was hard to ask."

Her explanation included flashing text, satellites, and being led to the warehouse. Killian didn't know whether to be impressed or horrified. "You're sure you don't know who's doing this?"

"I would have told you. Probably."

"Do you have any enemies or a stalker?" Was that how she'd come to the bomber's attention? Was the mystery hacker responsible for all of this?

She laughed.

He hadn't heard her laugh before.

It was earthy and husky and, with her eyes closed and her head tilted back, it was the most natural he'd ever seen her. Dizzie's laugh reached deep inside and affected him like no one else had.

That was silly. It was probably relief from the tension breaking.

And that was probably a lie.

When she finally stopped laughing, it took her a second to catch her breath. "That's ridiculous. Why would you say that? You're the one who probably has a stalker. All those girlfriends. And all the newsies."

The jealousy in her voice sent a flare of satisfaction through him. He shook his head. "No stalkers." Not in years.

Using his hands on her hips, he tugged her down onto his lap.

She resisted initially, then let her weight barely rest on his leg.

He missed the way she'd melted against him. She'd been so responsive. He forced those memories away. Not the time.

Ignoring how stiffly she sat on his lap, Killian recapped what they knew. "Let's review the last two days." He held up one finger. "You were chosen to deliver the bomb."

"That wasn't my fault!"

She almost bolted, but he anchored her in place with a restraining hand. Dizzie settled, but didn't fully relax.

"One, the delivered bomb," he said quickly. "Two, he contacted me while you were in custody. Three, he hacked your *eyes* after you left my house."

He paused and she nodded. Good, she was following his line of reasoning.

"Four, he led you to a hacker's hideout. All that hacking? Sounds like a stalker to me."

She watched him. "Yes, but no."

What? Killian stared at her, waiting for her to elaborate.

"I don't think it's a stalker," she said finally. "More like a guardian angel."

Her eyes sparkled as she spoke. Jealousy speared through him, making him uncomfortable. Jealousy meant feelings. He didn't have those. Did he?

Now was not the time to dive into that question. "A guardian angel?" he asked, skeptical.

"No, think about it this way. One, he convinced you to rescue me."

He was already shaking his head before she finished. "One was the bomb."

"We don't know it was the bomb."

He stared at her until she relented.

"Fine, it was probably the bomb. But," she hurried to add, "I don't think the guardian angel was involved."

She smirked at him, as if she knew how much he hated the idea of someone else rescuing her. "So, one, he sent you to rescue me."

"Fine, the bomb can be zero," Killian groused.

She laughed. "Two, he helped me avoid the newsies who saw me leave your place." Her eyes dared him to contradict her. "Three, he led me to a safe house where I could hide from the newsies and the Tremaine Corporation."

Killian stared at her, mulling over her version of events.

He wouldn't say that she was right—no way to know that until they found the mastermind behind the bomb. As a counterpoint to his own interpretation—well, it made sense.

Dizzie was much smarter than her position led people to believe. If she'd been born into his world, she'd be unstoppable.

She clicked her nails together.

"It's an interesting perspective." He held up a hand to forestall an argument. "There's only one way to know for sure—we need to find our mystery hacker."

Her mouth opened. Closed. He waited for her to lambast him for being wrong. Surprisingly, that wasn't her first objection.

She stared at him. "Do you hear what you're saying? Mystery. Hacker."

When he didn't respond, she sighed and spelled out her concerns. "Mystery hacker. Neither word describes someone, you know, easy to find. Unless you've been hiding some mad computer skills?"

He shook his head.

"Yeah, I didn't think so."

Ouch.

Killian had skills. Lots of them. Skiing. Dancing. Driving fast.

Dizzie was right. He was useless.

"I've got money." The minute the words left his mouth, he knew he'd fucked up. He was the world's biggest asshole.

She blinked several times. "Well, yeah, there's that. I'm not sure how that helps us. Unless you announce that you'll pay for information leading to the person behind the bombing."

The words hung in the air between them.

Killian watched the wheels turning behind her big blue eyes. She was considering the idea. So was he.

When he'd last spoken to Portia, the Tremaine Corporation hadn't intended to offer a reward. It had never occurred to him to offer one himself.

"That...could work," she said at the same time he blurted, "That's a good idea."

They looked at each other.

"Do you have any spare credits?" she asked.

Killian leaned forward to pull out his wallet. The move brought him close enough to see her pulse flutter in her neck.

"Untraceable credits, I mean." Credits that weren't linked to personal information or bank accounts.

He flipped through his wallet, though he already knew what he'd find. "A few hundred."

Small stuff. For bribing a maître d' or grabbing a bite from a food truck. It used to be a few thousand. Since the accident, he did a lot less partying and carried a lot less free money than he used to.

"That's probably not enough." Dizzie sighed, looking so lost that all he wanted to do was make it better. "How much do you think we need?"

He was used to throwing money at problems, but never in the form of a reward. "I have no idea," he admitted.

"Maybe the Jack could help." Dizzie paused. "That's where my money is. Maybe we can ask for help getting the word out. And ask how much we need."

He knew of the Jack. Shrewd and ruthless in business. Willing to provide solutions, for the right price, cash up front. "That could work." While Killian hated the idea of bringing an unknown into this mess, the Jack had shadier connections than he did.

"What if it's not enough?" She clicked her nails together. "Wait, why can't we use your money?"

Killian coughed. "Happy to. The problem is that you want untraceable credits so folks don't know who's asking, right?"

"I guess."

"I don't think it matters who's paying the reward." Her look told him to continue. "I don't see why it matters where the money comes from," he said. "Because you're right. I'm Killian St. John. *That* is my skill. No one will think twice if I offer a reward for information on the bombing that killed my best friend."

She shoved her hands in her pockets. "You think that will get the hacker to come forward?"

Killian shrugged. "The hacker. Anyone with information. I don't care who brings us the information as long as I get answers."

"If you're Killian St. John, payer of reward, what do you need me for?"

Of course, she'd picked up on the weak part of his plan. Technically speaking, he didn't. Killian could set up a reward—with or without the Jack—easily enough. Keeping her close was more about knowing her location than anything else. Except maybe it was also about keeping her safe from Portia.

"I'll need you to connect me with the Jack." Making that connection would give her a role to play.

She nodded. "Okay. If you're sure."

He was sure. He wanted this nightmare over. If throwing money at it worked, he'd be thrilled.

They had a plan. He had the feeling it was going to be a very expensive plan.

CHAPTER 26

"AND YOU'RE GOING to your bank to set up a reward?"

They'd spent hours in the blue-tinged room of computer monitors looking for answers online and finalizing their next steps. She hadn't heard a word from the hacker. Did he or she know that Killian was here too?

"Yes," Killian said. He took a bite of the meal Dizzie had thrown together.

It wasn't great, but the food in the tiny kitchen was their only option. Canned chili or stale cereal without milk. She'd chosen the latter, too damn tired, despite a second cat nap, to even heat up the chili.

"Because you don't trust the equipment here," she prodded.

He put down his bowl. "Yes, I'd prefer not to do my banking on equipment owned by a known hacker." He looked as tired as she felt.

She rolled her eyes. "We don't know that he'll track your information."

"We don't know that he won't either."

Valid. Dizzie chewed the soft cereal pieces and hard

marshmallows and forced herself to swallow. "You can access it from your house, though, right?"

"If you don't want me to leave, say so. We'll figure out another way." He studied her and she dropped her gaze to the bowl in her lap.

It wasn't a matter of not wanting him to leave, more that the hacker space was...cozy with him here. "No! I'm making sure we've covered all the details." There wasn't much to their plan and now that it was time to implement it, Dizzie was worried.

"I'll set up the reward with my banker and meet you at the Jack's. We'll find out how we can spread the word and we'll settle in to wait for anyone with information."

"At Razor Jack's." Going to the bar was the only way to make contact with the Jack.

"Yes." Killian sounded pained. He'd fought to convince her to come back to his house while they waited.

She'd vetoed that *and* staying here. Her winning argument, though, had been that people with information would be more likely to go to the Jack's rather than face the relentless newsies at Killian's house.

"Are you sure you want to offer that much in reward?" Dizzie cleared their bowls and tidied up the kitchen.

When Killian had named the amount that he intended to offer as a reward, the sheer number of zeros had taken her breath away. If only she had information on the bombing—that much money would nearly pay off her contract.

"It's only money, Dizzie."

Only money.

Theoretically, she knew that much money existed. In practice, like right now, that level of wealth wasn't a concept she could wrap her head around. She and Killian might both have ties to the Tremaine Corporation, but they came from opposite ends of the economic spectrum.

That he had more of this kind of money sent her pulse racing and not in the good way. The amount of power the man beside her wielded...it terrified her.

"It'll work," she whispered. It had to. She'd been in limbo for days and it was taking a toll. A future of running and hiding seemed unbearable.

Killian rubbed her arm and she leaned into the touch, needing the contact and the reassurance.

"I need to go," he said.

"I know." She pulled away even though a part of her—a deep part of her that she was trying to shush—wanted to beg him to stay.

A whisper of a kiss against her temple. A goodbye kiss.

Dizzie understood why he was leaving, but still struggled to believe he wasn't bailing on her or setting her up. Her heart said to trust him; her head was a lot more wary.

"Stay here until it's time to meet at Razor Jack's."

She nodded. Late afternoon couldn't come soon enough. She wasn't built for being cooped up like this. "I will. Probably."

"I mean it," he said. "If you run, you better hope I find you before Portia does."

She followed him to the door. She tucked her hands in her pockets, unsure what to say. "Um, bye," she murmured. Argh. She sounded lame.

A big smile crossed his face. "Um, bye," he echoed.

While she struggled with a witty comeback, Killian tugged her into his arms and lowered his mouth to hers. While they'd plotted this morning, they'd shared a few more kisses. His lips had quickly become her drug of choice. The circumstances were horrible, but without them, she'd never have met him, never had kissed him.

She grabbed his biceps and pulled herself up on her tiptoes.

The height differential put her at an awkward angle. She looped her arms around his neck and jumped. He caught her around the waist and she wrapped her legs around his hips.

He staggered back a step, but never broke the kiss. Instead, he deepened it, his tongue sweeping along the seam of her lips then darting inside.

One arm supported her under her thighs, the other curved around her waist, then dipped down to grab her ass.

He squeezed and Dizzie gasped, opening up further for his tongue's plunder.

More careful of her fingernails this time, she kneaded his shoulders, trying to get closer to him with every heartbeat.

He hoisted her higher and she took control of the kiss.

Took. And took. And took.

Killian pulled away, rested his forehead against hers. Beneath their harsh breathing, she heard mewing.

It was her. Her face flamed in embarrassment.

"I need to go." His voice was rough and sent shivers through her body, the same way his kisses had.

She nodded, too breathless to speak.

"You need to let me go."

This time, Dizzie shook her head.

To emphasize her point, she tightened her thighs around him. Toned and strong from riding, they easily supported her as she rubbed against the erection that said he didn't want to go.

"You're evil," he finally groaned.

She took it as a compliment. "I know."

He brushed his lips over hers again but pulled back before she could capture them.

Shifting their bodies until her back was against the wall, he gently pressed her against it. The movement ground her core against him. They groaned in unison.

With the wall supporting her, he reached back and unlocked her ankles.

She dropped her legs slowly, feeling around with her tiptoes until they touched solid ground. Killian waited until she stood on her own—mostly—before stepping away.

With a sound of displeasure, she said, "Party pooper."

He laughed. "You have no idea how much I want to stay. We have things to do. I want you safe before I take you to bed."

That was...unexpected, but the promise in his voice sent shivers through her. She had every intention of holding him to that. "Well," she purred, "in that case, you need to leave."

Dizzie stepped past him to open the door. Sheer force of will kept her legs from wobbling. Her arms swept out in invitation.

He laughed again. "Lock up behind me."

She managed to close and lock the door before her legs gave out. She slid to the ground and leaned back against the door.

What the hell had just happened?

CHAPTER 27

DIZZIE PASSED a few small shops that catered to non-corporate types, then crossed the street. She stood in the dim glow of the blinking neon sign above the bar. There was no bouncer at the door—you entered Razor Jack's at your own risk. With a deep breath, she pushed the door open. Chaos, music, and light spilled out.

This wasn't her first time here. Why was her stomach fluttering? She buried her nerves and walked in like she owned the place. It was the only way to not draw attention. She'd never been a regular, but she'd been to the bar enough to know how it worked.

Carefully picking her way through the main bar area on borrowed black heels, she sat down at a table near the back. Her feet hurt. Her boots were stowed in her bag and she missed their comfort and stability desperately.

Anyone on the lookout for a short blonde would be in for a shock. The curly red hair that spilled down Dizzie's back came from a pill. The dealer she'd bought it from had promised that the color-changing nanotech would only last a few days. The nearly see-through blue dress and the heels had belonged to a prostitute. She'd traded some of the clothes Killian had bought her.

The underwear was hers. She had to draw the line somewhere.

The only resemblance to her original self was her height. That couldn't be changed by taking a pill. Probably.

She shuddered. Convincing herself to swallow the hair-color pill had been hard enough. Hopefully the superficial changes would keep her from getting picked up by the recognition software.

"Get you a drink, hon?"

Dizzie looked up at the waitress who had appeared by her table.

She obviously took too long to reply, because the waitress spoke again, her voice low. "You can hang out here, hon, but you gotta buy something. The Jack ain't running a charity."

Dizzie ordered the cheapest coffee on the menu. The waitress continued to stare at her, so she added a protein bar. The stale cereal earlier hadn't been much of a meal.

The waitress stayed at her table until she paid. She swiped one of Killian's unregistered chips through the reader. Once the payment cleared, the waitress walked away, leaving Dizzie feeling like she'd failed a test.

While she waited, Dizzie pulled out her burner phone, another purchase from her street-side shopping spree. An unlocked older model that didn't require biometric data.

She checked the chip's balance. Blinked. The remaining balance was a lot higher than she'd expected.

Spending Killian's money felt weird. Outside of her Tremaine contract, Dizzie had always paid her own way. The Tremaine contract didn't count. That had been put into place when the company took her in as a baby. But until she could meet with the Jack to access her funds, Dizzie had to rely on Killian.

She'd wanted to go with him to his bank, but she appreciated the distance too. He made her feel things. Things she didn't know how to process. It shouldn't matter. Whatever was between them couldn't go anywhere. In the movies, the star-crossed lovers might end up together, but that didn't happen in real life.

His kisses fired up her body and she hadn't stopped thinking about it all day. Even when she'd tried to sleep, her mind had refused to shut down, imagining his hands on her.

The way he revved her body up was nothing compared to his acceptance of her nails. After the surgery, even Alice had given her funny looks. No one understood. Dizzie had learned to keep her nails to herself.

Until Killian.

The waitress delivered her coffee and protein bar, then studied her for a moment. Long enough to speed up Dizzie's pulse. Had she been recognized?

"Thank you," Dizzie said. She picked up her coffee and took a tentative sip.

"Gah!" It was awful. So bitter it nearly stripped the taste buds off her tongue. It wasn't like she was a coffee purist, but damn, this was vile.

She took another sip, trying to swallow without tasting it. She chased it with a bite of the nutrition bar. Better, but not by much. Needing a few minutes to get the taste out of her mouth, Dizzie pulled open a news app.

An overseas attack on a US-based multinational was the top story. Corporate espionage was suspected. Not surprising. The damn corporations constantly attacked each other.

Had the bombing been as simple as corporate espionage?

She focused on what she knew about Tremaine Corporation and its enemies. The company manufactured pharmaceuticals and other biologics. Its primary rivals were Takanachi, Arawa South, the Solveig Consortium, and Blether Brothers Manufacturing. Had one of them masterminded the bombing?

Opening a note app, she tapped out her thoughts using the awkward keyboard.

She couldn't wait to share her theories with Killian. Would he know the depth of Tremaine's Corporations rivalries?

"You need anything else, hon?" the waitress asked.

Dizzie hadn't noticed that the waitress had come back. She slid her palm over the screen.

"No, I'm, uh, good," she stuttered. Definitely not spy material.

"You sure?" The woman's tone made her look up.

The waitress waited until Dizzie met her eyes, then she flicked her gaze over to the bar where the Jack watched their interaction.

Shit. Dizzie sucked in a breath. "Am I going to be kicked out?" she whispered.

"Oh no, hon." The waitress looked horrified. "It's not that. Though it probably wouldn't hurt if you bought another cup of coffee."

Eager to stay off the Jack's radar, Dizzie nodded and slid her credit chip back into the reader.

"Let us know if you need any help." The waitress gave her another searching look as she walked away.

"Okay." Dizzie had the lingering sense the waitress was trying to give her a message, but she was completely missing it. As long as she wasn't getting thrown out, she wouldn't worry. Much.

Alone again, Dizzie researched corporate rivalries. All of them, not only Tremaine, in case the company tracked online searches. She didn't want to raise any red flags. Some of the stories linked to earlier news about the bombing. She clicked through a handful of links, curious what was being said.

She scrolled through the news, then gasped. The Tremaine Corporation had finally released her photo. Thankfully the newsies had yet to connect it with the grainy images from Killian's driveway.

That was a relief. If anyone linked Killian and Dizzie together, the backlash against him would be unimaginable. He didn't deserve that. She knew his loyalty to Portia was absolute.

To keep her hands busy, she sipped her coffee again and gagged. It was worse cold. She choked it down, then switched to the new cup the waitress had dropped off.

With her new baseline for coffee, the second cup didn't taste nearly as bad.

Dizzie tapped her fingers on the table. Stopped abruptly. Waiting sucked. She studied the room around her, swinging her foot to hide her fidgets. All dark wood and retro-biker décor, it smelled faintly of old beer and lemony soap. Dangerous, but not deadly. Comforting even, because day or night, the place never changed.

As she looked around, she tried not to make eye contact with anyone in the bar. She didn't want any trouble.

"Haven't seen you in here before." A guy set his drink on her table and leaned on the high tabletop.

Her stomach dropped. So much for going unnoticed.

She took a minute to settle her nerves before responding. "Never been here before," she lied.

"I come here all the time," he said.

Dizzie barely held back a snort. Dressed the way he was, she highly doubted it.

His dark pants and white shirt marked him as a corporate drone. Not Razor Jack's usual clientele. It was too lower class for middle managers and too rough for most office workers, unless they came on a dare or were slumming.

"That's nice." Dizzie kept her attention on her coffee. What would it take to make him go away?

He pulled out a bar stool and sat down next to her.

Ugh. She did not need this right now.

"Yeah, it's nice. I'm nice." His gaze crawled over her, giving her the creeps. "You look *real* nice."

She choked back the urge to vomit. "Sorry, not interested." She kept her tone as even as possible.

"What's your name?" He leaned close enough she smelled the beer on his breath.

"Not interested."

He laughed like Dizzie had said something funny, then waved the waitress over.

When she arrived at the table, it was Dizzie she addressed. "You all right, hon?"

"I'm fine. Just..." She searched for the right word, one that wouldn't cause trouble. "A little crowded."

"I'll take another beer." He slid his chip into the reader and selected one of the most expensive beers.

Crap.

"I'll be right back with your beer." The waitress looked between Dizzie and the creep and the chip. She turned back to Dizzie, apology in her eyes.

Dizzie nodded in understanding. It was up to her to get rid of this guy.

"So, how much?"

Startled, Dizzie looked at him. He slid his credit chip her way.

She shuddered. Sure, she was dressed like a hooker, but she hadn't expected anyone to take advantage of it. Gross. "I think you've got the wrong girl."

He looked her up and down. "I don't think so."

Her stomach churned and she knew it wasn't only due to the coffee. Sit here and hope he went away? Or run?

Neither option was good. Hope hadn't gotten her very far in life. Running wouldn't get her far, and definitely not in these shoes. Not to mention, she'd told Killian she'd meet him here.

"Excuse me." She slipped her phone into her pocket and got to her feet. She grabbed her bag and the new cup of coffee, intending to move to another table.

His hand wrapped around her wrist. "Where you going? We're just getting to know each other."

She tugged at her arm, trying not to cause a scene.

His grip tightened.

Fuck, that wasn't good. She stilled as her fight or flight instincts kicked in. "I gotta go."

"I don't think so." He pulled her toward him.

Screw avoiding a scene.

She stepped backward, trying to put as much space between them as possible. It wasn't much, given the grip he had on her arm.

Praying it was hot enough, she tipped the coffee onto his arm.

"You bitch!" He released her and she scrambled back, putting the table between them.

"You'll pay for that." He shoved a chair out of his way.

The high heels didn't offer much in the way of getaway

material, but Dizzie bounced on her toes, waiting to see which way he went, hoping to go the opposite way.

"We got a problem here?"

She dropped back on her heels in surprise. That voice. She knew that voice. The man it came from? Total stranger.

He was tall, with dark hair and muddy brown eyes. His clothes were... She didn't have the words for them.

His yellow shirt nearly blinded her, even in the dark bar. The skintight pants—which hugged a delicious set of thighs—were a completely unappetizing purple.

Dizzie stared at Killian in shock. She'd never in a million years expected him to come disguised as...whatever that was.

His appearance pulled the creep's attention from her. "Not your fucking problem."

"Yeah, she is." His claim sent a thrill through her.

"Oh yeah?" The corporate guy crowded Killian.

"You should leave. Now." Killian's voice was a low rumble.

Whatever the guy saw in Killian's face convinced him. He slipped in the puddle of coffee, righted himself, and practically ran to the door.

With Killian's attention on the other man, Dizzie took in his unexpected appearance. All clenched jaw and don't-fuck-with-me menace. This badass side of Killian was fucking hot.

Once the creep was out the door, Killian focused that growly attention on her. "Can't you stay out of trouble for a minute?"

"Did he recognize you?" They spoke at the same time.

Dizzie glared at him. "I was sitting here minding my own business when he came over."

"You should have told him to go away."

"Gee, why didn't I think of that?" Her words dripped with sarcasm. She stepped around the spilled coffee and settled at the second table.

Killian sat opposite her, angling his body to see over her shoulder.

She could still see past him and appreciated the consideration.

"Why are you staring?" he asked.

"I wasn't expecting...this." She waved her hand, indicating his entire outfit.

His smile broke through the disguise.

It wasn't his paparazzi smile, the one she'd seen at the gala or in videos. This was the real Killian. The newsies only ever caught this one in candid photos, pictures captured when he was having fun or hanging out with Tommy.

Her amusement evaporated. She shouldn't be having fun with Killian. Not when it was her fault his friend was dead.

He reached across the table and grasped her hand. "What's wrong?"

Curling her fingers around his was instinctive by now, though she tried to keep her touch light. It terrified her how easy it was to be with him.

"Sorry. I was thinking about..." Dizzie didn't know what to call him. *Tommy* seemed presumptuous. "Mr. Gilmore."

Killian's expression sobered.

Hands clasped, they sat in silence. She stared at their intertwined fingers, scarcely daring to breathe. Afraid to blink.

This couldn't possibly be happening. And she never wanted it to end.

The waitress delivered another cup of coffee and shattered the moment. Killian pulled his hand away. Dizzie experienced the loss of warmth and companionship immediately.

"What do you want?" The waitress glared at Killian.

The interaction was totally unexpected. His disguise must be working. No woman with a pulse would treat Killian St. John that way.

He pointed at Dizzie's coffee. "I'll have the same."

Oh no. Dizzie winced, but before she could warn him, the waitress was gone.

In a blink, the waitress was back. She set the cup on the table with enough force to send coffee sloshing over the side. "Anything else?"

"No, thanks." Killian looked confused. He turned his attention to Dizzie. "What did that guy want?"

Dizzie choked on her coffee. Seriously? She was dressed like a hooker and he had to ask? She chose the simplest answer. "Me."

He stared at her so long, she squirmed under his scrutiny. Was it that hard to believe?

Finally, *finally*, he spoke. "I don't know whether to compliment him on his taste or chase him down and beat the shit out of him."

The heat in his words shot straight to her core and she pressed her thighs together to keep from fidgeting.

On the run, dressed like a hooker in a seedy bar, and this was the most romantic moment she'd ever had. How messed up was that?

"Holy crap! What *is* this?" His coffee cup clattered to the table.

Lost in a sensual haze from Killian's frank statement, she'd forgotten to warn him about the coffee.

The outrage and shock on his face was priceless. He

wiped his tongue on his sleeve, making gagging sounds the entire time.

"Coffee," she gasped out in between bouts of laughter.

"No. This isn't coffee." He slid the cup across the table. "It's evil mutant coffee. Created when old coffee grounds mated with ancient beans and things went terribly awry."

He looked so horrified. It was easy to see the little boy he'd been as he exaggerated—sort of—the terribleness of the coffee.

Her heart stuttered and she pressed a hand to her chest. Over the last few days, he'd become more than a pretty face in the news.

"How could you possibly call this coffee? Why did you order this?" He continued his high-drama description.

"I had to order something," she said, trying hard not to laugh and failing. "It was the cheapest item on the menu."

"So you drank more than one cup of it? One I could understand, but two?"

She shrugged. "It's not the worst I've ever had."

His smile dimmed and they both stared into their cups of crappy coffee. They were straddling two worlds, with no idea how to navigate the distance between them.

She broke the silence first. "Did your bank visit go okay?"

"Fine. We'll have to lay low until word spreads."

"There are rooms in back, I think. I've seen girls come out of them. We can ask at the bar." They'd be safe enough, for a price. The bar was neutral ground compared to Killian's home and the Tremaine Corporation.

Dizzie wasn't naive. She knew why there were rooms in the back of the bar. Could she handle staying in one of them with Killian?

Maybe.

As long as she remembered it was business. They were together because they needed to catch the bomber. Not to soothe each other's hurts.

Find out who was behind the bomb, then go their separate ways.

No matter how much it hurt.

CHAPTER 28

"WE NEED TO SEE THE JACK," Killian demanded when they reached the bar. No one gave either of them a second look as they'd crossed the room. A few of the patrons had run their eyes over her, so apparently her disguise was effective.

The bartender looked from Dizzie to Killian and back again, an unreadable expression on her face.

Dizzie bit back a curse. You didn't see the Jack unless the Jack wanted to see you.

She reached back for Killian's hand. He took hers without hesitation. Dammit, now she felt bad for what she was about to do. Her fingers curled around his hand and she pressed her nails into his skin. Not hard enough to draw blood. It was a warning.

"Please," she said, looking straight at the bartender.

With the hint of what might have been a smile, the woman gave a sharp nod. "I'll ask," she said, then left them while she attended to other customers.

"What was that for?" Killian asked when the bartender

was out of earshot. He tugged his hand free and studied the little half-moon impressions she'd left.

"This is not *your* world," Dizzie said. "Being polite will get us a lot farther than being rude."

"Fine. What do we do now?"

"Now we wait."

It didn't take long. The bartender finished with her customers at the other end and drifted back their way. "Darryl will show you back."

They followed the Jack's security through a door marked EMPLOYEES ONLY and down a narrow hallway. Dizzie kept her head turned away from the camera mounted above the Jack's door. Though she'd changed her appearance, better safe than sorry.

Their escort rapped on the door and stood to the side.

The electronic lock released with a soft snick and he pulled it open for them. The heavy door didn't make a sound when it closed behind her and Killian.

The Jack sat behind a large, old-fashioned wooden desk. Dizzie didn't know anything about antiques, but she was pretty damn sure it was one. The desk wasn't the only old object in the room. Wooden bookshelves filled with paper books lined one wall. An old-fashioned globe sat on a coffee table between two chairs that were probably covered with real leather.

"What can I do for you, Dizzie, Mr. St. John?" The Jack's casual reveal of their names pulled Dizzie's attention back to the bar owner where it belonged.

She shouldn't be surprised that the Jack knew their identities. The Jack had a finger on the pulse of the city and was always informed. Probably why they were here.

Dizzie took a deep breath. "I was told you have rooms for rent."

"I would recommend a hotel if you're looking for a tryst." The Jack's voice was dry.

"Safe rooms," Dizzie corrected quickly. Her face burned and she knew she'd turned bright red.

"What have you heard?" An undertone of displeasure accompanied the mocking smile.

Somehow she'd said the wrong thing and she had no idea how to fix it. "Whispers," Dizzie clarified. "Quiet words in dark corners."

Killian stepped forward and stood between her and the Jack. "I have a proposition for you," he said.

"I did not see that coming," the Jack drawled.

Killian ignored the innuendo and barreled forward. "Here's what we need."

Lips pinched, Dizzie glared at him as he took over. Still, her way hadn't worked well, so what did it hurt.

"I'm listening."

"May I?" Killian gestured toward the chairs in front of the desk. The Jack nodded.

Dizzie took one seat, perched on the edge. The negotiations that were about to take place were outside her comfort zone. Hell, being in the Jack's office was outside it. Killian, though, appeared in his element. He leaned back in the chair like he owned it. The Jack watched them both with a smirk.

"We have some information that we would like you to share," Killian began. "We also need a room and we would like to use the bar to speak with anyone who responds to said information."

"You're offering a reward for information for the New Amsterdam Hotel bombing," the Jack said.

"How did you know that?" Killian asked.

"I have my sources. Given the bomber is sitting right

next to you, I'm not sure what other information you're expecting."

"Dizzie is another victim. I want whatever information people have," Killian said.

He believed her. Pleasure mingled with the guilt that she felt—and probably always would feel—when Killian defended her. His response had none of the hesitation he'd had when he originally questioned her.

The Jack and Killian continued to negotiate terms around her.

Killian tossed a credit stick across the desk.

The Jack swiped it through a credit reader and verified the balance. "This will get you three nights. You can meet in the bar."

"Perfect." Killian stood and extended a hand to help Dizzie to her feet.

"Not so fast," the Jack said. Dizzie held her breath. "My cut is 15 percent of the value of the reward. Plus, 1 percent for my staff if they broker the information that leads to capture."

Dizzie gasped. That was a lot of money.

Killian and the Jack stared at each other. "Fine," Killian said. "*If* the information leads to capture."

"Agreed," the Jack said as they shook on it. "See Dani at the bar. She'll get you a room key."

CHAPTER 29

THE CHAIN that the old-fashioned metal key the bartender had given them dangled from Killian's fingers as he led the way to the room they'd been assigned. Dizzie followed close behind, a presence that he was growing more and more accustomed to.

She was starting to get under his skin.

Killian had nearly lost it when that corporate asshole had put his hands on her. A wave of possessiveness had rushed through him and in that moment, he'd wanted to play hero. He'd wanted to be the one to save her.

When Dizzie had spilled a cup of not-coffee on the guy's arm, the spell had been broken and Killian had slowed his pace. She could take care of herself.

This driving need to keep her safe—was that how Tommy had felt about Portia? He stopped suddenly, struck by the thought.

Dizzie ran into his back. "What's the matter?"

"Nothing, sorry. I got distracted." True enough. No way could he explain the terrifying turn his thoughts had taken. "I want this to be over."

She stiffened and stepped back, so he hurried to add, "I want the waiting to be over." He didn't want his time with her to be over. That was part of the problem.

"Oh, right, me too." Her smile was tight, not nearly as open as the first one.

He'd done that. With careless words, he'd made her feel like she wasn't important. She was pulling away, when all he wanted was to pull her close.

"Let's go," she said. "What's the room number again?"

He was still distracted from her withdrawal. "Twelve."

The door closest to him was labeled with a small metal "1." The next one said "3."

"I think it's going to be on your side," he told her. "You ever been back here before?"

"No, never." Her red hair shimmied.

He missed the blonde.

In the bar, her big blue eyes had watched him from underneath unfamiliar red hair. The look was appealing—especially with the blue material hugging her curves—but it wasn't right.

It wasn't Dizzie.

They passed another few doors to reach room 12.

He positioned Dizzie to the side of the door. "Stay here."

Though technically she was better armed than he was with her metal nails, he wanted her safe.

She gave him a hard look. "Fine."

He wanted to kiss her, but the Jack had suggested—forcefully—that they get out of sight quickly. Kissing could wait until they were safely inside the room. He brushed his thumb over her cheek. "Thank you."

She leaned into his touch, then shifted her head to brush her lips against his hand.

The move was sweet and unexpected. He pressed his palm to her cheek then stepped in front of her and slipped the key into the lock. It opened easily and he pushed the door open.

No lights came on so Killian reached inside, groping along the wall until he found a light switch. The Jack took this retro thing to the extreme.

Crossing the threshold, he stepped into a small room. "All clear," he said after exploring the tiny space.

The room had a miniature bathroom, with a tiny shower and a tinier sink. The furniture fit the room. Small dresser, small table and chairs. Only the bed wasn't tiny.

Dizzie stepped into the room behind him and closed the door. Suddenly the room felt even smaller. "Cozy."

That was one word for it. At least three rooms this size would fit into his master bedroom.

"Three?"

"What?"

Dizzie slipped by him and sat on the edge of the bed. She kicked off her stiletto heels and sighed with relief. "Your bedroom is the size of three of these rooms?"

Shit, had he said that out loud? "Yeah."

"How many of these beds can you fit in yours?"

Killian pictured Dizzie in his bed and it took him a moment to parse her question correctly. "What?"

She gave him a cheeky grin. A grin that gave him all sorts of ideas.

Then she got quiet. "My room's about this size. A little less grim," she said. "Better lighting, too, but about the same size. Definitely better décor. It wasn't much, but it was home and I miss it."

"You have an apartment?" he asked.

Dizzie shook her head. "No. Well, kind of. I live in

Tremaine headquarters. They have dorms for people like me. I have a room."

Killian sat on the edge of the bed, careful to leave space between them. "But you could leave if you wanted to?"

"Sure." She looked at him, her expression serious. "It doesn't make sense, though. Why pay rent when that money could go toward paying off my contract."

"Contract? What contract?" He was missing a key factor of this conversation. That feeling was reinforced when she stared at him.

"You really don't know?"

"No," he said.

She shifted until she sat facing him, her knees curled sideways on the bed. "I don't work for the company, Killian. I belong to them."

He flinched. "What do you mean, you *belong* to them?"

"They raised me. Clothed me. Fed and sheltered me. Put me to work once I was old enough. And if I ever want to be free of them, I have to pay all of it back."

His stomach churned. Killian struggled to process her words.

"Some people don't worry about it. They do the work and live their lives and are perfectly content. The first time Tremaine put me on a motorcycle, I felt free. I loved it." Her eyes drifted closed and a smile played over her lips. "I loved it and wanted more. And that was when I was determined that I would be free."

Her blue eyes pinned him in place, her expression serious. Sad. "I take extra shifts whenever I can. That's what I was doing the night of the gala. There was a big bonus attached to that delivery if it was completed by midnight. So that's what I did." Her eyes glistened with tears. "That's all it was supposed to be. Some extra credits so I could pay off my contract."

Mind racing, Killian didn't know how to react. He'd already decided that she was a victim too. To discover the tragedy was so much deeper horrified him and strengthened his resolve to find the person responsible for the bomb.

When he didn't respond, Dizzie sniffed and wiped her eyes. "I'm sorry. It's not an excuse. I just... I just wanted you to know." She swung her legs over the side of the bed and started to slide off.

Killian placed a hand on her shoulder. "No, don't go. It's a lot to take in. How little I know about the people who worked for the Tremaine Corporation and the other companies my family hold stock in." He held her gaze. "I don't blame you."

"I do," Dizzie countered. "Portia does."

He sighed. Portia did blame Dizzie, and Killian wasn't sure anything could change her mind. Except maybe time. "You were trying to survive. Do other companies... I mean, is the contract common practice?"

"I don't know. Probably." She laughed softly. "I've only ever been worried about mine."

He scooted back until he leaned against the wall. His legs extended nearly to the edge. He ran both hands through his hair and squeezed the heels of his hands against his head. How had the system become so messed up?

"Will you tell me about it?" he finally said. "Growing up in the Tremaine headquarters?"

Dizzie tensed, her shoulders tight. Then she sighed and her muscles relaxed. She slid backward until she rested against the wall next to him. He noticed for the first time that her toenails were painted the same red as her nails.

"It was growing up. It was the only thing I knew," she

said, her attention on the shabby bedspread. "We ran wild through the tunnels beneath the headquarters. Had lessons in the crammed classrooms. All of us kids, we were friends. Family."

She paused and he held his breath.

"It wasn't really until we were older—thirteen, fourteen—that they give you an aptitude test and then tell you what you're going to be when you grow up, what you're going to do for the corporation."

"You don't get a choice?" Killian asked. He could have made a million choices, but he'd never made one.

"Not really," she said. Dizzie leaned toward him and bumped her shoulder against his. "Your turn."

"Turn for what?" He didn't think about his childhood often. Not since the accident. It made him miss his parents.

She looked up at him. "Tell me about your childhood."

What could he say about his childhood? "It was a lot like yours—"

Dizzie's snort cut him off.

Eyes wide, he looked at her. Her cheeks were flushed and her hands covered her mouth.

"Sorry. I'm sorry." Her words were muffled, but her eyes danced. "Did you just say that my childhood," she paused and pierced him with her gaze, "my childhood in the corporate orphanage was the same as yours in the glittering Seattle high society?"

"Okay, when you say it like that, I sound like an asshole," he said with a rueful smile. "It's true, though." He held up a hand to forestall any other interruptions.

"You were raised by strangers. I was, too. A series of nannies and other caretakers. You ran wild with your friends. Tommy and I were terrors when we were together." Killian smiled fondly as memory after memory flickered through his mind. He sighed. "We might have grown up differently, but the Tremaine Corporation controlled both our lives. Just in different ways."

"Fucking Tremaine." The venom in her voice wasn't unexpected.

He regretted bringing it up. But he couldn't deny that the company linked their lives together.

Dizzie dropped her head against the wall with a thunk. "If Portia's your best friend, can't you get her to back off?"

Killian shook his head. "No. Because of Tommy. Anybody else and I might have been able to. But Tommy... She loved him. There's no way she'll stop."

"You loved him too."

It wasn't a question.

He closed his eyes, breathed through the spear of pain his friend's name brought. "He was my best friend. Did you have a best friend growing up?"

"I do. Did." She shrugged. "It's complicated."

"Then you know what it's like. Spending all your time together. Tommy was a huge part of my life. Now there's a gaping hole where he used to be."

Dizzie flinched.

"I wasn't blaming you. It's why Portia won't give up. Tommy was my best friend and I can barely breathe through the grief sometimes. Imagine how Portia, his wife—his widow—feels. He was her best friend and her husband."

"I get that. Can't you tell her that there was someone else behind this?"

As much as he'd like to lie, he wouldn't give Dizzie false hope. "She's too focused. They've told her that the package you delivered contained the bomb. She won't let that go." Killian wouldn't either. He'd only been able—and willing—to shift his focus.

"That's what I was afraid of." Dizzie picked at the bedspread, slicing off little balls of lint with her nails and flicking them across the room.

He watched her for a minute, then reached over and wrapped his hand around hers. "Keep that up and there won't be anything left. We'll figure it out. We've got a plan."

The corner of her mouth quirked up, curving her lips into a faint smile. "You say that like it's a bad thing."

She was right. The pilled comforter had definitely seen better days. "The Jack would charge us for it."

A laugh bubbled out of her. "Yeah, probably call it an antique and charge you hundreds for it."

"Speaking of overcharging, want me to go grab us some food?"

"Are you sure it's safe?"

Killian didn't know how to answer that. She wouldn't truly be safe until the real bomber was apprehended. And maybe not even then. In her grief, Porta was a wild card. "Let me worry about that," he said finally.

CHAPTER 30

DIZZIE WATCHED Killian gather up the dinner dishes. "Can you cook?"

His head whipped around and he nearly dropped the plates. He set them gently on the dresser in the corner of the room then leaned against it, hands tucked into his pockets. Like nothing had happened. "No, why do you ask?"

"We wouldn't have to risk going out if this room came with a kitchen. I'm a master of heating things up, but I can't cook. At all." Living at headquarters, meals were included. Unless she had scored "cook" on her assessment, there was no reason for her to learn.

"We had a chef. Or ate out. Cooking for yourself," he paused and looked at the floor rather than at her, "isn't done."

She pushed off from the bed and stood in front of him. "You're super rich. I know that. Everybody knows that." Exasperation colored her voice.

He raised his head and looked at her. A blush tinged his cheeks.

"I don't want you to feel like I'm rubbing it in."

What started as a giggle, morphed into a full-blown laugh.

Maybe it was the stress of the last few days. Or his absolute sincerity. It didn't matter.

Once the first laugh escaped, she couldn't stop.

Dizzie stared at Killian while she laughed and laughed. The laughs turned into wheezes until she couldn't breathe.

A number of expressions crossed his face, ending with one that looked a lot like panic. "Are you okay?"

"You don't want to rub it in," she wheezed out between laughs. Dizzie dropped her hands to her knees. If she caught her breath, she might be able to speak. The words came out in fits and starts. "You're one of the richest men in the city. That and your good looks are probably the best-known facts about you." That hadn't come out right. "You know what I mean."

"Well, I'm glad I'm good for something." His words were stilted.

Had she offended him or was he still embarrassed?

"Yeah, well, anyway. Neither of us can cook. Luckily, we can afford meals because of your really big pile of money."

His jaw dropped.

Good, he needed to loosen up. No surprise that he didn't cook. He'd grown up in the lap of luxury.

"So, your folks weren't around much?" She probably shouldn't bring it up. He'd shared so little about his family and she wanted to know more. These were close quarters, so she wasn't surprised the conversation kept straying into more intimate territory.

Intimate. The word made her squirm.

Killian remained where he was, leaning against the dresser. He stood very still, tension radiating off him.

"I'm sorry. I shouldn't have asked. It's none of my business." She'd seriously overstepped. Now she didn't know how to make it right.

"It's fine. It's just..." He let out a long breath. "I never talk about this stuff. At least not with someone who isn't Portia or Tommy."

Shit. Her stomach was in knots. She kept reminding him of what he'd lost because of her. It must be killing him, to be trapped with the person who'd destroyed the strongest relationships in his life.

"How can you stand to look at me?" Her words carried all the anguish of the last few days. "I delivered the bomb, even if I didn't make it."

That broke his stillness but did nothing for the tension between them. He pushed to his full height and took her by the shoulders.

He stood close—too close—and stared down at her with such intensity that she felt naked and vulnerable. She wanted her leathers, her everyday armor, her bravado. Instead, everything had been stripped away, leaving her exposed.

He searched her face. Studying it? Or looking for something specific?

"It isn't easy," he admitted, so softly that she barely heard him.

The words, once they'd registered, hit like a slap. Her heart stopped and she tried to pull away.

His hands gripped her shoulders. Not tight enough to hurt, but she couldn't wriggle away either. "Would you rather I lie to you? It hurts." Killian released her shoulders.

Shaking—and shaken—Dizzie didn't move. If he could share this, she could take it. She owed him that and so much more.

"There's a hole in here." Killian rubbed his chest, right over his heart. "Where Tommy was. And another one from me and Portia. Our relationship is changed forever—even if you hadn't delivered the bomb. Death changes everything."

He paused and looked away, but not before she saw the glimmer of tears. "When my parents died, I suddenly had no family. I was all alone and the only reason I got through it was because of Tommy and Portia. And even then, I didn't come back all the way. A part of me is still trapped with Mom and Dad under that building."

Dizzie sucked in a breath. She'd forgotten that the St. Johns had been killed when a building collapsed during an earthquake. The bombing must have brought that all roaring back for him. Given his tragic past, she was surprised he could even be in the same room with her.

"When I see you, I see the woman who delivered the bomb."

She wrapped her arms around her middle to counter the chill of his words.

"But I also see a victim of the system. Someone who wasn't raised on corporate games, at least not the ones played at the highest levels. I know there's someone higher pulling the strings. Whether it's for corporate espionage or a power play—I don't give a fuck what the reason is. I'll find the person responsible and I will make sure they pay."

He looked at her then, grim determination in his gaze. "If you're a victim, I'll protect you. But god help you if you're not."

Dizzie could only stare at him. The illusion of Killian— the one crafted by the newsies and even the one she'd created over the last few days—had been stripped away. The man in front of her terrified her. The power he wielded. The way he could crush her. But his honesty gave her the courage to embrace hers.

Killian St. John in all his vengeful fury scared her, but he also aroused her. She may not get out of this situation in one piece, but she'd go down in flames with him.

Forcing all doubts and fears from her mind, Dizzie rose onto her tiptoes and kissed him.

CHAPTER 31

KILLIAN'S HAND slid around the back of her neck, holding her in place and warming her bare skin with his touch. His other arm wrapped around her waist, tugging her flush against him.

The kiss turned punishing as Killian took charge. And Dizzie loved every moment of it. She'd never tire of kissing this man.

His mouth devoured hers, but it still wasn't enough.

She stretched higher, wrapping her arms around his neck. Her balance failed and she fell the rest of the way against him.

His arm slid lower, just below her butt, and he hefted her higher.

Their kiss captured the sound.

She wrapped her legs around his waist, suddenly grateful for the terribly short dress.

Locking her ankles behind his back, she trapped his hips between her legs. Wanting, *needing* to press all of her body against him. His warmth. His strength.

They'd only be closer if they were naked.

That conjured up an image of their bodies tangled together, bare skin to bare skin.

Goddamn. She wanted that.

Now.

Dizzie rocked her hips forward, finding the ridge of his erection. She rubbed against him. Gasped as he rocked back.

Killian took advantage of her parted lips and deepened the kiss.

Her wrists crossed behind his neck and one hand slid into his hair. The other grasped him around his collar, careful to limit her nails to the fabric. Repeating the warehouse incident was the last thing she wanted.

He broke the kiss and Dizzie whimpered.

His knowing chuckle rumbled through her body, from her chest to the juncture of her thighs.

She wiggled against him, trying to get closer.

His mouth captured hers again. Holding her close, he moved, carrying her with him.

Her legs wrapped around him, each slow and steady step ratcheted up her desire.

Then she was falling.

She squeaked, pulling away from the kiss.

"Easy," he said against her lips. "I'm sitting down."

Dizzie recognized the bedspread over his shoulder. "Oh." She buried her face in the crook of his shoulder, trying to process this experience.

She was on a bed with Killian St. John.

On a bed. With Killian. St. John.

In his arms.

Killian paused, attuned to her movements. "Are you okay? Do you want to stop?"

"No!" She leaned back to look at him. "No. I mean…"

"No, it's not okay? Or no, you want to stop?" His smile had an edge that did nothing to ease the fire burning in her blood.

Two could play that game, though. "No stopping," she said, emphasizing each syllable with a light press of her nails to the nape of his neck.

"Anything for the lady," he rasped in her ear. His stubble brushed the sensitive skin below her ear and her whole body shivered.

Bracing her hands on his shoulders, Dizzie unlocked her legs from around his waist and shifted to straddle him. It still wasn't enough, but it was closer.

Killian's hands were firm but gentle as they slid up her back. He cupped her neck, gentler this time, threading his fingers through her hair. He tugged a little, locking his gaze with hers.

She read the question in them. "Yes."

Desire flared in his eyes.

In her body.

"Yes what, Dizzie?"

"Yes, to this." She raised her hand and traced a nail— gently—over his lips. "Yes, to you." Echoing his position, she moved her hand to the back of his neck. "Yes, to it all." She lowered her lips to his.

He let her control the kiss. Mostly. He used his hand in her hair to direct her, a tug here, a press there. But she did the same.

Give and take.

Push and pull.

It was a dance. A slow seductive tango made up of nibbles and nips. Darting tongues, breathy moans.

Dizzie swayed against him. Her fingers flexed on his

shoulders, but she remembered not to curl them. She didn't want to hurt him. Not again. Not ever.

The kiss was amazing. She never wanted it to end.

Yet, she wanted more. Never removing her lips from his, she pressed her hands against his biceps.

He resisted for a second before the tension in his abdomen eased and he slowly lowered them both to the bed.

His abs contracted as they sank—slowly, so damn slowly—to the bed until he was stretched out beneath her, her inner thighs pressing against his hips.

Killian felt so good beneath her. It had been a while since she'd taken a lover. Too much to do, no good options. She reveled in having a good option—a great option—now.

Dizzie shifted to get a better taste of him.

His hands tightened around her waist, his grip strong and sure. The way he held her made her feel feminine. Powerful.

Breaking the kiss with a last nibble on his lower lip, she pressed her hands to his chest and sat up slowly, exploring the different places her body rubbed against his. "I like seeing you at my mercy."

"At *your* mercy?" His look seared her, his voice huskier than normal.

She did that. She got him all gravelly and hot.

So she played with it.

She shrugged, deliberately rolling her shoulders. The movement emphasized her breasts. Normally, that move wouldn't do much. In this dress... Yeah, the flames in his eyes burned brighter.

"For now." Dizzie injected a teasing smile into her voice.

His answering grin aroused and terrified her. She knew

her way around a man's body. But this man? This feeling? It was bigger, more powerful than she'd ever experienced.

"For now," she repeated, "you're all mine."

Locking her knees against his hips for balance, Dizzie tilted her body forward and laced her fingers with his. She used their interlocked hands as a balance point and shifted her weight above him until they were face-to-face.

She brushed a feather-light kiss over his lips. Shifted to tiny kisses down his jaw.

Killian turned his head to capture her mouth in another of those devastating kisses, but she laughed and avoided his lips, continuing to pepper his jaw and neck with dainty kisses.

He strained beneath her.

Dizzie smiled. He could reverse their positions easily. Instead, he was letting her play. She nipped his jaw, then scattered kisses over it.

"You're killing me," he growled.

Her grin widened. She ducked her head and dragged her tongue over his neck.

This time when he growled, the rumble echoed through her whole body, igniting a blaze that might never be extinguished.

His body tensed and the tendons in his neck drew tight.

She kissed them too.

"Dizzie." So much strain and desire in that one little word.

Balancing on their palms again, she pushed upright and tried to tug her hands free. She needed them for the rest of her exploration.

Instead of letting her go, he tightened his grip. "Stay."

That damn sexy growl again.

"Killian," she growled back.

He released her hands, but his gaze promised retribution.

She trailed her nails over his wrist and his forearms. Lightly. So lightly, using just enough nail to make him shiver. Not nearly enough to break the skin.

Dizzie didn't have much experience with the playful side of sex, but she was loving every minute of it. Every minute of him.

While deciding what to do next, she shifted her weight and her core rubbed against the ridge in Killian's pants. "Oh!"

The contact, the friction, felt damn good, so she did it again.

The second time, his hips lifted to meet her, double the pressure. Doubling the intensity of her gasp.

He groaned in response.

Wanting skin to skin, she trailed her fingers over his chest, smoothing the garish shirt over the hard muscles beneath it. "Is this your favorite shirt?"

"What?" He stared up at her with desire-glazed eyes. "No."

"Second favorite?" She slipped her fingertip beneath the first button.

"No. Hate this shirt," he ground out.

"Good." The first button popped off. Her nail slid to the top of the small gap created by the missing button.

"Why do you own it?" Pop.

His shrug reverberated through her whole body.

Holy shit.

"Probably for a party."

Pop.

Her mind boggled. To have such a large wardrobe that you didn't remember where it all came from.

Dizzie refocused on her task, ignoring the reminder of their different worlds. The last few buttons were no match for her nails.

She peeled his shirt to the side, revealing his bare chest, and sucked in a sharp breath. Bruises mottled his skin with ugly purples and greens scattered here and there. She frowned at the reminder of the hotel bombing.

"It's okay," he whispered.

If he wasn't letting it bother him, she wouldn't either. For now.

A patch of dark hair in the middle of his chest trailed down to his lower abdomen. It was going to be such fun to see how far that went.

Her hands pressed against his warm skin while she decided what to do next with this beautiful man laid out beneath her.

Obviously, she knew what to do. Tonight felt different, though.

New. Special.

Two words that freaked her out.

Instead of thinking, she focused on feeling. His warm skin. Firm muscles. His rapid pulse.

Dizzie lifted her palms the barest fraction, enough to glide her hands over him and feel the tickle of his chest hair.

She smiled at the sensation.

"I can only take so much," he groaned. Desire coated his voice, sending a thrill through her.

"You sure about that?" Was that her voice? The soft husky one?

"Yeah," his voice rumbled. The room spun around her.

One minute, Killian was pinned beneath her. The next, their positions were reversed.

"You've tortured me long enough."

She blinked up at him, her heart racing. "Hi."

"Hi." He braced above her on his forearms, hovering in a partial pushup that kept most of his weight off her.

His shirt hung open, the loose sides curtaining her torso. She was surrounded by his scent.

Her hands had been on his chest before he'd flipped them. Now she slid them down his sides. His muscles quivered as she traced her nails along the length of him.

Dizzie's arms circled around to his back. She ran her hands up to his shoulder blades and back down. She traced the ridge of his spine as it disappeared beneath his waistband.

Her hands followed his musculature, which brought her back out to his hips. She curled her fingers into his belt loops and shoved down.

Killian stilled. Tension radiated from his forearms, his abdomen.

Dizzie stared up at him. She tugged on his belt loops again. "It's okay," she whispered.

His gaze searched hers.

Whatever he saw there must have reassured him, because he slowly lowered his body, pressing her into the cheap mattress.

His body was more solid than she'd expected. Muscle and bone and metal. He must have hesitated because of his cyber leg.

She pressed her cheek to his. "I want you," she whispered into his ear. "All of you."

She didn't care about his leg. In fact, she welcomed it. It gave them common ground.

Now they were nearly eye to eye, the rest of their bodies aligned. "Are you sure about this?" His voice was still husky.

She searched his gaze. For whatever reason, he was seriously concerned. "I promise."

"I wanted to wait until we were somewhere safe."

"The only way we'll be safe is if we catch whoever was behind the bombing. How about we settle for safe enough?"

He waited so long to answer, Dizzie wondered if he'd changed his mind. If he had, she'd survive. She'd be sad, but she'd survive.

Instead, he pressed his cheek into her hand. His five-o'clock shadow tickled her palm.

What would it feel like when he dragged his jaw across her body? She shivered in anticipation.

His wicked grin returned.

"Safe enough," he repeated and ducked his head to kiss her.

Every move echoed what she'd done to him. Whisper-light kisses down her jaw. Kisses he took a step further, tracing his tongue along the swirl of her ear and breathing on her damp skin.

Her next shiver only egged him on.

She'd pressed kisses to his arms and chest. Killian raised the bar, continuing the rain of kisses over her.

Even through her dress, wherever he touched her burned like fire. Fire that burned away the old and let a new Dizzie rise in its place.

Attraction and longing that she'd never experienced before coursed through her.

His hands slid over her breasts, his touch burning through the skimpy material of her dress.

"More," she gasped and rubbed against him.

Dizzie grabbed his shirt at the shoulder seam, curling her fingers into the fabric. She dragged the shirt down his arms until it tangled around his biceps. With a mew of complaint, she tugged again.

It wouldn't budge, not with his hands still on her.

"Not okay," she muttered.

He stilled instantly, staring down at her. "What's not okay?"

She tugged on his shirt. "Too many clothes."

"Yeah, that's a problem." His voice was gravelly, though she caught a hint of a smile.

She wriggled beneath him. *Why didn't he understand?* She wanted his clothes off. Now. "Fix it!" Her demand came out somewhere between a moan and a shout.

"Whatever the lady wants."

His weight eased off her and Dizzie whimpered, already missing him. Whose stupid idea was this?

Oh, right, hers. Dammit.

The bed shifted as he stood up.

She pushed up onto her elbows to watch him.

Killian stood beside the bed. Her gaze traveled up his body, taking in every detail. His erection bulged in his purple pants.

Her cheeks flushed. She flicked her eyes upward, taking in his muscled torso. The scruff on his chin, the sexy shadow that made him look a little dangerous. Her tongue slicked over her lips and another rush of heat flooded her sex.

Squirming, she pressed her thighs together. She'd never been this turned on in her life. If the foreplay was this good, how would she survive the main event?

When she met his eyes, the heat in them told her he'd enjoyed the way she devoured him with her gaze. The strength of her arousal overpowered her embarrassment and

Dizzie didn't look away. She was hungry for him and refused to hide it.

He held her gaze, his attention never wavering, as he shrugged out of his shirt. It dropped to the ground, gravity doing what she hadn't been able to do.

"Thank you," she whispered.

His chest was sculpted and her fingers tingled as she remembered how his muscles had rippled under her palms. She itched to touch him again.

Killian dropped his hands to the waistband of his pants. Dizzie moaned.

He popped the top button open. Then the next.

His fingers moved to the next one, but he didn't undo it. His hands fell away.

"Your turn." His voice was still rough. But tentative.

Dizzie sat up, trying to comprehend the sudden, subtle change in the atmosphere. His move didn't feel calculated. And she didn't think he was shy. Then it hit her.

Focused on making Killian feel comfortable, she crawled off the bed and pressed against him. She wrapped her hands behind his neck and tugged him down for a kiss.

The suddenness of the move caught Killian off balance and she used that to spin him around.

She pulled back from the kiss, breathless. She rose on tiptoes and steered him back.

"Bed," she warned before the backs of his knees hit the mattress.

He reached for her, but she stepped back, out of reach, and waggled her finger at him.

She watched him as she ran her hands over her breasts, taking pleasure from the texture of the lace, the whorls and loops soft and smooth against her palms. She skimmed her fingertips over her nipples and gasped out loud as the delicate fabric scraped over the tip.

Desire flared in Killian's eyes. "Come here." A command as much as a request.

Her hands skimmed over her torso, her hips, as she stepped closer, moving between his legs.

Killian reached for her and she guided his hands to her hips, placing hers on top. For several breaths they stayed that way, his hands under hers.

He moved his hands over her hips. Her body swayed gently under his exploration.

Dizzie raised her hands to the straps on the dress. She opened the clasp on the right shoulder first, then the left.

She lay her hands back atop his. Gently, she directed his caresses downward. The dress slid down her body until she stood in her underwear before the sexiest man she'd ever met.

Thank god it was good underwear.

She tried not to fidget as he sat there, his hands on her hips, looking at her. She had to be at ease with herself if she wanted Killian to feel comfortable enough to reveal himself.

It was damn hard. For the first time in her life, Dizzie was thankful that most of her modifications were on the inside.

Killian's hands began to move again and she stopped thinking.

"Pretty." He ran his fingers along the bottom band of the lace bra.

"Thank *you*," she replied. His eyes met hers and she added, "You bought them for me."

"You're very welcome." The fire in his eyes flared again, this time with an overlay of possession. "You should wear this color all the time." His gaze ran up and down her body, leaving heat in its wake. "Or better yet, no color at all."

He toyed with one of the straps. Dragged it off her shoulder and back on.

Down and up. The stroke of his fingers and the rasp of the lace as it shifted was hypnotic.

He slid a finger under the other strap, repeated the movement. Down and up. Back and forth.

Without warning, he slid both straps down to mid-biceps.

His touch danced along the lace until he reached the fabric that covered most of her breasts.

Killian curled his fingers over the edge of the cup, slid the material down. His knuckles grazed her nipple as he tugged the lace out of the way.

Her breath hissed and her nipple pebbled under his touch. Dizzie let her head to fall backward as he cupped her breasts and teased his thumbs over her nipples.

His palms slid over her shoulders and down her chest, then up into her hair. She swayed closer. The bunched fabric of the bra held her breasts up as an offering as he breathed on bare skin. "You're so beautiful," he whispered.

In that moment, she felt beautiful. Powerful. This amazing man was worshipping her, when it should be the other way around.

She arched toward him and he slid a hand to her lower back, supporting her.

His breath whispered over her breasts, even closer now, and her nipples hardened into tight peaks. Dizzie hovered on a knife's edge of need—delicious and terrible. She whimpered, the sound pulled from down deep.

She gasped at the first touch of his lips to the tight flesh, her head snapping upright again.

Killian looked up at her, a smile on his lips. His gaze never left hers while he licked and sucked.

With swift, smooth movements, he pulled the undergarments from her body, baring her before he continued to caress her breasts. She hummed in pleasure, squirming. Her legs encountered...pants. "Naked. Now," she demanded.

His chuckle was dark and deep and sent pulses of want through her system. He pulled back and she keened with the loss. "Patience, Dizzie."

"No." She pushed onto her elbows and watched as he dropped his trousers to the ground. His eyes never left her and she burned under his gaze, her body writhing.

She caught a glimpse of shiny metal and then the bed was dipping under his weight, his body warm and solid and big on hers.

He settled between her legs, captured her mouth with his, and slowly—so damn slowly—joined his body to hers.

CHAPTER 32

KILLIAN ROLLED to his side and gazed at the woman lying on her back next to him. Her red hair, tousled from his fingers, fanned out over the pillow. He played with a curl, watching it spring back into shape. The red was fine, but he wanted to see her blond hair spread over a pillow. His pillow. In his bed. In his home.

The possessiveness he'd felt earlier reared to life again. It didn't feel nearly as foreign this time.

Dizzie's cheeks were pink, and her chest rose and fell with her still-rapid breathing. Her neck and chest held the same hint of pink as her cheeks.

She smiled up at him, and his heart thumped hard in his chest.

His eyes trailed lower, looking forward to seeing the rosy glow on the rest of her form.

"My eyes are up here," she teased.

He dragged his gaze up from the enticing flush of her breasts to meet her shining blue eyes. They glittered with happiness. Or at least satisfaction.

"I know. I like the look of all of you." He dipped his head down for a kiss, a soft brush of his lips over hers.

She snaked her hand around his neck and pulled him closer.

Passing his free hand over her belly, he rested it on the mattress on her other side. Despite the advanced materials used in his leg, he knew it made him heavier and he didn't want to hurt her.

"This is a wonderful way to wake up." She rose to press her mouth to his.

Her tongue traced over his lips, then darted inside.

The pressure on his neck increased, accompanied by the slightest prickle of her nails. He shivered, remembering how they'd pricked his chest as she rode him to climax last night.

While the sex had been beyond amazing, the true marvel of the night was the way she'd accepted him. All of him.

Dizzie hadn't flinched when his cyber leg had been revealed. The opposite. She'd traced her fingers over the metal and pressed kisses along the length of it.

Killian drew back from the kiss. They were both breathing hard again. "If you keep that up, we're never going to leave this bed."

She traced her finger over his chest. "Is that an option?"

A beautiful woman wanted to spend the day with him in bed and he was about to turn her down. This situation was so fucked up.

"When this is all finished, we can spend a whole week in bed." It was easy to picture her in his giant bed. No scratchy, low-rent sheets. Soft cotton and a mattress that didn't poke them with springs.

Her blue eyes sparkled. "A whole week? That sounds like a challenge."

She draped her leg over his thigh.

He'd been semi-hard already, but the press of her soft flesh against him sent the blood rushing back to his erection.

"Why don't we make sure you're up for it, Mr. St. John?"

She began to move and all thoughts of turning her down fled.

CHAPTER 33

KILLIAN AND DIZZIE sat in a back corner of Razor Jack's. They were still in disguise but stayed in the shadows.

Now he wore shocking red pants with a purple shirt. Dizzie had laughed when she'd seen him.

On the other hand, his heart had practically stopped when she'd stepped out in her disguise. She'd paired leather pants with the heels. His buttonless yellow shirt was tied at her midriff. The open edges played peekaboo with her bra. Her breasts were lifted up like an offering.

It had taken an act of will to restrain the urge to keep her for himself. He'd settled for a deep kiss and the knowledge that she was wrapped in his clothes.

That primal need to mark her should worry him. It didn't. She was his. The lines between enemy and lover had blurred. He'd deal with that later.

"You haven't heard a word I said, have you?" Exasperation colored his voice.

Dizzie blushed. "I got distracted. Sorry."

He'd forgive any distraction that put that pink in her skin.

"Being out in public like this is a risk," he said.

"I know, but I can't handle being locked up in that tiny room any longer." She shook her head and the curls bounced around her face. "Plus, how else are we supposed to get information about the bombing if we're back in our room?"

Valid point. The bartender had informed them that information about the reward had been released last night. The Jack would act as intermediary.

She continued, her lips near his ear. "How about we stake out the bar a few hours at a time? Keep an ear out for any chatter."

His gut clenched at putting her in danger. Still, asking her to stay put didn't provide the desired results.

"Okay. We can always get a table in the back and we take meals in our room."

"It's a deal." She stretched her hand across the table.

He took it eagerly, curling his fingers around hers. He lifted her hand, intending to bring it to his lips.

The front door flew open, flooding the bar with light and killing the moment.

"Shut the damn door!" a patron yelled.

Killian released her hand and turned toward the door.

Someone else got up and crossed to the door. Shadows flashed in the band of light and there were a couple of thumps, then the man skidded across the floor on his back.

"What the fuck?" Killian jumped to his feet. The scrape of chair legs behind him indicated Dizzie had too. "Let's get out of here." He scanned for a nearby exit.

"Where?" She sounded calmer than he felt.

"Shit, I don't know." He propelled her toward the back of the bar, instinct driving him to get her to the safety of their room.

"We need to ask—"

"The Jack, I know."

They weren't the only patrons surging toward the bar. The sounds of a brawl behind them told Killian that leaving through the front wasn't an option. Once they reached the bar, Killian planted his body between Dizzie and the danger at the door.

The Jack stood with the bartender and watched the bouncers handle the fight, radiating displeasure.

"We need a back way out," Killian demanded.

"That's going to cost you."

No shit.

"Bill me." Killian didn't care about negotiating. At this point, he'd pay whatever the Jack asked to keep Dizzie safe. Whoever was at the door—and he would bet that it was Tremaine Security—was here for Dizzie. And maybe for him. Learning how they'd been discovered was a worry for later.

"A favor," the Jack said. "Anytime, anywhere."

"Done." Killian took the proffered hand and shook. He'd make a deal with the devil himself to get out of here right now. And maybe he had.

The Jack ushered them into another small hallway off the side of the bar. They took a sharp right and were blocked from view of the front of the business.

"Who is it?" Dizzie asked as Killian herded her in front of him.

"Tremaine Security." The Jack responded in even tones, though Killian detected an underlying anger. It was gone in an instant.

"This door leads to the alley. Your vehicle is parked a couple blocks away, as arranged."

Killian took in Dizzie's heels. Dammit. Her shoes would slow them down. "Got your bag?"

Dizzie nodded. "I didn't want to leave it in the room."

He turned to the bar owner. "Can you hold them off?"

The Jack looked offended. "Of course. But it—"

"I know. It'll cost me."

With a smile, the Jack retreated to hold off the invading forces.

Killian didn't know—or care—as long as he and Dizzie had time to disappear. "Change your shoes. We've got to move."

Dizzie nodded. She kicked off the heels and pulled her boots from the bag. With one hand on Killian's arm for balance, she wiggled her feet into the boots.

It was stupid to be so happy she chose to lean against him, rather than the wall. He missed her touch when she released him to shove the heels into her bag.

"Ready," she said.

Grabbing her hand, he tugged her toward the exit.

"Where are we going?"

He had no idea. "Does it matter? We can't stay here."

CHAPTER 34

THE BACK DOOR plunged them into an alley, one that was surprisingly well kept. That had to be the Jack's influence. Killian barreled forward, barely pausing to take in their surroundings.

Dizzie followed, grateful she'd ditched the heels. Even with them, she struggled to keep up with his longer legs.

He tightened his grip on her hand, practically dragging her with him. "Keep up!"

Her shoulder protested, but she didn't want to waste her breath arguing. Instead, she dug deeper and found more speed. "Where are we going?"

"The Jack said the car was waiting at the end of the block." He pointed ahead.

"What about the bike?" In her opinion, the motorcycle offered more flexibility, more maneuverability than a car would.

"What bike?" Killian glanced over his shoulder, but didn't stop moving.

Her breath heaved in and out. This pace was going to kill her. "Yours," she said. She couldn't keep up this conversation while running. Dizzie dug her heels in and pulled her hand free.

It took Killian a couple of steps to realize that she wasn't with him.

She placed her hands on her knees and sucked in air until he came back. "It's on the other side of the block." The alley might look prettier, but the air still smelled bad. Still, a girl had to breathe.

"You abandoned it?"

At his accusing tone, Dizzie straightened and put her hands on her hips. What kind of person did he think she was? "It's in a storage locker. Untraceable credit chip," she added, before he insulted her further.

"Oh. Good." His relief was tangible. "We can come back for it later." He nodded toward the end of the alley. "The car's that way."

He wasn't getting it. "What if they're tracking your car?"

He shrugged. "It's possible, but unlikely. Portia probably has them checking all the bars. Let's go."

"Sure, no one's going to notice an expensive vehicle in this part of town." She rolled her eyes. "Seriously, though, a bike gives us more options. Weaving in and out of alleys instead of running through them."

Grimly, Killian looked around.

She hadn't convinced him yet. They had to make a decision fast—she didn't know how long the Jack could hold Tremaine Security off. Sooner or later, security would come through that back door. They weren't far enough away. "Would anyone expect us to take the bike?"

He shook his head. "Probably not. I haven't been out on one in forever." His gaze skewered her. "You're the only one who's been seen on it."

Shit. She'd forgotten about the newsies. Still, people rode motorcycles all over the city. "I think it's worth the risk for the greater flexibility. And we might have a better chance of blending in."

Believing bone-deep that it was a better choice than the car, Dizzie turned and walked back the way they had come, toward where she'd stowed the bike.

Killian didn't immediately follow.

Shit. That wasn't good.

Finally, footsteps echoed behind her. Relief flooded through her and she released her breath on a slow exhale. He hadn't abandoned her.

"Fine. You win."

She didn't turn around. "It's not about winning. It's about getting the fuck away from Tremaine Security."

No response. Fine, let him have his tantrum.

They reached the end of the alley and Dizzie pointed in the opposite direction of the bar. "The lockers are around that corner."

"I don't like being out in the open. Security's probably looking for us." Killian's voice was as tense as his body.

"We've got this," she said, ignoring her own worry about the last fifty feet of wide-open sidewalk. "Put your arm around my shoulder."

He did as she asked and she snuggled into his embrace. Her arm circled his waist and she pressed her cheek against his chest. Her tension eased away, but Killian's didn't. If anything, it got worse.

"This is your plan? Cuddling?" Amusement and tension warred in his voice.

Dizzie closed her eyes and counted to ten, slowly. So easy to stay like this forever. But they couldn't. "Not exactly. Now, we walk down the street like a couple in love."

"Like this?" He tipped her chin up with his free hand.

She expected a soft kiss.

It wasn't one.

Fueled by aggression, it was demanding. Possessive.

She surrendered to it. To him. She wrapped both arms around his waist and leaned into the kiss.

They broke apart slowly. Her heart raced.

She raised her fingers to her lips. "Um, that was probably too much. In public at least."

"Or it made people uncomfortable enough they won't look too much closer."

Swallowing, hard, she nodded. The kiss made her feel uncomfortable things too. Made her want things she couldn't have.

"Ready?" he asked.

She nodded.

Arms wrapped around each other, they rounded the corner at a quick stroll, nuzzling and murmuring to each other along the way. She kept her face turned toward his chest and he nuzzled her neck, using her hair as a shield.

Crossing the half-block distance to the lockers, they didn't pass many people. The ones they did looked away from the public display of affection.

It was easy to pretend it was real, that they were in love. Disgustingly easy.

She sighed into his chest.

"What's wrong?" He kept his voice low.

"Nothing. Just thinking." Impossible thoughts. Dizzie reluctantly pulled away from Killian. She shivered, missing the warmth of his body pressed against hers. "Back here." She led him toward the street-side lockers.

The locker units were scattered all over the city. Made from repurposed shipping containers that had been divided into smaller and smaller sections, each with a digital lock, they were available to anyone who had the credits to rent one and provided a quick place to stash goods. She knew of more than one illegal enterprise that was run out of a streetbox.

This container had started life out a deep blue, but layers of graffiti and tags had changed the color of everything but the high corners. "Keep watch," she said as she circled around it.

She'd chosen one of the biggest lockers, on the side hidden from the street. Dizzie keyed in the code. The door creaked open and she ducked under the doorway to enter the storage locker. With no room to turn around, she grabbed the handlebars and gently pulled their ride out.

"Coming out," she warned.

Once clear of the streetbox, she set the kickstand and ran her hand over the gleaming metal. The freedom of the road was so close she could taste it. "Ready?"

Killian stared at the bike with a closed expression. "The car is still an option." His words were stilted. "A good one."

There was no time to explore his reluctance. They had to get out of here. "I'm taking the motorcycle. Your call." Dizzie released the helmet and handed it to Killian. "Put this on."

"No." His refusal was clipped. "You wear it."

Damn chivalry.

She pressed the helmet against his chest and released it. He caught it by reflex and glared at her.

She shook her head. "You're more important than I am. Take it."

The muscles in his jaw clenched.

"Dammit. We're wasting time."

Nothing. Just stony silence.

Fuuuck.

"You're either all in, Killian, or you're out." She stood on the foot peg and swung her leg over the seat. She turned the ignition key and the engine purred to life. Familiar vibrations flowed through her, bringing with them a sense of peace.

He stared at her and the bike for a long second. "This is a bad idea. A bad idea that's getting worse by the moment."

Kicking up the kickstand, she balanced on her toes. "Last chance. You coming?"

Without a word, Killian pulled on the helmet and swung his leg over the seat. As he settled in, his arms wrapped around her and she shivered at his touch.

She'd ridden with passengers before. None of them had affected her the way Killian did.

His feet were still on the ground so she took advantage of the moment to swivel around. "Where are we going?"

He shrugged. "It's your show now."

Dammit. "Okay."

She faced forward and considered their options.

The only places that came to mind were the hacker's hideout and back to Tremaine headquarters. Not much point in going back to the warehouse, unless they wanted to dig around the computers again. Or have sex on those small, uncomfortable beds.

Sex.

Oh, god. She shouldn't be thinking about sex with Killian again. Not when they were on the run from Tremaine Security again.

Not when he was pressed against her back and this beast of a motorcycle was thrumming between her legs.

Bad Dizzie. Don't think about sex with Killian.

Heat rushed through her veins. Well, that didn't work.

Think about safety. Some warm place to spend the night. She hadn't slept in a good bed since Killian's house.

Killian's house.

Dizzie clicked her nails against the handlebars.

That could work. Upside: Tremaine Security had no reason to look for her there. Downside: They'd have to cut across town without being noticed.

She laughed. Good thing she knew how to do that.

Should she tell Killian her plan?

Screw it. If she got a better idea between here and there? Well, quick direction changes were a hell of a lot easier on a bike than in a car.

"All right, hang on tight," she said over her shoulder.

Killian's weight shifted behind her. His grip around her waist tightened as he lifted his legs from the ground and placed them on the passenger foot pegs.

Dizzie shifted the bike into gear. Instead of the steady takeoff she expected, she fought to keep the bike upright.

"Shit!" She dropped her feet to the ground.

What was going on? She lived on her bike and could handle anything on two wheels. Why was this happening now? The only difference now was—

"That's what I was afraid of." Killian flipped up the helmet. "My leg messes with the balance."

Dizzie shook her head. "I should have thought of that. Thanks." No wonder he'd been leery of the motorcycle.

Less than twelve hours since she'd ridden Killian like a motorcycle and she'd already forgotten about his cyber leg. It might be made of lightweight advanced metal, but it was still metal. She'd factored in having a passenger, but not one who was unbalanced.

A laugh escaped. They were probably both unbalanced.

She wiggled the motorcycle experimentally.

Yep, there it was. A definite lean to the left.

Hands on the handlebars, she tilted the motorcycle again, this time a bit more steeply. She needed to have a sense of the difference before hitting the street.

Killian's hands tightened around her waist.

Keeping in mind how his leg would set them off balance, she hit the starter again.

CHAPTER 35

ARMS WRAPPED TIGHT AROUND DIZZIE, Killian was hyperaware of her muscles flexing and releasing, the subtle adjustments she made as they wove through Seattle streets. Her strength and confidence were sexy as hell.

For the first few blocks, he'd battled to stay relaxed, knowing his tension could throw off her delicate balancing act. He hadn't been on a motorcycle since he'd lost his leg. He'd been afraid of, well, everything. Feeling foolish. Crashing.

He was still wary, but Dizzie's mastery of the machine had allayed most of his fears. As long as he focused on her, he'd be fine.

Dizzie zigged and zagged, cutting across lanes and weaving through traffic.

The city flashed by. He glimpsed billboards and street signs. Familiar buildings blurred with ones he couldn't identify as they raced past.

No wonder Dizzie craved this freedom.

Killian recognized his surroundings as they headed up

Capitol Hill. What kind of safe house did she expect to find there?

Dizzie leaned into another turn, right past the surprisingly good neighborhood sushi restaurant near his neighborhood. His stomach sank.

His unease intensified as they passed by houses on his block.

The gates to his house swung open, automatically triggered by the keyfob in his pocket. What the hell were they doing here?

Killian was shocked that there were no newsies camped outside, but that was secondary to why they were here.

Blood pressure rising, Killian barely waited until they stopped and she'd set the kickstand before he pulled his helmet off. "What the hell are we doing here?"

After an ungainly dismount, he tucked the helmet under his arm and glared at her.

"We needed a place that was safe from Tremaine Security. Somewhere no one would think to look." Her cool voice and steady eyes reminded him of the night they met. The look of a woman doing her job. "Ta-da."

He couldn't fault her logic. He hated it, but couldn't fault it. "Why didn't you tell me?"

She rolled her eyes. "Would you have agreed?"

"No way in hell." He would have argued. Maybe even refused to get on the bike.

"Yeah, that's what I thought."

"Yes, it's secure," he agreed. "But that doesn't mean it isn't dangerous. What about the newsies? They're on the lookout for more information about my mysterious blonde."

"If there had been newsies anywhere around here, I would have kept going." She deliberately took a 360-view around the drive. "I think we're safe. Plus, I'm a redhead right now," she said with a toss of windblown curls.

"Because we're damn lucky." She didn't know what it was like. The invasion of privacy. The constant need to be on. He shuddered.

As a teenager, he and Tommy had made a pact to give the newsies the show they wanted. It wasn't until Portia and Tommy had gotten married that Killian realized he wanted to make changes. Less publicity, not more. "We need to get inside. They might have left a drone." Most of all, he wanted Dizzie inside where she would be safe.

"Fine," she said.

Killian reached out to help her off the bike.

An engine roared and they both turned toward the sound.

A shiny silver car pulled into the drive. He groaned. He'd recognize that car anywhere.

"Shit, someone else I wanted to avoid." Portia had left more than a dozen messages for him while he was with Dizzie. He wasn't ready to deal with the information about Tommy's funeral. "I told you we shouldn't have come here."

Dizzie looked away from the car. "What do you mean?"

"It's Portia."

Her nose wrinkled. "How did she know we were here?"

He shrugged. "No idea." They were about to find out.

Killian moved toward his guest parking. If he headed Portia off before she reached Dizzie, he might be able to control the confrontation. He wasn't looking forward to a showdown between the two women. If he had to choose...

Instead of parking, Portia drove past him, cutting it so close he had to jump into the yard to get out of her way.

As soon as he was clear, she gunned the engine and pulled the wheel hard to the right.

Toward Dizzie.

"Portia! Stop!" Killian raced toward her, knowing he wouldn't get there in time. He watched in horrified slow motion as the car sped toward Dizzie. "Hurry, Dizzie!"

She scrambled to get off the parked bike, but she didn't move fast enough. Just before Portia hit her, Dizzie managed to get her leg over the seat.

The car slammed into the motorcycle.

A pain-filled scream filled the air and rattled his bones. As long as he lived, he would never forget it.

The impact knocked Dizzie backward and toppled the bike on top of her. She landed in one of the flower beds that lined the driveway and lay there unmoving on crushed flowers.

Portia had stopped just after impact. Killian raced past her car, pausing to look inside. He exhaled in relief. The airbag had deployed and she looked okay—face pale, knuckles white around the steering wheel—but okay. She wasn't his priority right now. Dizzie was.

He ran and dropped to his knees next to Dizzie. Her face was a grimace of pain. Her head was bleeding. Fuck. Stubborn woman. She should have been wearing the helmet.

"Dizzie. Can you hear me?"

She groaned in response.

After the bombing, he'd hoped to never feel this helpless again. Those feelings flooded back, nearly paralyzing him with their intensity.

He stared at the bike pinning her down and at the leg that was bent in an unusual angle. What the fuck was he supposed to do?

Shit! Shit! Shit!

He didn't know.

Wait. There was one thing.

He pulled the burner phone out of his pocket. He fumbled the keys as he dialed Tremaine emergency services. They provided health and emergency services to Tremaine executives, investors, and a select clientele, and they would take her to the hospital where he and Portia had been treated after the bombing.

With his finger on send, he stopped. What it would mean for Dizzie? Was he delivering her to the people who were looking for her? Could he live with himself if he did?

She groaned again and the sound frayed his nerves. His heart. He'd have to find out, because he couldn't live with himself if she died and he could have saved her. He'd never come back from that.

She'd been hit by a car. He had to assume she was badly injured. The Tremaine facility was her best bet.

Hoping he wasn't making a mistake, he dialed the Tremaine emergency number. He'd find a way to protect her while she got the best care possible.

They picked up on the first ring. Killian gave his name and security number.

"Portia Tremaine was involved in a motorcycle accident," he told the voice on the other end of the line. "We need an ambulance immediately."

They would have tracked his position from the call, so he hung up. He didn't want to answer any questions, especially since it wasn't Portia he called about. They wouldn't show up for a courier, but they would for the heir.

"Why are you getting her aid, Killian? Why are you with her in the first place?" Portia kicked him, snapping him out of the past.

She stood next to him, nearly vibrating with fury. White powder from the airbag covered her face and torso. He flashed back to when she was pinned under the rubble. Killian focused on controlling his breath until he was back in the present.

While she yelled at him, Portia frantically searched in her purse, looking no worse for having intentionally crashed her car into Dizzie.

Portia smiled and pulled out her phone. "No ambulance for her. She can die alone, like Tommy did."

"Stop, Portia. You aren't thinking clearly." He rose to his feet and grabbed the phone. "You've done enough."

"Why?" Portia screamed. "She killed Tommy! Why do you care so much?"

Telling her that he'd developed feelings for Dizzie might escalate the already tense situation. "She's innocent, Portia. Just a pawn in a game someone else is playing."

He knew it. He'd accepted it. Reconciling his anger at Dizzie's involvement with Tommy's death game would take time, but it was time he was willing to spend.

"Prove it!" Her demand carried anger and grief.

"I can't, not yet. But I will," he promised her. Promised Dizzie.

Portia swayed.

Killian felt a flicker of alarm. She was still fragile from the explosion and, airbag or not, the crash hadn't helped. He stood and led her to his front steps. "Sit here until the ambulance arrives." His tone was no-nonsense, but not cold. He was pissed at her, with what she'd done, but still cared about her.

She glared at him but nodded.

He hoped she would keep her word, but she hadn't been herself these last few days. He needed to be with Dizzie. Once he knew she would be okay, he would figure out how to keep Portia from sinking so low she couldn't recover.

Killian approached Dizzie, making sure he was in her line of sight. Despite her ragged breathing, her pain-filled eyes were wide open. With the bike awkwardly laying on top of her, she looked smaller than ever.

Killian grasped the handlebars, intending to lift it off her. He'd barely moved it when she gasped in pain. He eased it down, helplessness washing over him.

"Killian?"

"I'm right here," he reassured her, dropping to his knees beside her. "Where does it hurt?"

"Everywhere." Her laugh morphed into a gasp.

The sound broke his heart and the urge to hit something nearly overwhelmed him. He ached to pull her into his arms, but wouldn't risk hurting her. That he hadn't been able to protect her made him physically ill.

"Shhh. Hold on. Help is on the way." He risked taking her hand with his free one. He couldn't just sit here and watch her suffer.

Her fingers wrapped around his, and he didn't even flinch when her nails dug into his skin.

CHAPTER 36

BY THE TIME the ambulance arrived, it had to drive through a crowd of newsies. Killian trusted his staff to keep them off the property and as far from him, Dizzie, and Portia as possible.

He comforted Dizzie while they waited and whispered soothing words of encouragement. He didn't let go of her hand until the medics exited the ambulance.

He stood and waved them over. "Over here."

Instead, they headed toward Portia. "Dammit. I'll be right back." He took off across the lawn to intercept them. Leaving her like this didn't feel right.

"We're here for Ms. Tremaine." They gave him a funny look and tried to go around him.

"No, over there. I called you." Killian grabbed a medic's arm and pulled him toward Dizzie.

The EMT resisted. "The call said Ms. Tremaine had been in an accident."

Fuck, he hadn't counted on them being stubborn. "Yes, she ran over someone. *That* person needs your help."

"She deserved it," Portia yelled from the step. She

hadn't made any move toward the EMTs. The crash must have shaken her up more than she'd admitted.

"You." Killian pointed to the medic who wasn't carrying the big medical kit. "Check Portia out."

The man nodded and dashed to her side.

Killian turned to the medic he still had a grip on. "You come over here and help her."

The medic ignored him and looked at his partner. The other man nodded, indicating, Killian assumed, that Portia was okay. Only then did he follow Killian to Dizzie's side.

"Car versus motorcycle," Killian said, though the medic had probably figured that out for himself.

The EMT knelt next to Dizzie and started his assessment. "We've got to get her treated now . Where should we..."

"Take her to the Tremaine hospital." When the medic started to object, Killian stopped him. "Do you know who I am?"

The EMT nodded. "I'll take responsibility, as long as you ensure she gets the best care," Killian said.

"Yes, sir."

Killian rubbed his fingers over his forehead. How many people would he have to browbeat to get Dizzie the care she needed?

CHAPTER 37

DIZZIE NOTICED THE BEEPING FIRST.

After that, it was the flare of pain each time she took a breath.

Where was she?

Opening her eyes took effort. She'd manage to do it briefly, then her lids fluttered shut again.

When she finally kept them open, all she saw was white.

White walls. White curtains. Bright white light. *Was she dead?*

No, not dead, probably, but this sure wasn't her room. She liked colors way too much. It wasn't the Jack's or the hacker's. Or Killian's.

Killian.

The last thing she remembered was sitting in Killian's driveway, arguing with the world's most frustrating man.

A car.

Portia.

Pain.

Lots and lots of pain.

She gasped at the remembered pain. The memories flooded back and she curled in on herself as she relived it. The beeping intensified.

Portia fucking Tremaine had hit Dizzie with her car. On purpose.

Dizzie sat up, ignoring the jaw-clenching pain. She was breathing hard by the time she managed and the incessant beeping was driving her insane.

She focused on the room. Medical equipment surrounded the bed. Some had big screens with bold numbers and lines and more data than she could focus on right now. Others had wires that led to the bed or to other machines.

Her heart monitor was the cause of the damn beeping. Every movement or moment of panic set the damn thing off.

The Tremaine logo—a caduceus with a cross bar to form a "T"—was attached to every surface in the room. She glanced down at the gown she wore. The logo was emblazoned on the chest.

Okay, she was in a Tremaine hospital, presumably in Tremaine custody. If she stayed here, her life could be counted in hours rather than days.

Dizzie looked down at the medical bracelet on her wrist. She had to get out of here. The beeping started again.

She swung her leg over the side of the bed. A wave of pain washed over her and she collapsed back onto the bed.

A nurse in a traditional white uniform bustled into the room. Her badge, complete with a big, bold Tremaine logo, indicated her name was Betty.

"Good, you're awake." She was cheery and chirpy. A combination made particularly annoying by the spinning room.

"What happened?" Dizzie croaked.

With that annoying blend of efficiency and cheerfulness, the nurse hurried over to her bedside, a glass of water with a straw in her hand.

"You were in a motorcycle accident." She handed Dizzie a pain pill then held the straw to her lips. "You weren't wearing a helmet, so you're incredibly lucky that you weren't hurt worse. The doctors were able to set the breaks and the nanomeds have worked their magic. You've been very well taken care of."

Concern passed over Betty's face. A flicker, then it was gone.

What was Betty hiding? Her mind leapt to the worst-case scenario. "Am I going to die?" Dizzie's heart clenched. The monitor raced again.

"Oh no," she laughed. "You're going to be fine." There it was again, something in her tone that said she wasn't telling Dizzie the whole story.

"I'll tell the doctor that you're awake. And Mr. St. John. He's been quite worried. Pacing the halls and keeping everyone but medical staff away from you."

She bustled out the door, leaving Dizzie alone with her fears. Maybe she wasn't dying, but what else could it be?

Killian would tell her. Right? Whatever was wrong with her, she wanted to know. Even if it meant that Tremaine Security was waiting to drag her away.

Dizzie sat on the bed, clicking her nails together. She wanted to move, but the first attempt made her rethink that option. She hated waiting.

Fortunately, she didn't have to wait long.

Killian slipped into her room. Dressed in scrubs, he looked tired. His beard scruff was heavier and he looked more casual than she'd ever seen him. So different...but she liked it.

When he sat on the edge of her bed, his thigh brushed hers.

Dizzie blushed when the rhythmic beeping increased.

He laced his fingers with hers. "Thank god you're all right."

"What happened?" She had to know, but that didn't stop the worry.

"There was an accident," Killian said slowly.

Dizzie tilted her head and another wave of pain washed over her. Her head throbbed in time with her pulse and she wished that the pain relievers would kick in soon. She lowered her head to her hands and groaned.

"I'll get the nurse."

"No, I'm fine." She didn't look up. "How did I get here? How long have I been here? What happens next?" The questions tumbled out.

She hoped Killian would be more forthcoming than the nurse.

"I called an ambulance. They brought you. About six hours."

"Six hours? When are they coming to get me?" The way her body ached, she was in no shape to outrun Tremaine Security. But she felt queasy knowing that this was it.

His lips tightened. "They won't be."

Dizzie didn't feel the rush of relief she expected at his words. "It's over?"

His face showed the same hesitation that the nurse had. "Not quite."

She was sick of not hearing the full truth. "What the hell does that mean?"

More beeping.

Killian squeezed her hand, then released her and pushed off the bed.

Oh shit. That wasn't a good sign. "Am I dying?"

Killian spun around, horror on his face. "What? No. No!" He was back at her bedside in an instant. "Why do you ask?"

Dizzie sat up fully, ignoring the pain around her ribs.

He reached for her hand again, but she pulled it out of the way. She didn't want coddling. "Why do I ask? Because no one is telling me what's going on. Much less the truth."

"The truth is..." he paused.

"Complicated?"

His laugh was harsh and lines of strain wrinkled his forehead. "That's one way to put it."

She snapped, "How about you put it in small words that even a simple courier can understand?" Okay, that was bitchy.

"What's that supposed to mean?" Killian sounded bewildered.

"Everyone here has a connection to Tremaine Corporation. I'm in the center of it all and you're all keeping a secret from me." And she wanted, needed, to know what it was. Had he turned her in?

He ran his fingers through his hair. The strands stood on end. "You were bleeding so much." His voice was quiet. "You were pinned under the bike. I was afraid you were dying. I called the emergency number for corporate families and investors."

He raised his head and looked at her, anguish in his eyes. "I didn't know what else to do. It looked bad." His eyes got a distant look in them. "There's been too much death and I didn't want you to die, too. I would have done whatever was necessary to keep you alive. I figured we'd deal with the security issue later. After they'd fixed you up."

Her fingers clenched in the sheet as he continued.

"They brought you to the hospital and ran a series of standard tests. Dizzie, they found an anomaly."

Her stomach dropped. This was it. She was totally dying.

He took her hands and looked deep into her eyes. Maybe it would be romantic if it weren't so terrifying. "They ran the tests again. The anomaly was still there."

Dizzie squeezed his hand. "What did they find? Tell me! I can take it."

"Your blood test indicated a match for the Tremaine family."

She heard the words but had no idea what they meant. "Portia bled on me? That's gross, but I don't see why it's a big deal."

He shook his head. "No. You've got Tremaine DNA. You're related to Portia. And her father. You're a Tremaine."

Her head swam. Killian wasn't making sense. "The second test showed that it was a mistake?" Did he hear the hope in her voice?

"No, Dizzie. It confirmed that you're a Tremaine."

Horror swamped her. She tugged her hand free and wrapped both arms around her middle to keep from shattering. Her voice was shrill. "That can't be right. It's a mistake. Make them run the test again."

"It's not a mistake, Dizzie." His voice was soothing.

"I don't want to be a Tremaine." The childish words tumbled out, but that didn't make them any less true. How could she be related to the very people she hated?

His smile was gentle. "You don't have a choice."

They'd taken everything from her, she wouldn't let them take her identity too. "My name is Dizzie. I'm a courier for the Tremaine Corporation."

"Your name is Dizzie. I'm not sure how, but you're also a member of the Tremaine family."

This couldn't be happening. The nightmare would end if she woke up. Dizzie pinched her left arm and gasped when her nails drew blood.

It was true. Her stomach churned.

The Tremaine Corporation already owned her. Being part of the family was another chain. Another way to keep her from her freedom.

He brushed his hand over her forehead. She leaned into his touch. A little.

"Are you okay?"

She didn't have enough left in her for a laugh. "No. Not really."

He wrapped her in his arms. "Do you want me to call the nurse?"

"No. Can you hand me that glass of water?" He held the glass while she sipped and considered this new information. "Do they know?"

He understood she was talking about the Tremaines. "I don't know. I wouldn't be surprised if the hospital alerted them."

"Are you going to tell them?" Maybe they would never know. She wished she could forget.

He ran his hand over his face. "We'll deal with that when you're feeling better."

"Sure." Her life was slipping further out of her control and she hated it. She wasn't strong enough to fight about this now. Clothed in a hospital gown, reeling from learning her life was a lie, she wasn't at the top of her game.

"Are you in pain? Do you want me to get the nurse?"

Dizzie almost said no. Then again, it was the perfect excuse to get him to leave her alone.

She didn't know how to deal with Killian right now. The day had started so well, waking in his arms. Six missing hours later and her life was over.

That caused a twinge in her chest on the left side. That was new. Probably a carryover from the accident. "Yeah," she said. "My head and chest hurt. Right here." She rubbed her chest right over her heart.

Killian looked at her, a question in his eyes. She turned away, unwilling to put a name to the emotion there.

"I'll get her." He was quiet for a moment.

Uncomfortable silence fell over the room, broken only by the hums and beeps of the machines. Dizzie closed her eyes.

He stood at her side. She couldn't see him, but she felt his presence.

He cleared his throat, but said nothing.

Dizzie held herself still, barely daring to breathe.

His footsteps and the door shutting were the only sounds that broke the steady rhythm of the beeping of her broken heart.

CHAPTER 38

THE NURSE ENTERED Dizzie's room. He wanted to follow but didn't think he'd be welcome. He settled for pacing up and down the hallway.

Dizzie was okay. That was all that mattered. The doctors couldn't tell him much, but they'd assured him she would be okay. As a Tremaine—how the hell was that possible?—she'd receive the best possible care.

Those tests results... Killian still couldn't wrap his head around them.

When he'd called Tremaine Medical Services, he'd intended to use the power of his name to protect her, although he hadn't been 100 percent sure that it would be enough to keep her safe.

Now... He shook his head. Now she was somehow related to one of the most powerful families in the world. And she wasn't happy about it.

Neither Killian nor the medic had believed it when Dizzie had triggered the top-level protocol in the ambulance. The second, more comprehensive test at the hospital had confirmed the relationship.

Ever since, Killian had expected someone from Tremaine to show up. What would it mean for Dizzie? Would they welcome her? Or arrest her?

A commotion in the hallway brought Killian back to the present.

"Where is she? I want to see the woman who killed my husband!"

Portia.

He had no idea what he was going to tell her.

She stormed down the hallway, flanked by a team of security guards.

Fuck. Portia wouldn't welcome a new sister.

If Dizzie left the hospital with Portia, he'd never see her again. He refused to let that happen.

Killian stepped in front of Dizzie's door and into Portia's path.

"Why am I not surprised you're here?" She spat out the words.

"You can't do this, Portia." Killian tried reason first. He kept his voice soft and split his attention between her and the guards. He couldn't stop four highly trained men, but that didn't mean he wouldn't try.

Anything to protect Dizzie.

"Do what? Have her arrested for murdering my husband? You forget, Killian, corporations police their own." She looked him dead in the eye. "You protected her, you bastard. Be glad I'm not here for you too!"

She hadn't forgiven him for putting Dizzie first at his house. Maybe she never would. He wasn't sure he'd survive losing both Tommy and Portia, but he wouldn't trade one Tremaine sister for the other.

"She didn't kill Tommy. Help us figure out who actually sent the bomb."

She moved until she was directly in front of him. A wave of her hand and her guards fanned out around her. "You and the courier?"

He nodded.

She considered him for a long minute. "There's nothing to find," she said finally. "I've had all the resources of Tremaine Corporation on the attack and they tell me that they don't have any idea who was behind it. Their best suspect is your little courier."

"But what was her motive, Portia? Why would she have done it?" Even before he'd gotten to know Dizzie, that had been the sticking point.

"I don't know. Maybe she snapped." Lips pressed into a line, dark circles under her eyes, Portia looked like a woman barely holding it together. "It doesn't matter. Security says she did it and Leopold agrees."

Killian had been afraid of that. They hadn't bothered to look for anyone else.

"Get out of my way," Portia commanded, glaring at him.

With a wave of her hand, the four men stepped forward. Two grabbed his arm. He dug in, bracing himself in the doorway. He wouldn't last long. There was only one more card to play.

"She's your sister, Portia." The words rushed out, louder than he intended.

Portia stared at him, searching for the lie. She threw back her head and laughed.

Any other time, he'd be happy to hear Portia laugh so freely.

Right now, he needed her to take him seriously. "It's true," he said, as soon as she paused to take a breath. "Didn't the hospital call you?"

"Why on earth would they call me?" she asked archly.

"Blood and DNA tests proved that Dizzie is a Tremaine. She's related to you and your father." That still sounded strange to his ears.

That wiped the laughter from Portia's face. "You're lying."

He shook his head. "I'm not. You can ask the administrator or the doctor. They made a call. Must have gotten your father. Or his assistant." Years ago, Portia had mentioned that she almost wished she wasn't an only child. This wasn't the way Killian had wanted Portia to get her wish, but he had to make her feel a connection. It might be the only thing between Dizzie and some dark room in the basement of the Tremaine headquarters. Or worse, a dark hole in the ground.

She blanched. "It's true?"

He nodded. "They ran the test twice."

Portia swayed

He surged forward, pulling away from the guards and catching her before her security team did. "Get a doctor!"

Security clustered around him as he held Portia. He stared down at her slack face, studying features that he'd seen his whole life, searching for Dizzie.

For days, Dizzie had reminded him of Portia. Now, as he catalogued their nearly identical noses and the matching dimples in their chins, he couldn't believe he hadn't seen the resemblance sooner.

When Killian had learned they were sisters, he'd believed that the Tremaine name would protect Dizzie and allow him to keep the two women who meant the most to him in his life. Given the way they'd both reacted, now he wasn't so sure.

CHAPTER 39

WHEN DIZZIE WOKE AGAIN, the room was dark. Even without the steady beeping, she knew where she was. Maneuvering to not quite upright, she braced for pain. It was miraculously gone. Without it, or the earlier pounding in her head, she could sit up. Whatever they'd given her, it had worked.

Raised voices nearby drew her attention. One sounded like Killian. Relief rushed through her. After the way they'd left things, she wouldn't be surprised if she'd driven him away.

She hadn't handled things well. He'd done nothing but care for her. In no world would she react well to finding out she was related to Portia and Phillip Tremaine, but it wasn't Killian's fault. She owed him an apology.

Dizzie turned toward the chair by the bed, expecting him to be at her side. He wasn't there. Had she imagined his voice? She strained to hear over the machines, catching snippets of conversation beyond the privacy screen.

"Hello?" she called.

"Are you okay?" Killian asked as he pushed the screen aside.

Her heart gave a ridiculous little jump when she saw him.

Portia followed him in, wearing a hospital gown like it was haute couture. "What's she doing here?" Dizzie snapped, scrambling away as far as she could.

Her newfound sister stopped a few feet away, crossing her arms. She looked as unhappy as Dizzie felt.

Killian crossed to her bedside. "How are you feeling?"

"Fine," she lied, like her happiness hadn't been crushed by her new archnemesis. Who was apparently also her sister. "A little disoriented."

The nurse entered her room and shooed Killian out of the way while she checked the monitor. "Looks okay." She focused on Dizzie. "Not unexpected when you wake up in a new place."

Dizzie nodded. It wasn't far from the truth.

The nurse smiled, then turned to Killian and Portia. "There's a visitor limit for a reason. You," she said to Killian, "need to decide who you're here to visit. And you," she pointed at Portia, "need to get back to your room. You're still under observation."

Portia looked like she was going to complain, but the nurse silenced her with a look. "Yes, I know who you are. No, I don't care. I work for the doctor and he wants you in that bed."

Forget Killian. Dizzie might be in love with the nurse.

Her stomach dropped.

She might be in love with the nurse, but she wasn't in love with Killian.

She couldn't be.

The monitor hiccupped with her momentary panic.

The nurse gave her another long look. Dizzie tried to smile reassuringly.

It must have worked because the nurse grabbed the room divider and pulled it, pinning Killian with a look. "Stay or go?"

He peeked his head around the divider to the side of the room Portia had disappeared to, then pulled back in. "Stay."

Dizzie's heart monitor did a happy dance. He'd chosen her over Portia.

At least this once.

"What was she doing here?" Dizzie asked again. She kept her voice low because she didn't want Portia to listen in.

"Your sister collapsed," Killian responded, emphasizing the relationship.

Dizzie curled her lip. "How sure are we about that?"

"That she collapsed? One hundred percent." He looked her dead in the eye. "I caught her before she hit the floor."

Asshole. He knew exactly what she meant.

"Aren't you the hero—two rescues in one day." Sarcasm dripped from her words.

Dammit, she had to stop lashing out at the one person on her side.

"Why are you acting like this? Aren't you happy to find out that you have a sister after growing up in the orphanage?"

He was absolutely sincere. How did he not understand?

"She wants to arrest me, possibly kill me, since she already hit me *with her car*. Did you see the look on her face when she did it?" She had to get out of here, and fast. "I'm feeling a lot better. When can I leave?"

"I don't know," Killian said. "That's a conversation between you and the doctor."

She looked at him warily. Could it be that easy? "If they released me today, I could just go?"

He looked pained. "No. There's still the matter of the bombing. And finding the bomber."

"Is security out there?"

His hesitation told her what she needed to know. "Are they here for me? Or for her?"

"I don't know. Probably both."

Fuck. Dizzie dropped her head back against the pillow and stared up at the ceiling. Every piece of good news was countered by bad. Her future looked bleaker by the moment.

Now she'd never be able to escape the Tremaines, not if she really carried their DNA. How had the hospital caught it? Why hadn't the health centers at Tremaine Corporation ever noticed it?

She'd worry about that later. Killian was talking again and she'd totally missed it.

She shook her head. "Sorry, what?"

"It's going to be okay," he repeated.

"I hope so." She sounded like a downer, so she tried to reengage. "Any nibbles on the reward?"

"I haven't been back to Razor Jack's."

She scowled at him.

"Been a little busy here." There were dark circles under his eyes, the product of worry and lack of sleep.

Dizzie sighed. "I can't point fingers. I lazed around in bed all day." She smiled to let him know she was teasing.

He didn't smile back. In fact, his expression turned serious.

Her stomach sank.

Killian grabbed her hand. His fingers were icy as he

laced them through hers. "I didn't want to leave you here alone," he said, his voice strained.

Her heart twisted at the pain in his voice. Did that mean he cared? He had every right to hate her for what she'd unknowingly done, but she hoped he didn't.

Dizzie brought their joined hands to her heart. "I'm okay. You saved me." She pressed her lips to the back of his hand. "If you hadn't called the medic, if you hadn't insisted they bring me here," she looked around at the swanky hospital room, "I could have died. Whatever happens, you saved my life. Thank you."

She kissed his hand again, then tugged. He resisted for a fraction of a second before he sat next to her.

"We're going to figure this out, right?" She was in his world now and she'd need his help to navigate it. To survive it.

"We will." He pulled her close. She rested her head against his chest, their linked hands caught between their bodies.

Killian shifted, stretched his legs out. Dizzie snuggled closer. His arms curled around her. For the first time since she woke up in the hospital, she felt safe.

CHAPTER 40

BY THE TIME Dizzie opened her eyes again, Killian was gone, but the indent on the pillow next to her was proof she hadn't imagined it. She'd slept well and felt rested. Her pain was nearly gone thanks to Killian and whatever miracle drugs they'd administered.

"I don't know what he sees in you."

Dizzie jumped at Portia's voice. Her heart monitor beeped. God, she was sick of that thing reporting her every emotion.

Swiveling, Dizzie found Portia perched on a chair between Dizzie and the door, the dividing curtain pulled back. That wasn't ominous at all. She wanted to respond to Portia's taunt, but what could she say? Dizzie wasn't sure what Killian saw in her either. And for someone known for being cool, calm, and collected, Portia had been showing some serious impulse-control issues.

Dizzie rubbed her legs. A lingering, painful memory from the last time Portia had let loose. She curled her fingers into the bedsheet in an effort to not take a swipe at her. Portia deserved it for trying to run Dizzie over.

For someone who had been similarly dressed in a hospital gown that last time Dizzie had seen her, the heir to the Tremaine Corporation now looked perfectly put together. Portia wore a somber black dress and black heels. Probably had a lackey fetch them for her. The only hint that Portia might be at less than her best were the shadows under her eyes and the pallor of her skin.

Dressed in a hospital gown and yesterday's underwear, Dizzie felt dowdy in comparison and more than a little vulnerable. She needed a shower and clean clothes. Where had her bag ended up? Had it made it to the hospital?

She itched to pull the sheet back up, but wasn't about to give Portia—her sister?!—the satisfaction of knowing that she intimidated Dizzie.

"I mean, he didn't bother to wait until you woke up." Her words and tone carried the same sneer that shaped her lips.

Dizzie had no idea where Killian had gone, but she hoped he'd be back soon. Until he returned, she'd have to let Portia's words roll off her back.

It was harder than she expected since the hits kept coming.

"He's probably off to get security to drag you back to headquarters to answer for your crimes. Since you killed his best friend and all."

Jesus. She got why they called Portia the Ice Queen. The other woman was a stone-cold bitch.

"Good morning, Portia."

Dizzie would be polite, though all she wanted to do was flip Portia off and have the nurses drag her from the room. Unfortunately, they would probably drag off the wrong Tremaine sister. "So happy you decided to visit," she said, channeling every interaction she'd ever had with high society ladies, hoping she got the fuck-you tone just right.

Portia glared at her.

Score!

"Why are you here?"

"You killed my husband. I want to see you suffer for it." Tears welled in Portia's eyes. Eyes that now reminded Dizzie a lot of her own.

"Fair enough." Dizzie swallowed. That was honest. Brutally honest. She was grateful for the other woman's candidness. The new world she was suddenly a part of was only partially built on reality.

"I'm sorry for my part in the bombing," Dizzie said. "I honestly didn't know what was in the package. It was just another job."

As soon as she said, Dizzie knew that she'd screwed up.

"Killing innocent people like my husband was a job? You're a killer and I can't wait to take you down."

Guilt weighed on Dizzie's shoulders. Maybe Portia was right. Maybe she did deserve to be punished for her role in it. But she shouldn't be the only one.

"Are you at least looking for who else was involved? Because I think the rumors were right and it was an inside job."

Oh my god. Why had she said that?

Portia's lips pursed. "Wouldn't you like to know?"

During their night at the Jack's, Killian had confided that he didn't believe Tremaine Security knew what they were doing. Personally, Dizzie thought they didn't care.

At the time, that hadn't been a concern. Now, if they didn't care and they knew where Dizzie was... She was pretty much screwed.

"Well, yes," Dizzie admitted. "But if you don't want to

tell me, I'm happy to hang out here." She shouldn't keep needling Portia, but she couldn't help it. The woman was determined to make Dizzie's life a living hell. If she let her live at all.

Portia rose stiffly from her chair and stalked toward the bed. Apparently, Dizzie had made the Ice Queen mad.

A squiggle of glee rushed through her. It lasted until Portia loomed over the bed, staring down at her.

"Enjoy your stay while you can." Portia's voice was cool and cruel. "This will be the last place you remember fondly."

Dizzie tensed every muscle to keep from leaning away when Portia bent and put her face close to hers. "You may think that Killian will get you out of this. You think that it matters that you're some castoff Tremaine bastard. It doesn't. Nothing can save you because you killed my husband and I'm going to make you pay." Portia straightened and ran her hand over the IV setup, the threat clear.

The door snicked shut behind her. Dizzie placed her hand over her heart. It was racing in time with the beeping.

Portia hadn't been subtle; she didn't have to be. As long as the Tremaine heir was in the hospital, Dizzie would need to be alert every moment.

Why had Portia allowed Dizzie to wake up? They'd been alone in the room. It would have been so easy to take Dizzie out while she was sleeping. And she would have gotten away with it. Why just deliver a threat?

Dizzie pulled up her sheet, but it didn't stop the shivers that raced through her. Portia's words echoed over and over again in her head.

Her—sister!— had been pretty damn clear that she didn't want Dizzie to survive this ordeal. Dizzie had her own concerns about the odds of her survival, but she wanted to live.

Not as a Tremaine. Not in Killian's fairy-tale life.

That was a lie. She'd take Killian's fairy tale, though she didn't see how it could possibly work out.

If she wanted the chance to find out, she'd need to save her own life. First step? Get out of the hospital.

Dizzie hadn't stepped out of her room yet, so she had no idea how many guards were posted outside. With any luck, they weren't worried about her leaving her room.

But this was a Tremaine hospital. Everyone here either owned stock in the company or was owned by it. Where could she go? How could she get out?

The monitors were part of her problem. All her vital signs were tracked through a wristband. She studied the plastic band that recorded her medical details. The medical staff would notice if she took it off. She slid her fingers under the plastic, feeling for the seam.

Deciding the monitors would have to wait, she pressed the button to call the nurse. Betty, the perky nurse, responded. Dizzie sighed.

"What do you need?" Her sunny smile brightened the room.

Dizzie smiled in return. The woman's cheer was infectious. "Do you know where my bag is? I need clothes. Real clothes, I mean. And a shower? I'm getting a little rank."

"Of course, Miss Tremaine."

The monitor picked up Dizzie's flinch, and the nurse looked at her in concern. "Are you okay?"

"Just not used to the name," she admitted. And if she had her way, she never would be. "I've always been just Dizzie."

"It must be like a fairy tale."

"Yes," Dizzie agreed with a forced smile. "Just like one." The old-timey kind, where people got their toes chopped off or otherwise got screwed.

The nurse opened the closet door and removed Dizzie's bag. She set it on the visitor's chair. "Do you want assistance with the shower?"

"I think I'm okay." Dizzie tested her claim by swinging her legs over the side of the bed. She braced for a wave of pain, but nothing happened. "Whatever you guys did to me really worked."

"Oh, aren't those nanomeds the best? They're limited to the really important patients. You're very lucky to get them."

Dizzie sobered at the reminder of her change in circumstances. If she hadn't been a Tremaine, would she have survived?

"Well, I'm very grateful for your care, Betty." It was true.

Betty beamed. "Press the call button if you need anything at all."

The smile Dizzie gave her in return was completely genuine. Betty seemed nice—maybe too nice for her own good—and Dizzie hoped she wouldn't get in trouble when she escaped.

"Thank you so much."

She bobbed her head. "Do you need anything else?"

"No, you've been amazing."

When the door closed behind the nurse, Dizzie dropped her head against the pillow. Her first problem— looking like a patient—was solved.

CHAPTER 41

AFTER A REFRESHING SHOWER with unlimited hot water, Dizzie studied her reflection. Her new clothes were out of her comfort zone and way out of her price range. The sleek black pants and collared shirt made her squirm, since she was used to T-shirts and leather. Sheer willpower kept her from tugging at the top buttons of the collar.

The woman in the mirror looked more corporate than courier.

She fussed with her hair until it hung down her back in a sleek ponytail rather than her regular braid. The nanomeds they'd treated her with had changed her hair back to its normal blond.

Did she really look like Portia? Dizzie peered into the mirror, searching for similarities. She didn't see any.

Killian had.

She wished he were here.

Dizzie shook her head. Now was not the time. It didn't matter whether she looked like a Tremaine or not. She'd never be one. She didn't want to be one.

She'd thought a lot about the test results while she

showered. How no one in the company had discovered the truth before. Whether she could use her newly discovered DNA to save herself. Based on the way Portia, an actual Tremaine, treated her, it was unlikely.

By the time she'd finished the shower, Dizzie had decided her best course of action was to stick to her plan. Fresh clothes had been the first step. The long shower had given her an idea about how to solve the wristband problem.

Satisfied that she had a starting place, Dizzie rolled up her leather pants as best she could until they hit her knees and slipped on her robe. The only shoes she had were the boots and the heels. She tucked the heels into the pockets with a grimace. Just the thought of wearing them again made her ankles ache, but the slippers would be noticeable once she left the hospital, and there was no way she could hide the boots under her robe.

Pulling the robe closed, she studied her reflection again. The clothes were for the outside world. Inside the hospital, she needed to look like a patient. Satisfied that she did, Dizzie took a deep breath and looked around the room.

Dizzie opened the door and found two guards standing outside. They weren't a surprise. Betty had mentioned them on one of her visits. Since she'd been chatty, Dizzie had also asked a lot of questions about the hospital and whether she could leave her room for a walk. She was going stir crazy. In her normal life, she never spent this much time indoors in one place.

Betty had eagerly confirmed that Dizzie could take a walk when she'd mentioned the walls were closing in. Eager to help out a member of the Tremaine family, she'd cleared it with Dizzie's doctor and the other nurses at the nursing station.

The guards, on the other hand, weren't in on it. They

immediately spun around when Dizzie opened the door. "Get back in your room!" one of them ordered.

She kept her eyes down and sagged against the doorframe. "Please, I want to walk around the floor. The doctor said I should try to put weight on my leg." The statement was true, except for the weakness she injected into her voice.

"Ms. Tremaine said—"

A passing nurse cut him off. "For pity's sake. Where do you think the girl is going to go? She's as weak as a kitten."

The nurse turned to her. "Are you sure you're up to it?"

Dizzie nodded, careful to look as tired as possible. "Yes, please."

The nurse pursed her lips, then nodded sharply. "Okay, but I want you to use a walker, just in case."

Dizzie could live with that. "Thank you," she whispered.

The nurse waved an orderly over and instructed him to get a walker.

Once he brought it, Dizzie wrapped her hands around the handles. "Thank you," she repeated.

She moved with a slow shuffle. It was harder than she thought to steer it with her elbows tight to her waist so no one would notice the shoes in her pockets.

As she passed a guard, he protested that he should accompany her.

Dizzie said a silent thanks when the nurse said, "Pfft, that girl won't last five minutes, tops."

They thought she was too weak. Good. That was what she needed for her plan to succeed.

The guards' glares were like a weight pressing down on her shoulders. She used the feeling, hunching over the walker and fighting to not go too fast.

Shuffle, step. Shuffle, step.

Every slow movement brought her closer to the corner and the stairway that would take her to freedom.

Her optical implant hadn't provided the hospital's blueprint, so she'd gained a basic idea of the building's layout from the nurses. She'd peppered them with questions, like how they evacuated the building in case of an emergency.

She turned the corner after what felt like forever. Despite her slow pace, her heart raced. If her monitor was reacting, Dizzie hoped they'd write off as overexertion. Until she got this bracelet off, she wouldn't truly be free.

Her gaze flicked down the hallway and up to the security mirrors on the ceiling and back again. A few orderlies and a nurse or two passed her, but no one took her for anything other than a patient out for a walk. Perfect.

The hallway cleared and she shuffled faster toward the stairway. Opening the door and maneuvering the walker through it was harder than she expected. Abandoning it here would tip them off.

She was breathing hard by the time she maneuvered it down two flights of stairs. The longer she was in the stairwell, the higher her chance of getting caught. She'd wanted to go farther, but there was no way she could drag the damn thing down more stairs. This was her stop, then.

Dizzie used the small window in the door and a security mirror to ensure the hall was clear before she slipped out of the stairwell. She left the walker in front of a restroom, then shuffled down the hallway as if she belonged there.

She needed to find a patient room for the final piece of her plan: leave her medical bracelet on another patient.

Dizzie had scraped her nail along the inside of the band over and over again, gently shaving away enough plastic to slide it off her wrist. The exchange had to be quick. Any interruption in her vitals and they might send someone to check on her. In order for her plan to work, Dizzie needed someone who wouldn't argue. Someone who wouldn't notice getting a second bracelet.

Trying to be casual, she glanced into the rooms that lined the corridor. Many were empty. Some she couldn't tell. Every few feet, Dizzie scanned the hallway. This floor had a lot less traffic than the one her room was on. The quiet was almost creepy.

Finally she found a room that had nothing but a patient lying in a bed. The beeping was too steady, the breathing too shallow. To her untrained eye, it didn't seem like a natural sleep. Were they in a coma?

Slipping through the door, Dizzie carefully closed it behind her. The scent of hospital disinfectants lingered in the air, but the smell of sadness was stronger. Besides the bed and the monitors, the only objects in the room were a small plastic plant on a corner table and a single chair in the corner. In case a visitor dropped by?

Was this what would happen to her? Would she die alone?

Dizzie sighed and struggled to ignore the aching sense of loss.

She ducked into the corner of the room, hoping she wouldn't be seen by anyone passing by. "Hello?" She spoke quietly at first. "Hello?"

Not a twitch from the bed. No beeps from the monitor.

This was it. Dizzie crossed to the bed and crouched on the far side. She grabbed the patient's fingers. They were warm but thin. Lifeless, even with a slow, steady pulse.

Lacing their fingers together, Dizzie tugged at her bracelet with her free hand. It slid along her wrist but got caught on the bump of her thumb. Dammit.

She released the patient's hand, but kept their fingertips touching. That provided enough wiggle room to slide the band over her own thumb and fingers and onto the woman. At least, she thought it was a woman. The patient was so skinny.

"Thank you," she whispered. "I hope this doesn't get you in trouble."

Her instincts screamed at her to leave, but Dizzie forced herself to wait. She had to make sure the presence of the second medical tag didn't cause any problems.

While she waited, Dizzie removed the robe and the slippers. She slid them both under the bed, hiding them in the shadows. Keeping an eye on the door, she perched on the edge of the visitor's chair and slipped on the heels. Then she twisted her hair into a low bun.

This was it. It didn't appear that anyone had noticed the switch, but she didn't dare linger. Dizzie crept to the door and opened it slowly. The hallways remained eerily empty. The kind of place where a new face would be noticed.

She followed the signs for the elevator. Peeking around a corner, she saw the elevator as well as the nurses' station. Only one person sat at the desk. That fit with the sad, abandoned vibe the floor gave off.

Though the nurse at the desk wasn't facing the elevators, Dizzie worried he'd turn around. He shifted slightly and she jumped back around her corner, her heart pounding a mile a minute.

Good thing she wasn't wearing that bracelet anymore. Otherwise, a nurse would have been rushing to see what was wrong with her.

Dizzie calmed down and looked around the corner. The nurse had barely moved. From this angle, she could see the screen over his shoulder. He was playing games.

Must be a cushy shift, just waiting in case someone woke up.

That would work in her favor. If he felt secure enough to game on the job, it was highly unlikely that anyone came to walk around this floor this time of day.

She watched him play and when he showed no signs of moving, she dashed across the floor to the elevator and punched the button.

The elevator button lit up, but there was no sound. She willed the elevator to come quickly. And to be empty.

When the elevator doors opened, there was one person already in it. He looked a little surprised to stop, but she stepped in as if she belonged and pressed the button for the lobby. She took up a position in the corner and kept the other occupant in her peripheral vision. The wall to her back provided her with the illusion of safety.

In her courier clothes, she was used to being ignored. Dressed like a corporate office worker, Dizzie kept waiting for someone to notice her.

Each ding signifying another floor took her one step closer to her freedom. Each stop also ratcheted up her tension. The closer they got to the lobby, the more she struggled to maintain a relaxed posture. The whole elevator ride, she waited to be caught.

When it stopped to pick up two more passengers, Dizzie held her breath. There'd be an alarm if they knew she was gone, right?

It took less than a minute for the elevator to reach the ground floor, but to Dizzie it felt like hours. The doors slid open and the noise of the lobby rushed in as the other passengers rushed out.

Dizzie exited last.

Two of the passengers veered toward the exit. She

followed at a steady pace. She struggled to blend in with the doctors and visitors who filled the lobby.

The closer she got to the outer doors, the more people joined the flow. It became easier to get lost in the crowd. With the same skills she used to thread between traffic, she slipped through the spaces between people, embedding herself in the stream of people.

The crowd narrowed as it approached the two sets of double doors. She pulled sunglasses out of her pocket and slipped them on before stepping outside.

A few feet outside the hospital, Killian approached the entrance from the other direction.

Her heart stuttered, then started again. Should she say hi? What if he told her to go back inside?

She couldn't risk it. Not after everything she'd done to escape. She kept walking when they passed.

"Portia?"

She ignored the spear of disappointment. She'd made the right decision. He might have seen her, but he didn't see *her*.

"Wait. Dizzie?"

Too little, too late.

Dizzie kept walking and melted into the crowd. When she reached the street, she stopped.

She needed a ride. She kept moving, drifting toward the valet stand as she planned her next move.

"Would you like us to bring your car around, Ms. Tremaine?"

She may have been pissed that Killian hadn't recognized her, but this was a gift. "Yes, please." She mimicked the cadence of Portia's speech.

A minute later, a sleek black car pulled up. This wasn't the one Portia had run her over in. That was a relief.

The valet stepped out and handed her the keys. Dizzie channeled her inner Portia and inclined her head.

Dizzie kept her expression flat and eased into the car. The valet closed the door behind her. The breath she'd been holding escape in a soft whoosh.

Boy, was Portia going to be pissed when she realized Dizzie had taken her car.

CHAPTER 42

KILLIAN STOPPED in the middle of the masses of people entering and exiting the hospital. People grumbled and shoved around him as he turned in a circle. He'd seen Dizzie in the crowd. He was sure of it.

Initially believing she was Portia, he hadn't been surprised when she ignored him. It wasn't until he'd passed her that he realized it was Dizzie. She was shorter than Portia and the crowds had swallowed her up. Portia would never have allowed that.

Why was Dizzie dressed like Portia? How had she left the hospital? Why had she ignored him?

As his gaze swept the street, Portia's car roared away from the curb. Killian swore that the woman he'd seen was Dizzie. But if it had been, was it only a coincidence that he'd also seen Portia's car?

If Portia had somehow convinced Dizzie to come with her, that was very bad.

Killian entered the hospital and stepped into an elevator, waiting impatiently as it ascended to Dizzie's floor.

Bypassing the nurses' station, he headed directly to Dizzie's room. The two guards stepped in front of him, blocking the door. "We can't let you in."

"I was here this morning. It wasn't a problem then," he countered.

The taller of the two smirked. "Still can't let you in."

Killian stepped sideways. They shifted to remain between him and the door.

He was considering his extremely limited options when a nurse approached.

"Can I help you?"

He gave her his most charming smile. "I'm here to see my friend. I was here earlier," he added to be helpful. "I'm Killian St. John." Surely he didn't have to add who he was.

She looked him up and down, a pinched smile on her lips. "Hmm," she murmured in a tone he didn't know how to interpret.

Killian looked down at his clothes. For the first time since the gala he wore his usual dark slacks and jacket, with a white shirt and no tie, so it wasn't like he looked like a slob from the street. Plus, there was the whole sexy eligible bachelor thing he'd had going on prior to meeting Dizzie. That usually got him in the door. Any door.

This was weird.

"She's not in there."

His stomach twisted. *Dammit!* He had seen her outside.

He looked at the guards to gauge their reaction. Given the shit-eating grins they wore, they'd obviously known. Assholes.

He turned his charm on full blast. "Where can I find her?"

The nurse frowned, suddenly looking nervous. "Oh,

she's gotta be around here somewhere. She insisted on a walk around the floor, though the poor thing looked about to pass out at any moment."

"How long has she been gone?" Killian had a bad feeling about this.

The nurse looked past him at the clock. Her face reflected surprise. "Why, almost an hour. I hope she hasn't had an accident."

His fists clenched. He'd known the hospital was a risk. He should never have left her alone. Had Tremaine Security taken her or had Dizzie slipped away?

How could they not know where she was?

A tiny voice in his head whispered that he knew where Dizzie was. She was heading somewhere in Portia's car. There had to be a way to track her.

"Well, there is a way to find out where she is," the nurse said slowly.

He'd apparently said that aloud.

"There is? Can you do that?"

She looked uncertain for a minute.

"What if she had a medical emergency?" he added, in case the nurse was wavering.

"We can check." With a decisive nod, the nurse headed for the central desk.

Leaving the smirking guards behind, Killian followed her.

"Well, that's strange," she said, studying the screen.

"What is?" His breath caught in his throat. He scooted around her until he could see the screen too. The charts and lines didn't mean a thing to him.

Ignoring him, she waved another nurse over. "You reading this the way I am?"

His view was blocked again when the other nurse rolled her chair over. "That is strange. Sure it's the right patient?"

"Yeah, I checked that first. Think it's a malfunction?"

Killian clenched and unclenched his fists. He couldn't contain his frustration as they volleyed questions and answers back and forth. If something had happened to Dizzie, he'd never forgive himself for bringing her here. "Will someone please tell me what's going on?"

The first nurse pushed up from her chair. "Excuse me? Who do you think you are?"

Trying to get his frustration back to manageable levels, he forced a smile. "I'm sorry. I'm worried about my friend."

More than worried, since both nurses agreed that something was wrong with Dizzie. What weren't they telling him?

"Your friend?" She glared at him and he knew the damage was done. "The one who came in with injuries from a car accident? That poor dear is probably better off without *friends* like you."

"Can you please tell me what's going on?"

"Are you family?"

He shook his head, but the pinch of her lips told him she knew the answer. "Can't tell you if you're not family."

Killian bit back a curse. What now?

"If you can tell family where she is, you can tell me." Portia's cold voice came from right behind him.

Fuck. He'd thought it couldn't get any worse.

"Ms. Tremaine." Both nurses were polite. The attitude he'd gotten had been replaced by respect and deference. And a little fear.

"Can you tell me what your relationship is with the patient?" The first nurse was brave enough to ask.

Portia ground her teeth together. Admitting to her relationship with Dizzie had to be killing her. Was Dizzie's relationship to the Tremaines in her records or had the hospital already hidden it?

The need to find Dizzie was almost a physical weight. Right now, Portia was his best option. So he stayed silent. All he wanted was to demand answers.

"I'm her...sister." Portia forced the words out through clenched teeth.

Killian looked at her, really looked at her. It was almost funny how alike the sisters were, though neither of them would admit it. Both stubborn to a fault. If they'd grown up together, they'd either be best friends or diehard rivals.

Why hadn't they grown up together? The hospital said there was no record of Dizzie before her hospitalization. Only the DNA test had revealed the relationship. And only because a fluke of fate had led a lowly courier to get treatment in the best Tremaine facility: her sister had tried to run her over.

"Does she have any other family?" The nurse didn't look up as she updated the records.

God, this had to be killing Portia. Poor little rich girl. Only daughter. Never the apple of her father's eye. Dizzie didn't seem in the running for that position either.

"Just me. Andmyfather." The words rushed out in a tangle.

Killian wished he could pull her into her arms and comfort her. She wouldn't allow it. Not in public. And maybe not ever after Tommy and Dizzie.

If the nurse picked up on her frustration, she didn't react. "Great, thank you."

When she finished typing, the nurse pulled the screen up so Portia could see it. "This is your sister's monitor."

Portia grimaced, but stepped closer to look at the screen.

Killian wanted to crowd in, but he was afraid that if they remembered he was there, they'd shut him out completely.

The nurse traced her finger over the screen. "This line is her heartbeat. It's steady but..."

"It's weird," the other nurse piped up.

"Weird?" Portia asked.

The first nurse sighed. "I hate to say it, but yes. It's healthy," she said, hurriedly placing her hand over Portia's to reassure her, "but it's too slow. Like she's in a coma."

"Oh dear, a coma, that would be terrible." Portia's voice dripped with sarcasm. She moved her hand away from the nurse's.

Killian cut her a sharp look. She ignored him and kept staring at the nurses' screen.

"I'm sure you don't have to worry about that." The nurse patted Portia's hand, clearly no longer wary of her. "Betty said your sister was a bit weak after her accident, but doing fine. I'm sure she's not in a coma. It's just a bit unusual."

"Why?" He couldn't hold back any longer.

Both Portia and the nurse looked him. He tensed, waiting to be sent away. Instead, neither did more than glare.

"I'm not sure," the nurse said slowly. "I think she might be on a different floor. The coma floor."

"There's a coma floor?" He and Portia spoke at the same time.

The nurse looked around, then leaned over the counter. "You didn't hear that from me."

An entire floor of coma patients? Who did that? And why? And why was it a secret?

As intriguing as that puzzle was, he couldn't afford to get derailed. "We need to find her first. Is there a way we can track her?"

"Maybe you aren't useless after all," Portia said. She stared at the nurses. "Is there?"

The nurse looked scandalized that they would ask. "Well, yes," she admitted. "We only use them in rare cases."

"I think this qualifies, don't you?"

"I suppose." One of the nurses swiped her badge over a drawer and pulled out a small object that looked like a tiny tablet. She pressed the power button and it flickered to life. She handed it to the second nurse, who typed something into the computer record. "It's set up for her tracker. The unit should have enough battery to find her."

Killian reached for the device, but Portia grabbed it first. "I am her family, after all. The little green dot is her?"

"Yes, it will get larger the closer you get to her."

"Sounds simple enough," Portia said. She looked over her shoulder at Killian. "You can go. I don't need your help."

He smirked at her. "Tough," he said. "I'm not leaving until we find her."

"You can't save her, Killian."

Not from Portia. That was his greatest fear. Though he wouldn't admit that to Portia. Instead, he addressed one more question to the first nurse. "Will it tell us which floor the signal is on?"

She shook her head. "Unfortunately not. But unless you're on the floor directly above her, the dot will stay small until you're close."

"Thank you for your help," he said when it became clear that Portia wasn't going to say anything.

He wished he could ask for a second tracker, but given

his lack of familial relationship, the odds of him getting one were slim. Instead, he needed to stay with Portia. "Shall we?"

"Eager to find your little bomber, aren't you?"

He gritted his teeth. It wasn't worth having this argument again. Plus, he didn't need her to know that, yes, he was eager to find Dizzie.

"Let's go." Ignoring the dig, Killian pushed away from the station and strode toward the elevator. He'd only gone about five feet before Portia laughed.

"Forget something?"

What could he have forgotten? Oh, right. They needed to know which floor the coma patients were kept on. "I thought you had it."

"Lucky for you, I do." She swept past him with a sniff.

"Great." Killian followed Portia to the elevator. When she picked up her pace, he did the same.

She rushed into the elevator and tried to close it before he got there.

He slid his foot into the track to stop it. The sensor recognized the obstruction and the doors slid open again. "Nice try." He stepped in behind her and pressed his back against the wall.

Neither spoke. He tapped his fingers impatiently against the wall. Dammit. It was like he was channeling Dizzie. Why wasn't she pushing the button for the floor?

"You okay?"

She shook her head. Blond tendrils shivered against her neck. "No. I hate this place." When she wasn't animated by anger, she looked wan. Sadness radiated off her.

"I'm sorry." He hated this place, too, and he hadn't spent nearly as much time here as Portia had.

"And I really hate the tenth floor." She looked directly ahead and addressed her words to the door.

"Is that where we're going?"

She nodded, but didn't press the button. He reached past her and did it himself.

"Dammit, Killian!" Instead of anger, her words carried anguish.

"We need to get moving." Since he was 99 percent sure he'd seen her outside the hospital, Killian knew it was a long shot that they'd find Dizzie on the tenth floor. There was still that 1 percent, though. He needed the certainty.

"I was getting there. I needed to prepare," Portia said as the elevator began its descent.

"For the coma floor?" He was being a dick, but he had to find Dizzie.

"For the floor where my mom died, asshole. Remember?"

Shit. He'd forgotten. When they'd been in middle school, Portia's mom had been diagnosed with an incurable form of cancer.

"I'm sorry, Portia. I didn't realize this was the same floor."

She shrugged, but there was no energy in it.

As he watched, her spine stiffened and she shed her memories, cloaking herself in her usual armor.

He'd forgotten that was how it started. She'd come by her Ice Queen nickname the old-fashioned way—by being a bitch—so it was easy to forget that the first time she'd needed the armor was when her mother had died.

"It doesn't matter." Her tone said otherwise.

The elevator stopped and Portia exited first. She moved slowly, as if her memories weighed her down.

"After my mom died, this whole floor was gutted and

completely remodeled. Dad didn't want any reminders." She turned and gave a bittersweet smile. "If he could have removed the entire floor, he would have."

Killian understood. His grief for Tommy battered at him. If the woman he loved had died here, he wouldn't want the reminder.

The tenth floor was surprisingly quiet. Only one nurse sat at the station. Otherwise, the floor appeared empty. It gave him the creeps. The sooner they finished their search and left this floor, the better.

"Where do you want to start?"

Portia was already moving, the tracker held stiffly out in front of her. She approached the nurses' station. "Excuse me. We need your help."

Killian trailed after her. The desire to search for Dizzie pulled at him, but Portia had the tracking program and he couldn't risk her finding Dizzie first.

The lone figure hunched over the computer didn't acknowledge their presence until Portia coughed. Loudly.

"What's your rush? These patients aren't going anywhere." The nurse propelled a small figure across the screen with his finger.

Wow. If he was playing video games at work, he should keep his eyes on the elevator and his screen facing the other way.

"I hate to interrupt," Portia drawled in full Ice Queen mode, "but we require your assistance."

"Seriously? Fine." He spun around to face them, his annoyance clear. "Where's the fire?" The words trailed off and his face paled when he recognized the Tremaine heir. Coming face to face with Portia tended to have that effect on Tremaine personnel.

The nurse jumped to his feet. The sudden movement

sent his chair flying to the other side of the enclosed space. It clattered against the station.

"Oh, shit. I mean, Ms. Tremaine. I'm sorry. I didn't know it was you," he stammered. His hands flippered at his sides.

Portia stared at him a long minute.

The more Killian studied her, the stronger the resemblance to Dizzie became. Portia's I'm-not-here-for-your-crap gaze reminded Killian of Dizzie's response to the guard at the gala.

"Well, now that you do," Portia said finally, "tell me everything that happened today."

His Adam's apple bulged as he swallowed repeatedly. "Everything?"

She nodded.

"Um, well, I woke up with, um, you know." He turned bright purple. "And since I was alone, I, um—"

Portia took a deep breath.

"What happened here. On. The. Floor. Of. This. Hospital?" The air around them chilled.

Killian swallowed a laugh. The guy was so clearly outmatched that it was painful to watch.

"Has anyone visited the patients today?" he asked to spare them all the awkwardness of the nurse trying to match wits with Portia.

"What? You mean, like visitors?"

"Yeah, like visitors." Good lord. Was the coma designation for staff too?

"No. No visitors." The nurse sagged in relief at being able to answer a question. He turned away to retrieve his chair.

"We aren't done." Portia's voice was a whip.

The guy froze, gulping audibly. "We aren't?"

"What about doctors? Other patients?" Killian cut through the babble again.

Every minute they wasted questioning this guy, the farther away Dizzie got.

The nurse looked confused, then his eyes widened. "Oh. Two doctors visited earlier. They came to check on the patients."

Dammit. The doctors were a surprise. Killian was sure he'd say that there had been a patient. "When was this?"

He shrugged. "I don't know. Half an hour ago. Maybe." He shrugged again. "I, uh, saw them arrive. That's it."

"You didn't see them leave?"

He shook his head. Killian wasn't surprised. The man had been totally absorbed in his game. If Killian and Portia hadn't approached the desk, he'd have never known they were there.

"What did they look like?" Portia asked. "Was one short and a blonde?"

Way to lead the witness, Portia.

"What? No. Two tall dudes." He stopped again. Killian could almost hear the wheels turning in his head. "A blonde? No. I mean, maybe?"

"One of the doctors?"

He shook his head. "Not one of the doctors. Maybe I saw blond hair. Out of the corner of my eye, you know? But when I looked, nothing was there."

This was it. Killian knew it. "Where?"

"Where what?"

Killian wanted to lunge over the desk, but he gritted his teeth and contained his impatience. Barely. How had this man gotten a job?

Portia took over the questioning. "The blond hair. Where did you see it?"

If Dizzie were the one asking questions, she'd be tapping her nails in impatience.

"I didn't see anything. Probably."

Killian cringed. This was painful.

"I know you didn't. But if you had, where was it?" Portia's tone was pure Ice Queen.

"Oh. Over there." He pointed down the hall.

Killian took off in the direction the nurse pointed, not caring if Portia followed or not. He opened doors down the hallway and hissed her name. "Dizzie!"

He heard footsteps behind him. Portia. Maybe the nurse.

"Dammit, Killian!"

Killian didn't stop. He had to find her, even though he had no fucking clue what he was looking for. She wouldn't have left a note.

The other two caught up to him after he'd opened a few doors.

Killian continued to ignore them.

Portia continued past Killian, tracker in her hand. She stopped two doors down.

The nurse stepped in front of him, blocking access to the next room. He was panting and his words came out in little puffs. "You can't go around opening all the doors you want! There are privacy laws and stuff."

Killian snorted. There may have been privacy laws on the books, but the only ones the corporations enforced were the ones they wanted to. He was pretty sure Tremaine Corporation wouldn't give a damn.

"You wanna enforce the privacy laws?" Killian turned to Portia, but she was slipping into another room. He barreled after her.

Although Killian wouldn't have believed it possible, this room was even quieter than the main floor. An air of melancholy hovered inside. The room's lone occupant lay in the middle of a hospital bed, body covered by a sheet.

Killian didn't know what he'd expected—to see Dizzie laying on the bed, maybe—but there was no sign of her. Disappointment and relief hit him in equal parts.

"She's here." Portia stood in the middle of the room, sweeping the tracker around.

He stepped close enough to see the screen. Sure enough, a large green dot pulsed on it. Killian gestured to the bed. "That's not Dizzie."

"Of course it isn't," Portia snapped. "But the tracker says she's here."

The nurse shuffled into the room, his steps the only sounds besides the slow beep of the monitor.

Killian studied the machines hooked up to the patient, their slow and steady beeps adding to the desolate air of the room. At least when Dizzie had been hooked up to monitors like this, the sounds had changed with her reactions. He peered closer to the screen, suddenly curious about the patient they were disturbing. "Sorry to disturb you, Hope," he whispered to the slim, still figure.

"Look under the bed," Portia ordered.

"Portia, leave the poor man alone."

She ignored him and repeated her order to the nurse.

He bent at the waist to peer at the edge of the bed. "There's no one under there."

He tried to straighten, but Portia put her hand on his shoulder and pressed him down. "Get on the floor and look all the way."

"Portia, you're being irrational. There's no one here."

Dizzie had been here, he was sure of it, but he had no way to explain his certainty.

She whirled and directed her frustration at him. "You insisted that she was in here. Are you trying to hide her from me now?"

"I was wrong. There's no one here but this patient. We probably shouldn't be here. Let's check the other rooms." He stepped out of the way of the nurse crawling around the bed.

"Get up." Killian grabbed the man's arm.

"No, there's something under here." The other man sprawled onto his stomach and his top half disappeared beneath the bed.

Portia shot Killian a look of triumph.

The nurse reversed his underbed wiggle. "Sorry, it's just a robe and some slippers." He cleared the bed and shoved the robe to the side. He braced his hands on the edge of the mattress to lever himself up and disturbed the blankets. A hand flopped out from beneath them, flapping lifelessly against his. His scream was earsplitting. "It touched me!"

Killian wanted to laugh but the guy was freaking out so badly that would only make it worse. How was this man a medical professional? Killian looked at Portia to share the moment, but she was staring at the clothes the nurse had retrieved.

"Relax, you're fine." Killian stepped forward and gently lifted the patient's thin wrist. As soon as the offending limb was moved, the nurse scuttled backward like a crab, then sprang to his feet and raced from the room.

The patient's arm weighed almost nothing as Killian laid it back along her side.

"Wait a minute!" Portia moved suddenly, until she stood at his side. "What's that?"

Killian frowned. "Her medical bracelet. So they can monitor—"

"I know that, Killian," she snapped. "Why is she wearing *two*?"

He felt a rush of pride and relief. Clever, clever courier.

Killian wished she'd asked him for help, but she'd very smartly gotten herself out of the hospital. Dizzie was proving to be as strategic a thinker as her sister. If the two of them ever worked together, they'd be formidable. If they didn't try to kill each other.

He shrugged, wanting to give Dizzie as much of a head start as possible. Not from him, but from Portia. She wouldn't be that far behind...

"The tracker says it's hers."

"Okay. She obviously isn't here, though."

"Dammit! She should have been taken into custody the moment I saw her. The moment you saw her." She glared at him.

"She's innocent, Portia." His rote response by now.

"For someone who's innocent, she went to an awful lot of trouble to escape the hospital." She stared down at the patient in the bed, a sad look on her face.

"Can't say I blame her. The company isn't that desirable. And you did try to run her over." He straightened the blanket over the patient's arm, then walked out of the room.

Portia followed him out. "Where do you think you're going?"

Killian stopped in the middle of the hallway and faced her. "We came here to learn why Dizzie's vitals looked like a coma patient's." He pointed to the door she'd left open. "We did that. Now I'm leaving."

He didn't wait for her to argue or respond. He'd spent

too much time with her and not enough time focused on clearing Dizzie's name.

Portia stomped her foot. "We're not done. Killian, come back here!"

CHAPTER 43

DIZZIE DROVE Portia's car into the executive parking lot in the garage. She circled the lot until she found a parking place with Portia's name on it.

Although the hospital was only a few miles from Tremaine headquarters, her heart had raced the entire drive over. The damn monitor would have gone crazy.

What had she been thinking, taking Portia's car? It could be reported stolen at any moment. Not that it mattered now. She'd voluntarily returned. She wanted—no, *deserved*—answers and this was the only place to get them. This building held the key to her identity and the identity of the bomber. She was sure of it.

Getting into the building might be a challenge given she had no idea what privileges or security the executives might face. She wiped her palms on her pants and then rifled through the glove box and the console.

All she found was a pair of sunglasses. Not very useful, but she placed them on top of her head.

No time like the present.

Knowing this was likely the dumbest thing she'd ever

done, and that included many motorcycle tricks she'd tried in her teens, Dizzie pushed the car door open and stepped into the parking garage. It was spacious and well-lit.

Portia's parking space was near the elevators, so Dizzie headed in that direction. Focused on keeping her stride even, she nearly ran into another person heading the same direction. She stopped abruptly enough that the sunglasses slid over her forehead and onto her face.

Too startled to say anything, Dizzie pushed the glasses up to sit properly.

"I'm very sorry for your loss, ma'am. Mr. Gilmore will be missed," the woman said.

Her words struck Dizzie like a well-aimed arrow. Did she know Dizzie was an imposter? It seemed very unlikely.

Dizzie studied the other woman from behind her glasses. She looked 100 percent sincere. "Thank you," she said, her words stiff.

The other woman swallowed hard. "I just wanted you to know." She looked like she wanted to be anywhere but here. Dizzie completely agreed. They approached the elevator in silence and Dizzie stepped in when the other woman did. "Lobby," Dizzie said, before the other woman could ask.

Her companion still looked terrified, so the ride was generally a quiet one. The other woman rushed out of the elevator as soon as the doors open.

Dizzie laughed softly. She'd been tempted to do the same.

She strode across the main lobby to the lifts that would take her to the highest levels of the company. This was such a bad idea, but it might be her only chance to get the answers she needed. She couldn't stop.

The elevator opened the moment she approached and

Dizzie slipped in. The door closed swiftly behind her and started to rise before she even pushed a button.

Top floor? The cursor in her ocular implant came alive.

Dizzie jumped. She hadn't heard anything from the hacker since the warehouse, so she hadn't expected any assistance once in the building. In the heart of Tremaine headquarters, the blinking letters felt like an old friend. She nodded.

Why here?

Dizzie shrugged. It was too complicated to explain quickly. Plus, you never knew who might be watching.

Only one person could provide the answers she wanted. Phillip Tremaine. Her father, apparently. She cringed.

She'd barely wrapped her head around her role in the bombing. Learning that she was the what—the long-lost daughter of a billionaire? That was crazy.

People told stories about missing heiresses. Made movies and wrote books about them. Surely if the Tremaines were missing a daughter, she would have heard about it. The newsies would have had a field day.

Killian had been adamant about the DNA tests. So if she wasn't missing—what was she?

Where better to find answers than the home for orphans at the very base of dear daddy's global empire?

The elevator stopped smoothly at the executive floor. Her stomach dropped.

Good luck

"Thanks." *Pull it together, Dizzie. You got this.*

Dizzie straightened her spine and wrapped every last shred of confidence she had around her. She'd talk her way past whatever guards Tremaine had. She'd get her answers.

The doors opened, revealing a sprawling reception area with striking views of Seattle and Puget Sound. The view from Killian's house had been amazing. This one put his to shame.

The floor, white marble with dark veins, was gorgeous, but it lacked the warmth, the sense of lived-in-ness that Killian's house had. It was beautiful, cold, and sterile.

Just like the Tremaines.

Ignoring what that might say about her now, Dizzie stepped out and took a closer look at the room. Three of the walls were clear, floor-to-ceiling glass. The fourth wall was frosted, probably hiding the offices.

A cold chrome desk sat in front of the frosted glass, clearly limiting access. Polished metal handles on the glass were the only indication of a door.

This had to be the place.

The desk's owner was probably Tremaine's assistant. Dizzie remembered the weasel from her time in the cells.

Dizzie shuddered. She'd love to forget those terrible hours in the cells.

Why wasn't he at his post? Somebody should be here. How on earth was this place supposed to make money if no one was in the office?

Oh, god. She sounded like a Tremaine.

Was a love of money genetic? She'd been saving to buy her freedom, not some deep-seated need to accumulate riches, but did that make a difference?

Her whole life had turned topsy-turvy.

She looked up toward the ceiling. "Do you know what's going on?" she said aloud. There had to be cameras, even here on the most sacred of floors. Maybe especially here. Anyone wanting to see Tremaine would surely be filmed— their every weakness discovered and dissected before they passed the big shiny desk.

No reply from her mystery friend.

Fine.

Dizzie wiped her sweaty palms on her pants and stepped forward.

Stopped.

Looked up at the cameras again. After this week's life-changing events, she didn't want to take another step into the unknown. There was no good answer that would explain why she had grown up in the orphanage. Maybe she should just leave.

Hesitating will only get her caught. She needed to move. Now.

One step forward, then another. And another. When she was parallel with the desk, she peered behind it, heart racing.

There was nothing there. She didn't know what she'd expected. Maybe a body on the floor behind it. She shook her head. Too many vids.

Still tense, she waited for something to announce her presence. An alarm. A secret password.

Was the whole situation a trap? She shouldn't be able to get this close to Phillip Tremaine's door without supervision.

There had to be *something*! She blinked to activate her optical display. Maybe it would show her what she was missing. Instead, there was absolutely nothing.

That had never happened in headquarters before. It almost never happened anywhere—unless a dampening field was installed.

It would make sense if there was jamming equipment on this floor to prevent surveillance. After all, this was the heart of the corporation.

Figuratively.

The Tremaine Corporation didn't have a heart. That

was pretty damn obvious since the CEO's daughter had grown up in the orphanage. The *onsite* orphanage.

Phillip Tremaine had never bothered to come see how she was doing. Had he kept track of her at all?

Dizzie had never questioned her file. The company made a pretty big production about giving the crèche kids access to their files when they turned eighteen. All the data they had, they promised. Most of the kids had the same story—found in the city, brought to the company. Reared and educated, trained and given a job. All the corporation asked for was complete loyalty. And your whole life.

Now, given the results of the DNA test, her history had to be a lie. Those "unknowns" that populated the form were obviously a lie. What else were they hiding?

If she survived this, she'd have to ask the hacker to find the real file—if it existed.

Or she could find those answers herself. That's why she was here. *Stop stalling, Dizzie.* The answers were right behind those doors. Everything she wanted to know was *right there.*

Fueled by anger, Dizzie circled the empty desk and took the final steps to the office doors. She reached for the polished metal and pulled. Expecting resistance, she stumbled backward when it opened easily. Regaining her balance, she pulled it open and stepped into the inner sanctum.

"Who the hell are you? How did you get in here?"

CHAPTER 44

THE BOOMING VOICE stopped Dizzie in the doorway. She recognized the voice—the man—from news stories and company announcements. She'd never been this close to the CEO before. Phillip Tremaine didn't associate with people like her. The ones who actually carried the weight of the company on their shoulders.

He sat behind a massive desk and glared at her. He had blue eyes and expertly cut dark blond hair. Sharp cheekbones that he'd passed on to Portia, but not Dizzie, and an angry set to his mouth. Phillip Tremaine looked like a man in his forties—he must've had work done.

"How did you get past my assistant?"

"There's no one out there." Her voice wavered.

Knees shaking, Dizzie moved forward slowly. Every instinct screamed that she didn't belong here. Her nails pricked her palms. All she wanted to do was turn around and run before this got worse.

The floor here had the same shine as the reception area. Her heels clicked on the surface and echoed in the large space.

"I do belong here," she whispered under her breath.

Dizzie tried to take in her surroundings while she studied the man behind the desk. He looked exactly like the pictures that adorned the walls and meeting rooms throughout the building.

The wall of windows behind his desk revealed another spectacular view of the city.

Tremaine pushed back from his desk and stood. "Leave before I call security."

Training demanded she obey. Instead, Dizzie shook her head and stepped closer. "No."

He reached for a button on his desk.

It was now or never. "I want a few minutes of your time." She paused for effect. "Father."

His hand stopped before he touched the button. "I don't know what you're talking about," he blustered, but the way he settled back into his chair told her otherwise.

"I had a very interesting hospital stay that says otherwise." Her words were as bold as his denial had been. Without waiting for an invitation, she took the chair directly in front of his desk. Lower than his, it accentuated the power differential between the CEO and the people seeking his favor.

It didn't bother her. She had grown up so far down the food chain, everyone above her played power games.

Her time with Killian had taught her that there was nothing special about him, Portia, or anyone else in the highest levels of society. The only difference was money and opportunities.

Now that she had a connection to the highest levels of power, those opportunities could be hers.

His hand edged away from the button. "What do you want? Money?"

Dizzie didn't stop the laugh that bubbled out. Money.

Until today, yes, that was exactly what she'd wanted. Enough money to buy out her contract and set herself up with a comfortable lifestyle, doing whatever she wanted, whenever she wanted.

Everything she'd worked so hard for and now the CEO was offering it on a silver platter. But today, it wasn't enough.

"I want answers." Until she spoke, Dizzie hadn't known what she would say.

Tremaine laughed. Not the evil villain laugh she'd half-expected. Just an average laugh, only special because it came from a man running one of the top corporations in the world. "Answers? To what?"

Was everything too much to ask? She chose her words with care. She couldn't show weakness—her position was precarious as it was. "How did I end up here, in the orphanage?" There. That should get the conversation started.

He shrugged. "You were probably left on the doorstep or found in a drug den the way most of the kids were. Is that all?" He returned his attention to his computer screen.

Asshole. "Fine. Let's cut the bullshit. DNA says I'm your kid. I'm guessing you weren't all that careless with your..." she paused, trying not to think about old man sperm. "Your baby-making materials. You had to be involved with me ending up here."

Oh god. She was going to throw up.

"You're smarter than you look. How did you end up a courier?"

He sounded proud. She didn't want that.

Did she?

"Took the Tremaine skills test, and it said courier.

Who's my mother?" She asked another question quickly so he wouldn't dismiss her.

"Some girl from the Solveig family. Where's your ambition?"

Dizzie dug her fingers into the arms of her chair and struggled not to react. If he meant the Solveig Consortium, she had not one but two parents from the corporate class. Her whole life they'd drummed into her how much she owed the corporation that owned her and now...

Now, *they* owed her. Owed her for her lost childhood and the parents she never knew.

Anger surged and she tamped it down. She couldn't afford any distractions, not even her mother's identity. Not while she and her father were involved in this bizarre answer-for-answer dance.

"My ambition is directed solely at paying off my contract. Wanna take care of that for me?" As soon as the words escaped, Dizzie knew they were the wrong ones.

"Is that why you're here? You think you can blackmail me into canceling your contract?" His voice barely changed but she heard the sudden disinterest.

Dizzie was tired. Tired of the corporate games. Tired of pretending to be someone else. "I have no fucking clue why I'm here." She leaned back in the chair. "I'd love to have my contract paid off. Working it off is a shitty way to live and I want my freedom. But I also want to know who the hell sent the bomb that killed your son-in-law." Her brother-in-law. Grief for the family she'd never known welled up.

She'd gone from having no family to having a crazy dysfunctional one.

"Right now, though, I want to know how and why I ended up in the crèche."

"Why would I give you those answers?" Phillip

Tremaine—she would never consider him her father—leaned back in his seat. This was a man used to getting his way. Closing deals. Making money. Winning at all costs.

And she was facing him with no cards.

Sure, she could threaten to go to the newsies, with the DNA results to prove her story. That wouldn't protect her from the might of a multinational corporation. And she could "mysteriously" die before she could tell her story.

Throwing herself on his mercy wouldn't work either. Everything she knew about him indicated that he didn't have any. She needed to give him a reason to keep her alive. She went with honesty. Maybe she'd surprise an answer out of him.

"I don't know," Dizzie admitted. "But I've got nothing to lose by asking."

She barely breathed. She was so far out of her league here, it wasn't funny.

He stared at her. Then, to her surprise, he started talking. "Your mother was from Solveig Consortium. One of the younger daughters. I met her on a business trip to Sweden. She was careless, got pregnant."

This time his laugh was pure villain.

Shivers raced up her spine. Dizzie held herself rigidly still, afraid any movement would distract him.

"Somehow she got it into her head that I would leave my wife for her." He looked directly at her, daring her to challenge him. His eyes were blue like hers, but infinitely colder.

Dizzie gulped. Her need for answers had blinded her and she'd underestimated him. Would she leave this room alive? "What happened to her?"

A cold smile curved his lips. "She believed a baby

would bring the companies closer together. It was...unfortu-nate...when she died in childbirth."

The lack of feeling in that statement chilled her.

"I already had a wife and an heir. Solveig had nothing to offer. I'd already made significant inroads into their geographic market. I didn't need closer ties with the company. I needed new revenue sources."

He paused his story and looked expectantly at her.

Throat dry, she asked, "And you found them?" She wanted to ask what had happened to her mother. Likely not a safe conversational direction.

"Oh yes, I found them." Again, that smile. "You. You were the beginning of a very profitable revenue stream."

Her blood ran cold. He sounded eager to tell her all about it. That couldn't be good. "The courier business?"

He laughed. "No. It started with umbilical cells when you were born. Then I realized that I had my own source of healthy young organs."

Her hands dropped to her torso, her stomach. She had all her organs. Right? Her medical records said she did, but she knew those records had been manipulated.

"Organ donation?" The words were oily on her tongue.

"Less donation. More," he paused, and she watched him search for the right word, "insurance."

"Do you mean..." The concept was so terrible she could barely force the words out. "Spare parts? For Portia?" If Portia had been injured and Dizzie hadn't delivered the bomb, would they have tried as hard to find her? To save Portia?

His laugh sent chills up her spine. "Not for Portia." He waved his hand dismissively. "I can always have another heir. But I won't live forever. Yet."

Ohgodohgodohgod! Bile surged in her throat. She choked it back.

She'd trapped herself in a room with her long-lost father, an egomaniacal madman. This was the kind of story the crazy gossip mags published. The ones with alien babies and science gone wrong. Stories so crazy, no one believed them.

"Oh," she said, because he seemed to expect a response. If he was waiting for hysterics, well, she was trying very hard to keep that from happening. Her nails curled into her palms and she focused on the pain, not the panic.

"Yes, oh." He clasped his hands together on the desk and smiled.

"So, um, you're pretty healthy right now, right?" Dizzie hadn't heard otherwise, but couriers weren't on the need-to-know list.

"I'm generally healthy, yes."

"That's good." She scooted to the edge of her seat. "Thank you for your time. I should probably get going. I'll be sure to keep myself healthy, in case you, uh, need me." She stood, dying to run, hoping it wasn't obvious.

"Aren't you the conscientious daughter?" He sounded almost...touched. "Unfortunately, I can't let you leave."

Dizzie froze but didn't sit back down. She had to keep her wits if she were going to make it out of here alive. "You can't?" Her voice squeaked.

"Unh-unh. There's still the little matter of the bombing."

Right. The bombing. She hadn't forgotten about it, but it suddenly seemed a lot less important in light of everything she learned. "I had nothing to do with it."

"I don't care. You'd be more interesting if you had. It's a

good thing I'm more interested in your body than your mind."

Gross. Her stomach churned, but she ignored it. *Don't show weakness. Don't show weakness.*

"Portia wants me dead." Why had she said that?

"As she should." Tremaine didn't sound concerned at all that his heir wanted to kill his back-up plan.

How was she part of this family? She wished she could take back the last two days, pretend she didn't know.

"Still," he said, "since it's in my best interest to keep you around, I may be willing to help find the person behind the bombing."

For days, that had been what she had wanted. Now, when it was so close, she wondered what the cost would be. Did it matter since he already owned her?

"I was never going to be able to buy out my contract, was I?" It was a moment of clarity she'd never expected.

"Probably not." He clasped his hands on the desk in front of him. He looked thoughtful, rather than apologetic. "I hadn't decided. I enjoyed watching you try. You were very industrious and I respect that. Maybe you'd have done it if you outlived me. But since I was keeping you on hand to extend my life..." His words hung in the air between them, a threat she'd never known existed.

"So that's it? I'm a Tremaine courier for the rest of my life?" She'd loved her job, the freedom it allowed. Now it was just another cage. One she'd never escape.

Dizzie couldn't square the man who was keeping her around for spare parts with someone who was willing to let her risk her life as a courier. "And if I wanted a different position? A desk job?"

He stared at her a long moment and she struggled not to squirm. His gaze was empty. Cold. Calculating. He was obviously gauging her worth. "You took the same exams as every other corporate orphan, right? Looks like that's all you were good for."

What an asshole. Dizzie dropped back into her chair. What did it matter now? With a few words, he'd destroyed her hopes and dreams. There'd be no escape from the layers and layers of Tremaine family machinations.

Dizzie swallowed hard. She was trapped. But maybe not everyone had to be. "The, um, other kids in the orphanage. Are they...are they all like me?"

"My children?" Tremaine laughed. "Oh, no. Only you and Portia are mine. The others? Some are like you, bastards of others loyal to me kept around for emergencies."

"And the others?"

"Spare parts for those who can afford it."

His ominous omission hung in the air between them. The older kids that they'd been told had bought their freedom...had it all been a lie? Dizzie thought of Alice and her heart broke. There had to be a way to get this story out, to save them. Pulse racing, she asked, "What happens now?"

"Now? I can make this all go away." He waved his hand dismissively.

That sounded too good to be true.

"I don't think Portia is going to like that." *Why, Dizzie, why did you say that?* Why remind him that his other daughter—his heir! — hated her?

"I'll take care of Portia."

Yeah, that didn't sound ominous at all. "And me?"

"I think we've come to an understanding. Haven't we?" Again, that piercing look.

Sure. If knowing that her life would never truly be free could be called an understanding. "Yes." What else could she say?

She didn't know what to do next. Leave? Wait to be dismissed?

The office door flew open with enough force to hit the wall. Dizzie jumped and whirled around.

The click-click-click of heels identified the newcomer. Portia. She looked pissed, her lips pinched, her eyes narrowed. Dizzie was petty enough to take some pleasure in knowing her "escape" probably contributed to the irate look the other woman wore.

A contingent of heavily armed Tremaine Security personnel followed her into the office. "Seize her!"

Portia had barely spoken before Dizzie was surrounded. Two guards grabbed her arms, pulling them tight behind her. She didn't struggle. She was too far outnumbered.

Dizzie wanted out of this office. If that meant leaving with security, she'd take it. Man, things had changed.

Phillip Tremaine stood. His presence dominated the room in a way she hadn't noticed before.

"What do you think you're doing, Portia?" He didn't raise his voice, but Portia shrank under his attention.

Then his heir shook off the effect and asserted herself. "What am I doing?" Her voice was incredulous. "What are you doing? Having tea with the woman who killed my husband?"

Dizzie was impressed in spite of herself. She couldn't imagine what it had been like to grow up with this man. The security team had formed a ring around Dizzie, forcing her to stand on tiptoes to watch the conversation. She was a little pissed that she hadn't gotten the height that Portia and Portia's father had.

"What Dizzie and I were discussing is none of your concern." Tremaine's words dripped with dismissal.

"Dizzie, is it?" She snapped out the words in disbelief.

"Don't be tedious, Portia. A mere courier is no threat to you."

Should she be insulted? She didn't disagree. She was surrounded by security with no place to run.

"She killed Tommy!" Portia's voice rose, driven higher by a keening pain.

Tremaine waved Portia's concerns away. Dizzie felt almost bad for her. Almost. The man was an asshole. She'd heard stories about how he treated Portia, but seeing it first-hand was a real eye-opener.

"No great loss."

Dizzie's eyes widened at the harsh words. No wonder Portia was such a bitch if she had to deal with him every day of her life.

Dizzie barely saw Portia's hand move. The slap echoed around the room.

Her grudging respect for Portia grew.

"How can you say that? Why would you say that?" Pain laced her sister's words and guilt speared Dizzie. Even though she hadn't known what the package was, she was responsible. She'd never forget that.

"Grow the fuck up, Portia. There's more going on here than you know."

"Then tell me. I'm your heir. I should know everything there is to know about the business."

Dizzie strained to see what was happening. Tremaine seemed to be considering Portia.

"Clear the room."

Everyone moved to obey his command. Dizzie tried to hold her ground. She dug in her heels, but she was easily overpowered and dragged toward the door.

"What about me?" she yelled before they hauled her out.

Portia sneered. "Take her down to the holding cells."

Dizzie waited for Tremaine to countermand the order. After all, he'd brokered a deal with her. All he did was wave them all out of the room.

"Take a seat, Portia," was the last thing Dizzie heard before the doors closed.

CHAPTER 45

PORTIA HADN'T WASTED any time bolting from the hospital after Killian told her that Dizzie had taken her car. He'd followed as quickly as he could. He didn't know what the hell Dizzie was doing, but he didn't want her to face the company alone.

Reporters were clustered around the front of Tremaine headquarters when he pulled up. Security tried to divert him along with the rest of the traffic.

Shit. That wasn't good.

He ignored the direction to move and stopped in front of the guard. He rolled down the window. "Do you know who I am?"

"Do I look like I care?" The guard was obviously overwhelmed.

Killian's temper flared and he gripped the steering wheel tightly. "You'd better care or I'll ensure you don't have a job the instant I get inside."

Normally he wouldn't have threatened first. But with Dizzie's safety on the line, he'd do whatever was necessary.

A simple threat was nothing compared to the lengths he would go to protect her.

The guard paled as he focused and identified him. "Sorry, Mr. St. John. No one told me you'd be here."

"No problem." Killian smiled. No reason to keep being an asshole now that he had what he wanted. He waved his hand at the chaos surrounding Tremaine headquarters. "What's going on?"

"Ms. Tremaine called a press conference. Rumor is they captured the bomber from the other night."

Killian managed to keep his expression steady. They'd caught Dizzie. How had she allowed that to happen?

"That's big news." It also explained the newsies surrounding the building. "Who was it? How did they capture the person responsible?"

"I don't know, sir."

Killian wasn't going to get any more out of him. "Thanks for the info. I'll ask around when I get inside. Can I go in?"

The guard blushed. "Of course, Mr. St. John. Go on through."

Killian thanked him, his mind already focused on his next moves while he drove past the perimeter erected to contain the crowd.

What the hell was happening? And how was he going to get Dizzie out of there?

CHAPTER 46

"LET ME OUT OF HERE, DAMMIT!" Dizzie pounded against the glass wall. She knew it was useless, but it gave her a focus for her anger.

They'd tossed her in the same cell as before and left a couple of guards. Killian probably had no idea where she was and her hacker had ignored her recent attempts at contact. She was on her own.

She was still innocent. A pawn, maybe, but not a mad bomber. At least this time she had the added bonus of being a Tremaine. Which didn't mean a damn thing. No one here would believe her, especially not the guards who followed Portia's commands.

"I didn't do it!" The guards didn't even turn around. Could they hear her?

Tremaine had hinted that he'd get her out of this. He was a slick businessman and Dizzie had no reason to trust him. She'd seen the way he treated Portia, the daughter he actually claimed. Dizzie was less than nothing to him.

Who was to say that he wouldn't let Portia get her

revenge and keep Dizzie on ice until he needed her for spare parts?

She slapped her palm against the glass again. "C'mon, guys. Seriously, I didn't do it."

Neither budged. Okay, the easy way was out. Now to come up with a real plan, since she was pretty sure Killian wasn't coming to rescue her again.

She tapped her fingernails against the glass. If this were the movies, her nails would be sharp enough to cut a hole in the glass. Maybe that was possible—if she had time. But not today.

Dizzie paced back and forth in the small space, losing count of the number of times she circled the small room as she tried to find a way out.

She was still pacing when the guards turned toward the glass cube and stood at attention. Then Portia strolled down the corridor outside her cell like she owned the place.

Which she did.

Well, shit. If Portia was here, Tremaine had abandoned Dizzie to the mercy of her long-lost sister.

Portia was her father's daughter and heir. She'd have no mercy for Dizzie. And maybe she didn't deserve any for what she'd done. Knowledgeable or not, involved or not, Dizzie's actions had cost lives. She'd spend the rest of her life trying to make amends, but she had to be alive to do it.

"Dismissed." Portia paired the word with a wave of her hand.

That sent a shiver of fear up Dizzie's spine.

"If you're watching," she whispered with a glance toward the ceiling, "now would be a great time to help me out."

Nothing. What had she expected, for the cell doors to fly open?

Fine. On her own.

Again.

Security took their sweet time leaving. They sort of argued with Portia, but Dizzie couldn't tell if they were more concerned about leaving her alone with Dizzie or leaving Dizzie alone with Portia. She didn't know if these two answered to Portia or to their father. In either case, they didn't answer to Dizzie.

All Dizzie had ever wanted was to be free of this company. That dream had never seemed farther away than this moment, when she was bound to it by blood and circumstance.

Portia keyed in a code on the clear glass wall and the door swung open. She stalked into the cell.

Dizzie studied Portia. Surely security wouldn't leave Portia alone with her with no way to protect herself.

"Now that we're finally alone, I think it's time we had a little chat, don't you?" Portia's smile was predatory.

Dizzie tensed for an attack. As far as she knew, Portia had no enhancements. Still, the last few days had taught her that the upper classes kept secrets from the paparazzi. Like Killian's leg.

And her.

Portia dragged a chair into the cell. She pulled the door closed behind her, then positioned the chair right in front of it. She sat, one leg neatly crossed over the other. If it weren't for the dark circles under her eyes, there would be no way to tell this Portia from last week's pre-bombing version.

Dizzie sat back down on the bunk, mimicking Portia's position. It wasn't a perfect imitation. Then again, neither was she.

A sense of déjà vu overtook Dizzie. It hadn't been that long ago that she'd sat in this cell and faced Killian. Dizzie hadn't convinced him of her innocence then, but she had in the days following. Unfortunately, she didn't have days to convince Portia. She might not even have an hour.

"Didn't we do this already?" Dizzie asked. "At the hospital?"

Portia's smile was pinched and didn't reach her eyes. "Ah, the hospital. You made quite the impression there." Her tone was biting.

"As the good Tremaine sister?" Dizzie smiled sweetly. Portia may want her dead, but Dizzie would make her work for it.

"No, as the ungrateful piece of trash who took advantage of nurses who just wanted to help."

Dizzie winced. If Portia peddled that story to the newsies, it wouldn't be a hard sell. She really hoped that the nurses hadn't been blamed for her escape. "Don't blame them. They didn't know."

Portia continued. "Killian was pretty pissed that you left without telling him." Lips pinched, she studied Dizzie.

Dammit. If they'd grown up as real sisters, maybe she'd have learned to read Portia's expressions.

"He's way out of your league." Portia struck again.

No shit. Dizzie knew that, but her heart refused to listen.

She sighed and pulled her knees up, hugging them. "What's your point, Portia? You're not telling me anything I don't already know."

"You're not my sister." The snapped words came out of nowhere.

God, if this was what having a sister was like, Dizzie was glad she'd never had one. Even Alice had never been this bad. "Well aware. Looks like I dodged a bullet with that."

"How can you make jokes?" Portia pushed off her chair, sending it clattering into the door as she lunged at Dizzie. Portia was faster than she'd expected.

Dizzie uncoiled her legs and moved, but she didn't get completely clear.

Portia caught her around the middle and they both landed on the bed.

Dizzie was on the bottom, trapped between Portia and the thin mattress, while the other woman punched her in the side.

"Ow. Dammit! Get off me!" Her mostly healed ribs didn't appreciate the attack. Dizzie slapped Portia's shoulder. She didn't want to hurt her, just make her move. Only Portia, Phillip Tremaine, and a few security guards knew she was down here. It would be easy to make Dizzie disappear if Portia actually ended up hurt.

"Is this your big plan? Squish me to death?" She slapped at Portia's shoulders again. Dammit. If only she could bring her legs into the fight. Instead, they were trapped under Portia too.

Dizzie jabbed Portia in the side with her nails. Not hard enough to draw blood.

Probably.

"Ow!" Portia yelled and rolled off Dizzie.

Freed, Dizzie stood, though she wobbled a bit. After she regained her balance, she kicked off her heels. She was too inexperienced wearing them to fight in them.

Too slow.

Portia's slap came out of nowhere.

Dizzie's head whipped to the right and her left cheek stung almost immediately. "Ow!" Portia could hit harder than Dizzie had expected.

Dizzie stepped back out of range. She curled her fingers

into her palm and balanced on the balls of her feet. She turned her left shoulder toward Portia, to protect her head from Portia's longer reach.

Portia stared at her hand, shaking it.

Dizzie hoped Portia's hand hurt as badly as her cheek did. "You fight like a girl," she taunted.

Portia lunged again. Dizzie took advantage of her impulsiveness and swung her right fist, striking Portia in the jaw.

Portia's head swiveled and she dropped to the mattress.

Thank god. Dizzie's hand hurt like a motherfucker and she really didn't want to have to punch her again.

"You hit me!" Portia brought her hand up to her lip. It came away bloody.

Dizzie experienced a sense of satisfaction. "You hit me first!" It was a reply better suited to the playground. Or actual sisters. "What do you want from me?"

Portia didn't answer. She sat up and stared at the blood on her hand. "They wouldn't let me see him. I don't even know how much he suffered." Portia's pain was palpable, striking Dizzie harder than any physical blow.

What was Dizzie supposed to say to that? "I'm sorry." It would never be enough.

"You're sorry," Portia snarled. "You delivered the bomb that killed my husband but you're sorry. You nearly buried me alive. Oops, you're sorry. You nearly buried Killian—the man you're fucking—alive. But you're sorry. That's supposed to make it all better?"

Portia's words—her pain—rained down on Dizzie like blows. She flinched, but didn't hide. She deserved it.

"If it's any consolation, Portia, you were both supposed to die."

The voice sent chills down Dizzie's spine. She knew

that voice. The last time she'd heard it, she'd been locked in this same damn cell.

She whirled around, her hands curled into fists. Leopold Brunswick stood in the cell's doorway, looking ruffled. His hair was mussed and his usually pressed suit appeared slightly rumpled. He wasn't even wearing a tie.

"You two are really acting like sisters."

Portia pushed off the mattress and faced her father's assistant. "Did my father send you, Leopold? Are you here to tell me to go back upstairs like a good little girl?"

Apparently, Portia thought the guy was an asshole too. Bonus points for her.

"Oh no, Portia. Your father didn't send me. If fact, if he knew why I was here..." He laughed.

The sound gave Dizzie the creeps. She wished Portia hadn't dismissed the guards.

"If he knew what?" Portia taunted him. "I know you like to throw my father's power around, Leopold. It makes you feel special. Makes you feel like you're a part of the family, right? When you do my father's bidding?"

Portia laughed. It was cold and bitter. The perfect Ice Queen laugh. "Well, guess what? The courier here has more of a shot at being part of the family because, news-flash, she already is." Her voice carried a tinge of hysteria.

Hadn't her sister heard what the man said? Taunting the man who wanted them both dead didn't seem like a good plan.

Dizzie's gaze volleyed between the two of them. Trapped as she was in a cell between two of the people who ran the Tremaine Corporation, her lack of power had never been more evident.

This was a private battle. There was obviously bad

blood between the two of them. Maybe Dizzie could use that to her advantage.

The fight with Portia had positioned Dizzie close to the door. Unfortunately, Leopold blocked the doorway.

"You are such a bitch, Portia. I wish the bomb had taken you out, the way it was supposed to. Both of you."

Dizzie's jaw dropped and she took a step back, hitting the glass wall. *What the hell?* Had Leopold just confessed to being behind the bombing?

"You set me up with the bomb?" The words flew out before her brain caught up.

Leopold turned his attention to her. "You're definitely not the brainy sister, are you? It was so simple to take the package to business services. And you're so predictable, taking whatever extra shifts you can."

"Why would you want to kill us?" Portia asked. "Kill *me?*"

Leopold scowled at her. "I only can take over if your father dies without heirs."

Portia laughed. "You think you'd become the heir if I died?"

"Since I've already taken care of your father."

"What?"

Taking advantage of their shock, Leopold reached into his pocket and pulled out a gun.

Dizzie gasped. Or maybe Portia did. The sound echoed in the suddenly quiet cell.

Dull black, the weapon seemed to absorb light. He aimed it at Portia, then Dizzie, shifting back and forth between them.

The muzzle wavered. He couldn't seem to decide which of them to shoot first.

Dizzie kept an eye on the gun, too afraid to look

anywhere else. Her palms were sweaty, her pulse racing. There were cameras in the cell. Someone had to be watching and send help. Right? Now would be good.

Portia laughed again.

"Stop antagonizing the nice man with the gun," Dizzie hissed at her sister.

If they kept him talking, maybe he wouldn't shoot them. "You're not going to shoot us in front of the cameras," Dizzie said quickly. "There will be witnesses."

Leopold smiled. It wasn't a pleasant sight. "That's the best part. Portia wanted to get rid of you alone, so she had the cameras turned off. There won't be any witnesses."

Dizzie looked at Portia. "You bitch! You were going to kill me?"

Portia shrugged and didn't deny it.

Fuuuck! This day just got better and better.

He waved the gun again and that was when Dizzie noticed his gloves. "It's unfortunate that Portia, blinded by her grief, killed the person responsible for her husband's death," Leopold explained. "Then, unwilling to live without him, she turned the gun on herself."

Actually, that was...a pretty convincing plan.

His hand might be shaking, but Dizzie didn't think he was going to change his mind about killing them.

She slowly shifted half a step to the left. Hopefully it wasn't enough for either Portia or Leopold to notice. The closer she was to the door, the better. She'd take any advantage she could.

"I get why you'd want to take out Portia," Dizzie said. An offended gasp came from beside her. "I don't understand why you wanted me too. I'm nobody." Her parentage seemed to be a tightly held secret.

"Nobody?" Leopold laughed. "Do you think Phillip

Tremaine had secrets from me? I was his right hand. He *relied* on me. Hell, I helped bury the bodies. I know exactly who you are and why he kept you close."

Well, that explained why he wanted to take her out too. She may not be an heir, but with her innards, Tremaine could be around for a long time.

"You didn't do this all by yourself, did you?" After days of not knowing how she'd become a bomb-delivery service, Dizzie wanted answers. Before she died seemed like a good time.

Leopold aimed the gun at her. Dizzie's stomach churned and she fought the urge to flee.

"Oh no. I had help," he admitted. "One of Tremaine's captive computer specialists was more than happy to uncover company secrets. Especially after I told him it would bring down the Tremaine family so he'd be free."

A hacker was involved? *Her* hacker? Why had he been helping her? "Your partner will know what happened. Why you killed us."

"I'll tie up that loose end as soon as I finish with you." His voice took on a manic edge.

Dizzie didn't think they had long until he pulled the trigger.

"Why didn't my father tell me about that project?" Portia asked.

"Oh, Portia. You try and try, but you'll never be the heir that your father wants." His smile had no sympathy in it. No pity. "But you don't need to worry about disappointing him anymore. You'll be dead in a minute." He pointed the gun at Portia.

"You can't do this!" Portia threw up her hands, as if that would stop him from shooting her.

"Yes. I can."

The gunshot was crazy loud in the small room. Ears ringing, Dizzie jerked back and hit the glass wall. She ran her hands over her body frantically. Nothing hurt, but that didn't mean she hadn't been shot.

"Help me!" Portia lay on the ground, her right shoulder bloody. There was a bullet embedded in the glass wall a few feet behind her. Leopold stepped forward, aiming the gun at Portia again.

His movement opened Dizzie's path to the doorway.

This was it. Her opportunity to slip out. Maybe Leopold would turn the gun on her, maybe he wouldn't. But shouldn't she take the chance to escape?

"Help me." This time Portia's voice was closer to a whimper.

Dizzie looked at Portia from her position by the door. The open door.

Blood flowed from Portia's shoulder, probably not enough to kill her. At least not from that first shot.

Leopold stood over Portia. He looked almost as surprised as Portia that he'd actually shot her. It must be different when you did the killing face-to-face rather than with an anonymous bombing.

Dizzie looked at the door again. Leopold and Portia were both distracted. She could get away. Maybe get deep enough into the company's lower floors to hide for a short time.

Dammit. If she were the one lying in a pool of blood, she knew Portia and Leopold would leave her there. But Dizzie couldn't do it. Killian would never recover if he lost Portia. And he would never forgive her if she cost him both his friends. She'd never forgive herself.

Dizzie may not be able to save Portia, but she had to try.

"Not as easy when you have to do the killing in person,

is it?" Her voice barely wavered even if she wanted to throw up for taunting the murderous assistant with the gun. What was she thinking?

"It was a stroke of genius having you deliver the bomb." His self-satisfied smile turned sour. "You've turned out to be more resourceful than I'd imagined. It's almost like you had help disappearing." The gun drifted away from Portia as he turned to face her.

He was digging. Waiting for her to betray someone. The hacker?

Probably. And although she was livid that she'd been used, Dizzie understood. That was the system she lived under.

It was what the Tremaine Corporation turned people into.

Dizzie batted her lashes. "Yes, Killian has been incredibly helpful keeping me off the grid."

Leopold snarled and lunged at her. That distracted him from Portia, leaving Dizzie to face him.

This was such a stupid idea.

She ducked to avoid him and spun to the side, moving away from the door. He crashed into the wall where she'd been standing.

That had to hurt. It took him a second to turn around. The hit hadn't disoriented him as much as she'd hoped.

She balanced her weight on the balls of her feet, ready to move quickly if she needed to. She was glad she'd kicked off the heels, since there was no way she could move fast in those or maintain her balance, but she missed her boots. Any kick she landed would do more damage to her than to him.

Dizzie kept her eyes on Leopold, who pushed away from the way, gun still in hand. His head was bleeding. She hoped the blood trickled into his eye and messed with his vision.

"That was a mistake," he drawled.

Dizzie shrugged. Yeah, maybe. Especially since she was now farther from the door. But she wouldn't regret it for as long as she had left.

"You're not going to save her. You can't even save yourself." He swung the gun up and pulled the trigger.

She hadn't expected him to be that fast. Dizzie tried to lunge out of the way.

Too slow.

Her legs slipped out from under her and she fell on her hip. A whisper of heat kissed her ribs as she tumbled to the floor.

The heat turned to fire. Dizzie scrambled to her knees and pressed her hand to her left side. "Fuck!" Her fingers skimmed over an open wound.

That had been a kill shot. How had she ended up with only a flesh wound? Was his aim that bad?

Leopold's shadow fell over her. It didn't matter how she was still alive. She needed to keep moving. Her knees slipped and she looked down. She knelt in a slowly growing puddle of blood. One that traced back to Portia.

Portia had saved her life, however unwittingly. Now Dizzie needed to save hers.

"Stop." Portia's voice was weak, but it was enough to catch Leopold's attention. He turned toward her. Dizzie scrambled toward him on her blood-slicked knees.

She'd only get one chance.

As soon as she was close enough, Dizzie swiped at the tendons behind his knee with her nails. She ignored the sensation of cutting through skin. Instead, she concentrated on seeing Killian again as she forced her nails deeper.

Leopold screamed and tried to turn toward her. He dropped to the ground between her and Portia. Dizzie swiped at his torso from behind, her nails tearing through flesh. She caught him on both sides, leaving deep scores. Every movement of her arm sent pain sparking along her side.

Finally, he dropped the gun. It hit the floor with a clatter.

Dizzie scrambled on her hands and knees to grab the gun. She stuffed it in the back of her pants. Hopefully Leopold would stay down, because Dizzie wasn't sure how much more she could take.

Panting for breath, she stared at Leopold. He twitched and moaned on the floor. One swift kick to his head or his side with her boots and she would have been able to knock him out. Barefoot, that wasn't an option.

Painfully, Dizzie pushed to her feet. Her side throbbed. Her hands and knees were sticky with blood.

She circled around him to get close to the door. What could she use to tie him up? She couldn't see anything. The room was sparsely furnished, intended to keep prisoners locked up with no way to hurt themselves or escape.

The gunshot wound in her side burned. The magic drugs from the hospital would be welcome right now. Were the nanomeds still in her bloodstream? It would be awesome if they kicked back in. Her whole body hurt.

Dizzie studied Portia. Her shoulder appeared to have stopped bleeding, but there was an awful lot of blood on the floor beside her. Dizzie's pants were drenched with it and she didn't want to think about her feet and hands.

Help still hadn't arrived and Leopold could wake up at any moment. She had to find a way to restrain Leopold. Or did she?

Dizzie started to laugh.

Maybe shock had made her brain slow. Maybe it was the loss of blood. She didn't have to tie Leopold up. She could lock him in instead. Safety was just outside the door.

Now to get Portia out of the room. She was conscious, somewhat, but Dizzie didn't think she'd be able to walk.

"This is probably going to hurt," Dizzie warned, then bent and slid her hands under Portia's shoulders. Fire raced up Dizzie's side when she strained to move Portia's weight. Step by slow step, she dragged her backward, inching toward the door. Dizzie tried not to think about the blood squelching under her feet as she tried to keep her footing.

Portia was semiconscious and mostly dead weight. Dizzie's back and side screamed as she hunched over, dragging Portia inch by inch from where she lay on the floor bleeding.

Dizzie paused to catch her breath. Portia roused slightly. "What are you doing?"

"Getting us out of here." She wrapped her fingers under Portia's shoulders again and pulled. Portia screamed.

"Ohmygod that hurts! Stop!"

"I can't." Dizzie dragged her another few inches.

"I demand you stop!" Portia screeched.

Her cry was loud enough to make Leopold twitch. Dizzie didn't like that. "Shut up! We don't want him to wake up."

Dizzie couldn't see Portia's face, but she was sure she was staring at the man on the floor. "Fine," Portia finally said.

"Good."

It was too late, though. From the corner of her eye, Dizzie saw Leopold twitch again. She had to move faster, but it wasn't easy. She took another step and met resistance.

"This would be a whole lot easier if you helped," she muttered.

"I'll help, little girl." Leopold rolled over and grabbed Portia's foot.

Portia screamed again and shook her leg to dislodge him. "Get him off! Get him off!"

Dizzie kept pulling and they moved, but not very much.

Portia yelled again. "You have the gun, don't you? Shoot him!"

Yeah, that was easier said than done. If Dizzie pulled out the gun, she'd have to let go of Portia. Nothing would stop Leopold from getting her then.

Dizzie couldn't believe that help hadn't come yet. Leopold must have been telling the truth about the cameras being turned off.

She'd process her feelings about her sister's apparent plan to kill her later. For now, she had to get them both out of this alive.

"Hit him with the shoe," Dizzie instructed. Her abandoned shoes were within reach.

"That's stupid!" Portia yelled. Still, she grabbed one and swiped at Leopold.

It didn't do much but it looked like she still got a few good hits in. And it bought Dizzie some time.

She dug her bare heels into the floor and bent her knees. Then she straightened her legs and pushed off with all the strength she had left.

Dizzie landed on her butt right outside the door and she gasped to catch her breath. The effort had been enough to tug Portia's leg free. If it were only Dizzie, she'd be free and clear. But Portia was still mostly in the cell.

Shit.

"Keep kicking," she said, gasping.

"Get me out of here," Portia demanded as she kicked.

With slashed tendons, Leopold wasn't able to get up. He inched across the floor on his hands and knees, his mouth a rictus of pain.

Despite that, Leopold was gaining on them. He grabbed Portia's foot again.

Portia had landed in the vee of Dizzie's legs. Dizzie wrapped her arms around Portia's waist then braced her feet on the edges of the cell door and shoved off again. She didn't get nearly the distance as before, but it was almost enough.

The same trick wouldn't work a second time. Dizzie tightened her arms around Portia's middle and threw their bodies sideways.

Fire burned up her side, so intense she wanted to pass out. But they weren't home free yet.

As soon as they were fully clear of the door, she released Portia and scrambled back toward the cell.

Leopold had steadily gained ground, leaving a trail of blood behind him. He cursed continuously as he crawled across the floor.

Dizzie reached the door before Leopold could and slammed it shut. She knew from experience that he wouldn't be able to open it from the inside.

Breathing heavily, she dropped to the ground and let the last few minutes sink in. "We did it, Portia."

No response.

"Portia?"

Why wasn't she answering?

Once again, she scrambled over to Portia's side. She gently rolled her over. Her first close-up look at the wound was obscured by the blood that coated the front of Portia's shirt.

Dizzie pressed her fingers to her sister's neck. Portia had a pulse, but it was faint. Shit, what now?

On the other side of the glass, Leopold laughed and pounded on the wall. "At least I got one of you this time." He mimed shooting a gun. "You're next!"

Dizzie pulled Portia into her arms and tried to keep pressure on her wound. "Please don't die. Please don't die."

She fought to keep her panic at bay. If Portia died, Dizzie had no way to prove it wasn't her fault.

That was how security found them, Dizzie cradling the unconscious Tremaine princess and her father's assistant screaming that it was all her fault.

Two security guards extricated Portia from Dizzie's arms and radioed for immediate medical assistance. The rest of the squad arrested Dizzie.

They tugged her hands behind her to secure them. The sudden movement pulled at the wound and pain burst through her whole side. After the confrontation with Leopold, it was too much for her system to handle. She sagged in their grip.

CHAPTER 47

KILLIAN STOOD in front of Tremaine headquarters, waiting with the newsies who were getting antsy. Portia had never showed, and the PR person was running out of excuses. He'd spent the whole time creating and discarding plans to get Dizzie out of the building—and out of the city, if he had to. He had enough money to set them up somewhere else.

The thought made him ill. Not the living with Dizzie part. But the fact that he'd be betraying Portia.

That had been the problem with most of his plans. Too many of them ended with Portia never forgiving him. Especially the one he'd decided to go with: releasing Dizzie's identity as Tremaine's daughter might be the only way to get her safely out of the building.

And if he took that step, it was possible neither woman would ever forgive him. He could live with that if it meant Dizzie was safe.

His phone rang. Killian pulled it out. Was it Dizzie? He hadn't spoken with her since last night.

Caller ID was blank, the same as the call he'd received

in Dizzie's cell. Killian's stomach sank. He turned away and answered. "Hello?"

"Dizzie's been captured." The robotic voice delivered the message emotionlessly.

Killian paled as a wave of emotions rushed over him. Fear, anger, worry. He turned away from the crowd so the newsies wouldn't see his sudden panic as a story. "How? What? Why?" His questions tumbled out.

"The original bomber attempted to kill both Dizzie and Portia. Both were wounded and Portia's still unconscious, so they didn't know what to do with Dizzie."

Killian had questions, so many questions, but he limited himself to the most important one. "Who was it?"

There was a pause on the other line. A long pause. "Tremaine's assistant."

Holy shit. Leopold? "Is he talking?"

Another pause. "I don't know. I can't get any more information. I need to go. It's up to you." A long pause. "Tell her I'm sorry."

There was a click and a dial tone. Killian was left staring at his phone.

Tommy's killer had a name now. One that still shocked him. But instead of the relief that Killian had expected to feel, his stomach churned with a sense of failure. Dizzie had been wounded and once again, he couldn't do anything to save someone he loved.

Love her? Was that what this feeling was? The realization should have been a surprise. Instead, it was a relief. He spent years after his parents' tragic accident living half a life, never allowing himself to feel anything too deeply. Dizzie had broken through that shell and freed the man trapped inside.

He could do no less for her.

Killian stared at the podium. The newsies had gotten restless and were drifting away. It was now or never.

Hardening his resolve, Killian made his way to the front of the crowd. No one tried to stop him. They were trying to corral the newsies, but it wasn't working.

The panicked PR person stepped aside, quickly ceding the floor to him. What was he doing? He'd spent most of his life avoiding these people. Now here he was standing up here to speak to them willingly.

For Dizzie.

He leaned toward the microphone and dropped a bomb of his own. "Leopold Brunswick, Phillip Tremaine's assistant, has been arrested for the New Amsterdam Hotel bombing."

Silence. Pure, golden silence.

The questions came fast and furious. Why? What about the courier? Who else was involved?

He sucked in a deep breath while the newsies fired questions at him. He exhaled slowly and cleared his thoughts. Killian raised his hands. It took a few long seconds for them to quiet them down, but they finally stopped shouting.

"No, there is no information on Mr. Brunswick's motive at this time. Tremaine Security is working to identify it.

"Yes, a Tremaine Corporation courier had been a person of interest, but no longer is.

"No, at this time, it is not known if any other high-level Tremaine personnel were involved.

"Yes, there will be a thorough investigation.

"No, the courier will not face disciplinary action. Her role was unwitting."

He paused and studied the crowd. Some of the newsies were still shouting questions, but several were already breathlessly streaming the information to their audience. He didn't even know if most of what he had said was true, but the important parts were: the bomber wasn't Dizzie.

He had one further piece to share, if he dared. His relationships may never recover, but granting Dizzie her freedom was the right thing to do.

"In the course of the investigation, it was discovered that the courier was, in fact, Phillip Tremaine's daughter. She was raised in the company orphanage and was unknown to her sister, Portia Tremaine. The two were introduced in the hospital and are working to figure out their relationship."

"No further questions." With that, he turned and walked into Tremaine headquarters to find his courier.

CHAPTER 48

DIZZIE WAS surprised that she was still in the infirmary instead of back in a cell. Her wound had been treated and the pain muted. The medical staff had cleaned off some of the blood and provided her with a set of scrubs since her clothes had been covered in blood. So, things were looking up. Of course, there were still guards stationed outside the door.

Neither the doctors nor the guards had asked her any questions. They wouldn't believe her anyway. Killian was the only one who had and it was unlikely he knew she was here. Her only hope was that when Portia woke up, she'd confirm that Leopold, not Dizzie, was behind the bombing and the attack in the cell.

At this point, Dizzie didn't care if the truth about her role in the bombing came out. She'd deal with whatever consequences came her way. Mostly, she wanted to forget that she was part of this completely fucked-up family that kept children around as potential organ donors.

That was the truth she wanted out in the world. The truth she would fight to expose. Somehow.

Dizzie thought about the other Tremaine orphans, the people she'd grown up with and the kids who were still part of the system. How many of them were part of Tremaine's scheme? How many of the orphans who'd disappeared, the ones they'd been told had paid off their contract, how many of them had been killed to supply organs to a wealthy person?

There had to be a way to dismantle the program. What would happen to the kids? They deserved a chance at a normal life.

Activity outside her door drew her attention. She pushed off the bed. Whatever happened, she wasn't going to take it sitting down. She wasn't going to take any more Tremaine shit sitting down.

The door opened and a guard entered. Dizzie stared in shock at Alice. And cursed the part of her that still wanted to share everything that had happened with her once-best friend.

"Leading me to my execution?" The words were bitter and sarcastic.

Alice flinched. "You're free to go. Ma'am."

Ma'am? What the fuck?

"Free to go?" This had to be a trick.

Alice nodded but didn't meet her eyes. "Yes. Free and clear."

That was the last thing Dizzie expected. "Did Portia send you down here?"

"I don't know, ma'am. My orders are to release you."

Dizzie stopped. "What gives, Alice? Why are you calling me 'ma'am'?"

She was still pissed at Alice and she wasn't sure if their friendship could be repaired, but it was totally freaking her out that Alice was treating her with deference.

Alice raised her head, but still didn't meet Dizzie's gaze. "Because of what they're saying, ma'am. It's all over the news."

That didn't tell Dizzie a damn thing. She did her best to stifle her frustration. "What are they saying?"

"You know."

Dizzie gritted her teeth. "No, actually, I don't know what they're saying. I've been stuck in here for hours."

Alice finally looked directly at Dizzie, surprised. "Oh. Well, the newsies are saying that you're a, well, a Tremaine. So, um, we're treating you like a Tremaine."

How had the newsies found out? "Where did they hear that?" she asked, not wanting to confirm it just yet. Acknowledging that she was a Tremaine came with a lot of baggage Dizzie wasn't sure she wanted to deal with.

"Mr. St. John said so at the press conference."

"Oh." A press conference? What the...

"I'm, uh, sorry about last week, ma'am."

Last week. Crap, so much had changed since then. Once, Alice would have been the first person Dizzie told about this crazy change in circumstance. From becoming a Tremaine to her relationship or whatever it was with Killian. Now? She still couldn't see past Alice's betrayal.

"Okay. Thanks." What else could she say? "I'm free to go?" She was tempted to ask for it in writing. Proof that this wasn't a cruel trick.

Alice looked as though she wanted to say more. Instead, she nodded. "Yes, ma'am." She gestured at the door.

Dizzie stepped out, hesitantly at first. She was still waiting for this to be a trap.

One step out of the room.

Another.

When she exited the infirmary, Dizzie's shoulders relaxed a fraction.

She was still in hospital scrubs. She turned back and looked at Alice, who wore a strained expression. "What's the fastest way back to the dorms?"

She'd kill for a shower and her own clothes. A nap. If the news of her parentage was out, Dizzie had the feeling this was the calm before the storm. A big shitstorm composed of Phillip Tremaine, Portia, and Leopold.

Killian wasn't part of the problem, but he had spilled the secret and she wanted to know why.

Footsteps echoed in the hall behind her. She tensed and spun around, afraid she would see guards.

She brightened. "Killian!"

Her fear of guards evaporated and she ran toward him, intending to launch herself into his arms.

As she neared, though, she had second thoughts. Would he be happy to see her?

She skidded to a stop in her slippered feet. He was close enough to touch. "What are you doing here?" she said, her voice wavering.

"I came to rescue you. But it looks like you rescued yourself." He studied her. His brows furrowed and his jaw clenched. "How badly were you hurt?" Anger and an emotion she was afraid to identify colored his words.

"It was just a graze." She lifted her top and showed him the bandage on her side. "It barely hurts anymore."

Killian closed the distance between them and, careful of her wound, pulled her into his arms. "Thank god you're safe."

Safe. Yes, that was exactly it. His arms were her safe place.

Dizzie leaned into him, absorbing his strength. His presence. Finally able to relax, she started to shake.

"Hey, it's okay. I've got you."

She burrowed closer, while Killian whispered soothing words. His chest was warm beneath her cheek. She wrapped her arms around his waist and held on. "He was going to kill us," she whispered.

Killian tensed and his arms tightened around her. "Brunswick?"

She tilted her head back to look at his eyes. "You know?"

"Just the basics." He pressed a kiss to her forehead. "Will you tell me what happened?"

Dizzie blew out a slow breath. "I... Just a little, okay? I was in the cell—the one where we met." She smiled, trying to add a bit of levity, but it fell flat. "Portia came in—"

"Why?" Killian asked.

"She wanted to see me." Dizzie pressed her forehead to his chest so he couldn't see the turmoil in her eyes. She wasn't going to mention that Portia had had intentions like Leopold's. Dizzie still didn't know how Portia had planned to do it, since she hadn't brought a weapon. She chalked it up to Portia's deep grief and a spur-of-the-moment thought. She was already responsible for so much damage to his relationship with Portia, she wasn't going to make it worse. "Leopold followed her in. He said we were both meant to die in the explosion." The terrifying memory of that moment shuddered through her.

"I'll kill him," Killian growled.

"He shot Portia and shot at me." The wound in her side throbbed in reminder. "I couldn't leave her there. He was going to kill her. So I attacked him and..." she swallowed hard. She'd never forget the feeling of rending flesh and muscles with her nails. "And we got away."

Killian's hands landed on her shoulders and he eased her back enough so he could look at her. Dizzie avoided his gaze until he rested a finger beneath her chin and tilted it up. "Thank you for saving her, Dizzie."

The look in his eyes, the warmth in his voice. She nodded.

"Will you tell me how?"

Dizzie looked away. "I attacked him with my...with my nails."

He sucked in a deep breath, but didn't say anything.

"It was... It was bad. There was a lot of blood."

Cupping her face between his hands, Killian said, "I'm so sorry you had to do that. But I'm so glad you made it out of that cell alive."

The kiss began gentle, reverent. A kiss of gratitude. Relief. Love. At least on her end.

She loved him.

Whoa. She *loved* Killian.

Dizzie wrapped her hands around his wrists, levered up onto her toes, and poured every ounce of herself into the kiss.

A throat cleared nearby. Dizzie broke off the kiss reluctantly.

"Excuse me, Mr. St. John?"

Killian released Dizzie and shifted so his body was between her and the newcomer. "Yes?"

A young man, wearing a suit that didn't quite fit, stood a few feet away. "Sorry to bother you, sir, but there's an issue in Mr. Tremaine's office and, well, we don't know what to do about it."

"Why are you coming to me?"

"Well, sir. You handled the reporters really well and there's not really anyone else we can go to at the moment."

"Give us a minute," Dizzie said. She grabbed his hand and pulled him down the hallway.

"Why do they want me to deal with this?" Killian looked puzzled by the turn of events.

"Portia is out of commission. So is Leopold. They're the closest to Phillip Tremaine and they can't fix whatever the problem is." Dizzie tugged him closer because she didn't want this part to be overheard. "When we were fighting Leopold, he said he'd already taken care of Phillip Tremaine."

Killian's eyes widened.

"I don't know what that means," she said, "but it might be related to the problem in Tremaine's office."

"But why me?"

"Why *not* you?" Dizzie asked, exasperated. "Apparently you're good with reporters—I understand you told them about me—we'll talk about that later. The company needs someone to step up to the press again, and the company wants you." She gestured to the man who was fidgeting down the hall. "If it's not you, it might be someone without the care and personal touch you'll bring."

"But you've been hurt."

"And I'll be fine. You need to do this. For Portia and Tommy."

"And for you." He raised her hand to his lips for a kiss.

"And for me," she agreed with a sigh. Her whole life had been tied to the company.

"I love you, Dizzie Tremaine." Killian pulled her close for a kiss, but she resisted.

"No, nope, never." This needed to be settled once and for all. "I'm never ever taking that last name. I didn't have a last name before. I don't need one now." She'd had one name her entire life. She wasn't going to take a family name now. Especially one she was so conflicted about. She might have been a Tremaine by DNA, but she'd never claim to be a part of that family.

"I love you, Dizzie, no last name." Amusement threaded through his voice.

She laughed softly. "I love you, too, Killian. St. John." She pressed a kiss to his lips. "Now go save your best friend's company." Dizzie gave him a little push.

"I'll find you later," he said.

"You better."

DIZZIE LOOKED around her room for the last time. Well, it wasn't her room any longer. She'd packed up her belongs and moved in with Killian once everything had settled down at the Tremaine Corporation.

Well, "settled" was being polite. Phillip Tremaine was missing and there were signs of a struggle in his office. Blood and Leopold's tie had been found near his desk. Everyone assumed that Tremaine's assistant had done him in, but the other man wasn't talking. In the meantime, Killian was helping Portia transition into the CEO role and root out her father's corruption.

Personally, Dizzie didn't care what happened to the company, though she was curious about the hacker who'd helped save her life.

But even that question took a backseat to her concern for the other orphans. She was determined to discover how many of the others had been kept or, in the worst cases, created for Phillip Tremaine's organ donation program. And she now had the funds to do it. It had been one of her demands from the company, instead of dragging Portia to court for her share of the company, while the court of public opinion was firmly on Dizzie's side.

When Killian had released her identity, her entire life had changed. Instead of calling her a bomber, the newsies referred to her as the lost Tremaine daughter. They'd wanted interviews and to talk about her feelings. Everything but her mother's identity, her father's location, and the identity of the hacker was out in the open.

She'd hated every moment of it. But she'd used the newsies and the interviews to gain her freedom. With all the attention on her, the Tremaine Corporation had no option but to release her. Her emancipation had been done through an intermediary Killian had recommended, since she'd never have trusted someone appointed by the company. She was free of her contract and had enough money to never have to work. She'd even freed her bike from Tremaine control. It waited for her in Killian's garage, right next to the Turbosmith Excel.

The bombing had turned her entire life upside-down. She was no longer a courier for Tremaine Corporation. It still freaked her out if she thought about it too long.

For years she'd dreamed of freedom. Now she had it. The price would have been too high if she didn't have Killian.

Her new status was isolating. People treated her one of two ways.

Old friends like Alice treated her with the same deference that they did Portia. Nothing Dizzie said or did convinced them that she was still the same person. They didn't see Dizzie anymore. They saw a Tremaine.

The other group treated her with suspicion. She'd heard whispers that they believed that she was guilty. That she'd gotten lucky and had blackmailed the family in order to be recognized.

Wiping tears from her eyes, Dizzie looked around the empty room again. By next week, it would be someone else's room. "Thank you," she whispered, and with that, she cut the last string that tied her to her old life.

Killian waited in the hallway. "Ready?"

She nodded and grabbed his hand. "Let's go home."

The hacker watched the empty room for a long moment before he turned off the camera. He felt a glimmer of hope. Dizzie had landed on her feet and escaped the situation he'd accidentally dragged her into. Good. That was good.

There might be hope for him.

He had to leave shortly for his shift on Tremaine's cybersecurity team. It wouldn't be long before they started searching for Leopold's accomplice. The hacker had to free himself from the Tremaine Corporation and the mess he'd made before they learned his identity.

THE END

ENJOY THIS BOOK?

Reviews and ratings encourage other readers to try out a book and I'd love your help spreading the word! If you could take a quick moment to rate or leave a review for this book on your favorite book site, I'd be forever grateful!

Once she stopped being stubborn and learned to read, Heather always had a book in her hand. Or in her bag. Or under the pillow.

Anne McCaffrey, Nora Roberts, Agatha Christie, and Tamora Pierce. Heather devoured anything and everything, from sci-fi and fantasy novels to historical romance and Harlequins. Her favorites, though, were the stories that combined swoony romance with fantastic adventures.

Now she creates her own worlds and plays "what if...?"

Heather lives in Seattle with her husband and two cats. When she's not writing (or working her day job), she can be found reading, traveling, or enjoying a quiet cup of tea—sometimes all at once!

ACKNOWLEDGMENTS

Releasing a book into the wild is scary and I couldn't have done it alone. There are so many people to thank!

Thom, who's supported me from the start! Love you!

My mom, who made me learn to read and bought me books and supported me no matter what!

Christina Sol, friend and longtime critique partner, thank you so much for all your support, whether it was for life in general, the story, or this crazy writing adventure!

Shelli Stevens, friend and cheerleader, thank you!

Eve Silver, who graciously mentored me after this book won the Catherine contest Golden Ticket! I truly appreciate the time you spent and all the knowledge you shared.

All the contest judges who read Dizzie's book and especially the ones who scored it high! Your comments and insights made this a better book.

Danielle and Jen for beta-reading!

Michelle and Tim for reading and proofreading and general encouragement!

Family, friends, and fellow writers too numerous to name who have supported and encouraged me over the years!

If I missed you – I'm so sorry! It wasn't intentional and there's always next book!

(Special thanks to the exclamation mark. I couldn't have written this section without you!)